LOVE FORMS

| a novel |

Claire Adam

HOGARTH
LONDON/NEW YORK

Published in the United States by Hogarth, an imprint of Random House, a division of Penguin Random House LLC, 1745 Broadway, New York, NY 10019.

HOGARTH is a trademark of the Random House Group Limited, and the H colophon is a trademark of Penguin Random House LLC.

LIBRARY OF CONGRESS CATALOGING-IN-PUBLICATION DATA
Names: Adam, Claire, author.
Title: Love forms: a novel / by Claire Adam.
Description: First edition. | London; New York: Hogarth, 2025.
Identifiers: LCCN 2025006919 | ISBN 9780593230923 (hardcover) | ISBN 9780593230930 (ebook)
Subjects: LCGFT: Novels.
Classification: LCC PR9272.9.A33 L68 2025 | DDC 813/.6—dc23/eng/20250224
LC record available at https://lccn.loc.gov/2025006919

Printed in the United States of America on acid-free paper

penguinrandomhouse.com
randomhousebooks.com

2 4 6 8 9 7 5 3 1

First Edition

Book design by Susan Turner

The authorized representative in the EU for product safety and compliance is Penguin Random House Ireland, Morrison Chambers, 32 Nassau Street, Dublin D02 YH68, Ireland, https://eu-contact.penguin.ie.

Love
forms in the human body.

—Louise Glück, "The Fortress"

LOVE FORMS

1

IT WAS MY FATHER WHO MADE THE ARRANGEMENTS. MY UNCLE helped, since he lived down south, where all this kind of business is carried out. I'm talking south-south: down past the airport, past the swamp, past the oil fields, everything. Way down at the bottom of the island, down where Columbus landed, long ago. There's hardly anything down there, just fishing villages. Peaceful, old-time places: a few ramshackle wooden houses, and children playing marbles in the shade under the trees. Everywhere you look, in those places, you see pirogues pulled up onto the sand: little wooden boats, fishing boats, supposedly—although how much fishing the men really do nowadays is anybody's guess. The boats are very basic. Open-topped, maybe twenty feet long, with just a plank of wood to sit on and a boat-engine clamped onto the back. But somehow they manage to make the journey across those seven miles of ocean between Trinidad and Venezuela—and carrying all kinds of things, not just fish. It's a dangerous journey, though, even when special arrangements are made, as they were for me.

My father brought me the clothes I was to wear: black T-shirt and long-pants; a big long-sleeved men's shirt to wear over the

T-shirt, also in black, and with the buttons cut out. We'd be traveling by night, and anything that might catch in torchlight had to be covered, including my own skin. The Trinidad and Tobago Coast Guard was one difficulty, the Guardia Nacional on the Venezuelan side was another, but the worst problem was bandits. Bandits would steal the engine off the back of the boat and leave you out there to drift, or they would take the whole boat, and throw you in the sea. I also had a pillowcase to go over my head: the reflection of torchlight against things like eyeballs and teeth had been known to give people away.

The shirts, the trousers, the pillowcase—all these things were cheap, cheaply made; they weren't things I would normally have worn, or owned. Probably, they came from some roadside vendor in central Trinidad. I doubt my father bought them himself: more likely, he sent one of his men out to do it—someone unimportant and unknown, who wouldn't be recognized and connected to our family. I'm only guessing, of course. I didn't ask about these details at the time. If I had asked, I'm sure someone would have said, "Dawn, girl, the less you know, the better."

It was early August when I made the journey. In my room, alone, I changed out of my shorts and T-shirt, into the black clothes my father had brought. My knapsack was already packed, hidden at the bottom of my wardrobe. I set it on the floor at the foot of my bed, looked through it, then zipped it closed again. I was full of a nervous energy; I would have liked to tidy up, or clean the room, but there was nothing left to do—the bed was made, the floor swept; the desk and bookshelves, still full of my ordinary school things, were tidied and dusted. I took my posters down from the walls. (The posters showed close-up photos of boys from music bands that were popular at the time. I sat at my desk and pulled the tacks from my little pink-framed corkboard on the wall. All my revision schedules, exam schedules, my friends' phone numbers, my motivational sayings handwritten on little scraps of paper—I took them all down from the corkboard, and crumpled them up. Then with nothing else to do but wait, I sat on the floor, my elbows on my knees, leaning against the side of the bed.

Only my mother was at home with me that afternoon. I don't know how she passed the time; we didn't speak. At some point, I heard her footsteps downstairs: she slid the patio doors shut, and then turned the key in the lock. I heard her pull the curtains shut too. I don't know what made her do that—it was only afternoon—but maybe she was possessed by the same feeling of shame as I was, and the sense that a part of our lives was coming to an end. Or maybe she was just like me—filled with the same nervous energy, her hands searching for things to keep busy with, to help pass the time. I don't know. After that, it went quiet: I heard nothing. I imagined her sitting on the sofa in the living room, her arms folded, her handbag and car keys waiting nearby on the kitchen counter. In any case, for quite a long time, maybe half an hour, we stayed in our different parts of the house, each thinking our own private thoughts, and watching the hands of the clock tick forward.

My mother drove. I sat beside her in the front seat: we wanted me to be seen, to look as if I were on my way to the airport. We went down the hill, first, along the road that my father had cut through the forest, then along the bumpy, potholed road by the golf course. A pause at the bend, waiting for a chance to merge onto the main road, and then the same old sharp acceleration as always—first gear, then quickly into second, then third—as she turned onto the stretch that runs alongside the Maraval River. Nowadays, there are gated communities all along that road, low-rise apartment blocks with pools and tennis courts, but back in 1980, on the day that my mother and I set out, it was still just bush. The picture I have of it in mind now is not so much from that day, as from all the other ordinary days that had gone before: thick wild grass grown to shoulder-height; forest trees, branches heavy with ripe fruit; bright flashes of birds among the green leaves.

The first handover was made in midafternoon, somewhere between the university campus and the airport. An unfamiliar road, and one I've never been able to find again. I remember squat brick houses sparsely placed, the rain just fallen, rising again now as vapor from the hot asphalt. My mother slowed outside one of the gates, and then pulled over in front of a parked car. A man appeared at her window: clean-shaven, neatly dressed; probably black nylon trousers and a light-colored shirt-jac. I can still bring to mind something of his manner: courteous, eager, important; full of reassurance that his mind was only on the task at hand. "Right, Mrs. Bishop," he might have said. "Right, right. Everything good. Everything done fix up. We ready."

My mother got out. I waited alone in the car, watching them through the front windshield. She and the man walked together to his car, just ahead, and he opened the door on the driver's side and she ducked down to look inside. I don't know what she was looking at. She came out again, and the driver pushed the door shut, and she bent down and pressed her thumb against the tire. Then they walked around the front of the car and she tried the other tire, and the driver opened the other doors, one by one, and she looked inside, and checked the other tires. They came back around to the back of the car and the driver opened the trunk, and my mother looked inside. My mother reached into her bag and took out a small brown envelope and handed it to him. He took it quickly, and put it in his pocket. Then she turned and beckoned to me to come. I got out of my mother's car. As I walked the short distance to the car in front, I was aware of being observed from the windows of the houses all around; I suppose people must have been watching from behind their curtains. I remember sweating in my hot black clothes and trying to hold my knapsack over my stomach.

"Go in the back, go in the back," the man said.

I thought he meant the trunk, and I stopped, unsure. He came around and opened the door of the backseat for me, like a chauffeur.

"In here," he said. "You'll have to get down. Not right now. I'll tell you when."

I got into the man's car. The windows were covered in dark film. My mother and the man were behind the car, out of sight. I looked out the window to the side, instead, toward the man's house. A hibiscus hedge; a metal gate, painted white, with a red metal letterbox. Beyond the gate, a front lawn; croton plants growing along the border of the driveway. On the upstairs veranda of the house, a hanging birdcage, a large bird moving slowly inside the cage.

The car sank as the man got in the front and started the engine. I remember him as energetic, eager to set off. He pressed a button to wind the window down on my side, so I could wave to my mother as we left. But I didn't want to see her: I was afraid of what I would do. Instead, as we drove away, I slid down to the footwell so I was out of her sight, and I arranged myself there, my thighs pressing uncomfortably against the front of my body. Later, I stretched my legs out across to the other footwell so I could breathe more easily.

I must have been in that car for three or four hours. I'm only guessing, based on the distance I know we traveled, all the way down the southern main road. I didn't look out the windows: the road was familiar enough, and I could tell where we were just by the smell. The stink of the swamp: unpleasant but not unnatural. The fuel smell of the airport: sweetish, volatile, dangerous. A different petrochemical smell as we went farther south: the thicker, dirtier, heavier smell of the oil fields as we passed Pointe-à-Pierre. After San Fernando, the road became less familiar, everything more confusing; I couldn't picture the exact road we were on. But then, eventually, there was the cleaner air of the sea, and a narrow, bumpy road; and through the car window I saw the tall bushy heads of coconut trees thickly packed together.

It was dusk by the time we stopped, and I unfolded my body from the footwell of the car, and stepped onto uneven, sandy ground—a cool, breezy place, shaded by small trees. I was grateful for the fresh air. I felt dizzy; I had to sit down on the ground. The man walked a short distance away. When he came back, I followed him along a path through the trees. I wasn't afraid of him. We had become accustomed to each other on the long drive, even though we hadn't spoken much. Now, he swung his keys in his hand, and walked with a calm self-importance. He might have been thinking with pleasure of whatever money he'd earned.

I went to a lady's house to wait. Not really a house—more like a shack: one of those on stilts, covered with patches of galvanize. I'd seen houses just like it all over Trinidad, but I'd never been inside one before. In the main room of the house, there was a brown velour couch against one wall; I sat there to wait. I was there a long time, and all I remember is the couch, and that the room was very bare. No television, no pictures, or even other furniture that I can remember. I think there was an overhead light; I think it must have been electric: a bulb, rather than a kerosene lamp. There was a length of fabric across the window—like a curtain, except that it was nailed at all four corners, and didn't flap in the breeze.

It wasn't a nice house: I'm ashamed to say that. The woman wasn't unkind, but she didn't want me there. She was an old woman, heavy; she walked with difficulty. She brought me food on a Styrofoam plate, and a plastic spoon wrapped in a paper napkin. I asked if there was a phone. At first the woman didn't reply: maybe she was thinking that conversation wasn't part of the arrangement. Eventually she said no, no phone. She said my parents knew I'd reached. I asked for water. I offered to get it myself, but she said she would get it. I think she didn't want me moving around her house. As she went through the beaded curtain to the kitchen, I caught a glimpse of a rusted chair, and fly tape hanging from the ceiling, stuck with black flies. After she brought the water, and took away the Styrofoam plate, she settled back there, on her side of the beaded curtain, on the chair under the fly tape, to wait.

I was there from around six P.M. until midnight—this is my guess anyway: I'm recalling this as best I can, you understand. The truth is that I only remember impressions—images, sounds, feelings. The sequence of events is just my reconstruction, based on what I know must have happened. However many hours it was, the time in the lady's house passed slowly. The lady was old, black, poor; I was white, young, rich—she must have known who I was. We passed the hours in near-total silence. There was a dog tied up under the house: occasionally I heard the sound of it digging in the dirt, or the clank of a chain. Meanwhile, outside, the night grew deeper.

The next thing I remember is seeing two men standing outside in the dark. I think this must have been outside of the lady's house that I just described; I can't remember being at any other house on the Trinidadian side. The men were black, and dressed in black, and with black cloths covering the lower half of their faces. I only saw them by the little bit of light cast from the doorway of the house. I didn't want to go. For the first time, it crossed my mind that my father and uncle might have lied to me. From the doorway at the top of the stairs, I looked to the woman for help. I asked, "Go with them?" She nodded, lips pursed. I looked at the men, and then I looked to her again, and she looked back at me without speaking.

One of the men was impatient. "Come, come!" he said. "We don't have time to waste, you know." He wasn't really in a hurry, he just wanted me to move. He was that kind of man.

"You know who I am, right?" I said. I was trying to sound bold, but who knows how my voice came out. "You know who my father is?"

"Yes, yes," he said. "Don't frighten. We know where you going. You will arrive alive." I remember those words—he said them in a jokey, rhyming way, like the TV advertisement for seatbelts: Arrive alive! "Come, come. The boss-man done give all the instructions. Mr. Bishop and them. We know what going on."

The other man hadn't spoken yet. Now he said something in Spanish, and the first man answered him with a shrug.

"Come on!" the first man said. "Come onnn! You don't know time waits for no man? Man, woman, cat, dog! We have a window, you know." He tapped his wrist. "Everything arranged. Is now for now we hadda go. It have all kinda people crossing that water tonight. And we don't want to bounce up nobody. Now for now. Come."

Shakily, I went down the steps. The Trinidadian man walked in front; the Venezuelan one followed behind me. My legs were stiff from sitting, and it was hard to walk in the deep, soft sand. The Venezuelan tried to take my arm to help me, but I shook him off. In the darkness, the fallen coconuts all around us glimmered like skulls.

There was a jetty, and a boat knocking against a wooden piling. The first man sat at the edge of the jetty and then disappeared. Then the other man held me under the armpits and pushed me to the edge. I struggled. Below, the other man was reaching up from the boat, grasping at my legs. I landed on something solid. Then: gaps, darkness; I just don't remember. The other man must have got into the boat, they must have untied it from its moorings. The lurching was terrible. I must have been focusing on clinging on to whatever I could hold. Then we were moving; we were away from the shore.

"You brought the hood?" the man asked. "Put on the hood."

"You're not wearing one," I said to the man. I looked at the other man, at the other side of the boat, but if he understood me, he gave no sign. "He's not wearing one," I said. I was suspicious, and afraid. We were still close enough to the shore that I could have jumped out and swum back.

"I hadda see to be able to drive the boat," the man said. "And him, he's a lookout." He pulled the scarf up so that it covered his mouth and nose, and he looked even more like a bandit than before. He called out to the Venezuelan man, and the Venezuelan man did the same.

"Hood, hood," the man said, gesturing. "You brought it? Put it on."

I was going to jump out. You grow up in Trinidad, you learn how to smell danger: I wanted to get out. And then someone's hands were around my head, or throat, or over my eyes; I tried to fight. Then I was being pressed against the bottom of the boat, and everything was dark. I stopped struggling. It would have been so easy for him to twist the pillowcase around my neck and strangle me. I let him put it over my head instead, and then I didn't move again. We must have crossed the gulf like that, in the dark, the little boat lurching and smacking against the big ocean swells.

I REMEMBER ARRIVING, AND HAVING to climb up onto something wooden, maybe a jetty. It was muddy; I remember slipping, and someone holding me by the arms. There were other people there, but I couldn't see them in the dark. I don't know who they were. Then there was another car, a jeep, with open windows. I got down into the footwell again, automatically, or maybe because of the wind. I was hardly awake. I didn't know what time it was, or how long I'd been traveling, or where I was being taken. At some point I had to change cars, and I think I might have been sick by the side of the road. The image I have of the place where this happened is like an ordinary open highway, the road wide and smoothly paved, all in darkness except for the occasional headlights of cars traveling in the opposite direction, on the other side of a low railing.

At some point in the journey, in one of the cars, there was a woman in the back with me. I don't know when she appeared. It was too dark to see her clearly: I remember just seeing her face in silhouette as she looked out the window. She was older than me. My impression was that she was thickset, sturdy. And she was calm—that's what I remember, mostly, that her presence was calming. I think now that she must have been one of the nuns from the house, but I didn't know that then. She must have come in order to guide us to where we were going.

It was daylight when we arrived at the place where I would stay. We had driven up a hill, past other scattered houses. All around us was green, the same deep dark forest green as in Trinidad. When the driver switched off the car, I was aware first of the green forest all around, and the clear jeweled voices of birdsong. Then a dog arrived at the gate, sheepishly, as if apologetic for being late. The dog was of no clear breed—brown, slender; knee-height, with a shaggy tail—a nice-looking dog, gentle and welcoming, barking politely, as if to let someone know we had arrived. She was like any other dog who would run up to a gate in Trinidad: even the bark, and the meaning of the bark, was the same. I was disoriented; I thought I might be in a dream. I looked at the woman who had gotten out of the car with me, and I touched her arm to see if she was real. She was sweating—along her forehead and on her cheeks, under her glasses. I said, "Venezuela?" Because I thought that maybe there had been some confusion, and that somehow I was back in Trinidad. She didn't understand. I said, "Venezuela? Or Trinidad?" And again, the other way: "Trinidad? Or Venezuela?" When she understood, she smiled, and she said, "Venezuela." She lifted her hands, palms to the sky, and said some other words, and among the words I didn't understand, she said again, "Venezuela."

She put an arm around me as we walked to the house. The gate was unlocked, all we had to do was open it, and we walked straight in, up the drive, with the little dog ambling beside us.

I remember quite clearly what the house looked like from the outside. It was an ordinary two-story house, painted white. There were flowerpots lining the driveway. There was a garden all around, dotted with ordinary fruit trees. The fence was diamond-meshed galvanized wire in some places, or brick wall in others, about four or five feet high. There was a big black PVC water tank just behind the house, up a slight slope.

I'VE SPENT MANY HOURS TRAWLING through images online, trying to find this place again. But Venezuela is a big country. If you look at a map, you'll see: it's gigantic, nearly a million square kilometers. And outside of the big cities, the place is just forest. Try it. Look at a map, zoom in. Everywhere you look is forest. Even now, over forty years later, I still don't know exactly where I was.

2

I FEEL I SHOULD CLARIFY ABOUT THE NUNS. WHEN YOU SAY "NUNS" nowadays, people think of evil, cruel women who starve girls and make them scrub floors—Caribbean nuns aren't like that. For the most part, they're cheerful women, busy, active. They run schools, they teach, they find housing for the destitute; they manage kitchens, they pray with the sick, bring food to the poor. And in Trinidad, it used to be the nuns who coordinated the relief efforts—for example, when there were floods, or when an island had been hit by a hurricane.

I have very clear memories of how it used to work. Our school chapel used to be commandeered as a sort of hub: schoolchildren took part in the effort, and it was like a military operation, organizing huge piles of donations into categories; laying out cardboard boxes at the ends of the pews, and distributing items among boxes. There were other adult helpers—some men, some other religious women—but it was the nuns who were in charge. They wore gray knee-length dresses and simple black veils that covered their hair; and sensible shoes—shoes suitable for walking long distances in any terrain. When hurricanes were coming in, there was a sense of working against the clock, but the nuns were fearless, tireless: they strode up and down the aisles, directing operations, their veils fluttering in the wind. Later, I learned that those same nuns used to take the donations to the airport themselves, and as soon as the sky was clear, they would be out on the tarmac getting the boxes loaded onto the plane. Who knows, maybe they even flew the planes; I wouldn't put it past some of them.

They weren't all particularly devout: I think now that they were just capable women—women who saw what needed to be done, and rolled up their sleeves and got on with it. Priests were a little different: they were more inclined to sit and complain about the country going to the dogs. But the nuns did the legwork. Nuns got things done. And nuns were trusted: I don't know if they even needed things like passports to travel from one island to another, or if they just showed their faces and they were waved through.

In that house in Venezuela, the nuns were all called "Hermana," pronounced without the *H,* like ear-*man*-a. I'm sure there was at least one Hermana Maria: I keep returning to the name "Maria-Theresa," but I could be making that up. I can't remember the names of the others. I think there were four of them, or sometimes five; other local women came and went too. I have a recollection of a woman who I now think must have been a midwife, or maybe she was a doctor or nurse. In any case, they were all decent. We were fed; we were looked after. One Hermana was a stern sort of person, but there was none of the cruelty I've heard about in other places. And some of the girls cried now and then, but it wasn't because of the nuns.

I was there for four months, from August to November—long enough, you would think, to still have a clear picture of the place where I stayed, but I only remember fragments. One of the rooms had a black-and-white tiled floor, like a chessboard: I remember that clearly. In the nuns' office downstairs, there were leafy plants on a windowsill that made the light in that room dim: I remember shade and shadows where there should have been bright sun. And the house smelled of bleach and insect spray, just like Trinidad. In fact, many things were just like Trinidad. There was burglar-proofing over the windows, and beyond the windows there was a view of the crisscrossing flanks of the hills, much bigger than the hills at home, but carpeted in the same dark green as at home, the same thick, wild forest. There were the same noisy, squawking parrots as there were at home, and golden orioles, and hummingbirds who came frequently to the hibiscus; the same thick ropelike vines hanging from branches of the tall trees; the same peeping, whistling frog-calls that went on through the same hours of the night.

From the garden, you came up a flight of steps and arrived at a sort of covered walkway, almost like a long balcony or gallery that ran along the high flank of the house. The bedrooms were up there, with doors onto this long balcony or walkway. Two or three beds in each room; mosquito nets over the beds. A crucifix on a nail hammered into the wall.

When I first arrived, I shared a room with a girl called Salomé. I remember her name because it made an impression on me: I thought it was a name that existed only in the Bible. She was from Peru. I remember her sitting cross-legged on her bed, brushing her hair. I remember that part vividly: the long black hair; thick, shining hair.

The floor on that covered walkway just outside the bedrooms was tiled, and very slippery when it rained. I was there in rainy season: it rained often. Girls picked their way along carefully, barefooted or in rubber flip-flops, pressing their clothing flat against their bellies so they could see down to the floor.

I slipped on that floor on my first morning there. I think it was my first morning: everything was still new and unfamiliar. Probably, someone had spoken a warning about the wet floor, but I hadn't understood it in Spanish, or maybe hadn't heard above the noise of the rain beating against the corrugated iron roof. I had followed the other girls out of the bedrooms, but then for some reason I had fallen behind, and when I ran to catch them up, I slipped on the wet tiles and fell. I slid some way along, and crashed into the balcony railing. I began to examine my leg, and I saw, now in daylight, the bruises and cuts that had appeared on my body during the long journey the day before. Inside my body, the baby kicked vigorously. I could feel the sickening gliding movements of the small body pushing against my own organs.

One of the Hermanas came up looking for me—not the stern one. I remember her as being rosy-cheeked and energetic, with glasses; brown-skinned, with very sparse gray hair. She might have been in her fifties. She linked her arm through mine and helped me downstairs, plucking occasionally at my wet clothes. Downstairs, I heard the other girls' voices, and smelled food—good food: coffee, fried eggs, toast. The nun took me to a room, and opened a cupboard and pulled out clothes on hangers. She held them against my body to see the size, talking cheerfully all the while in Spanish, exclaiming at how nice they would look.

A hot feeling of humiliation spread over my body, thinking of having to strip off in full view of the nun to change out of my wet clothes. She must have understood, because she led me to a bathroom nearby. I remember a toilet cubicle, smelling strongly of bleach, and very dark once the door was closed. There was just enough light from the breeze blocks near the ceiling for me to see what I was doing.

In the dark bathroom, I changed into the dress the Hermana had given me, and folded up my wet clothes. When I came out, I held the little wet bundle out to the nun, as if to ask, What shall I do with these? I must have been crying, because she took my face in her hands and wiped her thumbs under my eyes, and she hugged me and spoke gently in Spanish. And after I had calmed down, she took me to the kitchen, where five or six other girls were seated at a long table. I took my place with them, and someone set a plate of food in front of me.

I KNOW NOW THAT I was in Venezuela for nearly four months, but while I was there, it was hard to keep track of time, when every day seemed just like the one that had gone before. The only day that was different was Sunday: when a priest came and said Mass to us in the little prayer room downstairs.

And there were other visitors: we weren't exactly sealed away from the world, or locked in a prison, or anything like that. A man came to cut back the bush in the garden; a different man came and pushed a lawn mower around. There might have been a different man again who came with a ladder and took away a jack Spaniard nest from the high ceiling, but it's possible that he was the same man who cut back the bush. (I have a vague recollection that one of the men was deaf, possibly the one who cut the grass. But maybe he wasn't really deaf; maybe I just misunderstood what someone said as we looked out the window at the man, in black rubber boots, and a bandanna over his mouth and nose, diligently pushing the lawn mower, green flecks of grass flying up and sticking to his clothes.) And the nuns went out in a car sometimes, on some business or other. Once, a girl had to go to hospital: I don't know where the hospital was, or how they got her there. The girl didn't come back.

I had brought schoolwork with me: I was supposed to be doing work for my A-levels. I remember sitting at a table somewhere in the house and trying to study. One girl did workouts from a VHS tape. There was a room with a sewing machine; the sound of the sewing machine whirring. And we made beaded jewelry—once, or many times, I can't remember. We might have been on a patio, or in some open sort of room. On the table, the beads were in plastic packets, and we had to open the packets and empty the different colored beads into bowls, and the girls sat around the table threading beads in patterns onto fine nylon thread, like a fishing wire.

Sometimes children came to the house, and we played clapping games with them, and ran races with them on the grass. And newspapers arrived—not daily, but just from time to time—in big stacks, pressed into cardboard boxes or paper bags. Several times, I was given the job of packing these newspapers away, into the bottom of a cupboard in the nuns' office, or, when that was full, into an unused bathtub in the bathroom downstairs, the same one where I had gotten changed in the dark on my first morning at the house. I barely looked at the papers: they were all in Spanish, and, in any case, whatever politics or events they talked about seemed to bear no relevance to me, or, in fact, to any of us in the house.

I had never been near a woman in labor before. Whenever it happened, the rest of the girls gathered in one of the bedrooms upstairs—to stay out of the way, or just to be together, I'm not sure. That screaming: it was like listening to someone trapped in a fire. At first we tried to play cards together, but then girls lay on their beds with their pillows over their heads, or prayed, or paced around the room.

The first time, I remember the feeling of relief when the girl downstairs finally went quiet. And then the surprise at hearing the new voice, the baby's sudden wail. One of the girls in the bedroom closed her eyes and clasped her hands. We went downstairs, quietly, huddling together as we walked.

In the room where it had happened, the girl on the bed was covered with a sheet up to her chin. She looked like a corpse. One Hermana was bundling up some dirty sheets. Another woman I didn't know was on her hands and knees, wiping the floor with wads of newspaper. Another Hermana was holding the baby in her arms. It was a real baby: you could see movements from within the bundle of blankets. The nun smiled and touched her forefinger to the baby's cheek. The girl just lay on the bed, under her sheet. She was so still that I thought that she might actually be dead. Her head turned very slightly on the pillow, and her eyes followed where the baby moved.

When my turn came, the pain was worse than I imagined. I don't know who was there; I don't know if they gave me anything for the pain. At a certain point, after it was over, I became aware of a rasping sound, like the sound of a saw being pushed back and forth: it was a shock to realize the sound came from me, that it was the sound of my own breath. On the bed, and on the newspaper laid over the floor, there were huge splashes of deep dark red, and footprints made with the same dark red, as if someone had been careless with a can of paint. It was hard to believe that I had been at the center of all this. Not far away, a Hermana was wiping the baby with a towel. The baby was purple-gray-colored, in blotches; wet, smeared in blood and what looked like whitish wax. The legs were folded at the knee, and the folded knees pressed right up against the belly so that they made a dent. The feet were curved, like birds' feet might be. The fists were loosely clenched, but the fingers moved.

As for myself, all I remember is a sense of shock—that I was still alive, when death had seemed so close. And a bigger, deeper shock too—the same one that many women feel after giving birth for the first time, I think: that sudden dawning of understanding.

The night after the baby was born, I stayed in a different room upstairs on my own. The other girls brought me food, and mugs of hot sweet tea. Downstairs, the baby cried all night. I knew that another lady would come in a car, sometime soon, and take the baby away: I'd seen the lady several times by then—a nice-looking lady, well dressed, efficient, organized. She came with a helper, and in the trunk of her car she had things like boxes of diapers and baby clothes and tins of Klim—all the things you needed for a baby.

When one of the Hermanas came to get me the next morning, I was dressed and ready, waiting to be told what to do. A car was outside the gate, its engine running. The Hermana hugged me and said to go quickly, not to keep the driver waiting. She looked exhausted, with dark bags under her eyes. I remember thinking that with her hair uncovered, she looked just like an ordinary woman.

I set off down the stairs and down the drive, walking slowly. I still looked pregnant, my stomach still bloated and round from where the baby had just been. In fact, when the driver saw me, he switched off the engine and he went inside the house to find the Hermana, to make sure he was taking the right girl. I stood by the car to wait. It must have been early. The morning was fresh and cool, the dew not yet burnt away, and full of birdsong. The house was quiet. The little dog waited with me by the gate, wagging her tail gently. The man came back, hurrying down the drive, and gave me a thumbs-up. Quickly, he got into the front seat and started the car. We had better go, he said; we had to catch the tide, and it was a long drive.

I started getting into the passenger seat in the back, but I hesitated, the car door open, one foot still on the ground. Many times have I returned to this moment in my memory. I was still so close to the baby then: I was only just outside the gate of the house, a matter of forty or fifty yards. The man looked over his shoulder and smiled a reassuring smile, saying in Spanish that it was okay, that I would be safe; that he was going to take me to the coast as the nuns had instructed him; that I had nothing to fear. I mumbled something in response. With one hand, I grasped the back of the passenger seat in front, the warm plastic sliding under my sweating fingers. Doubtfully, I pulled my other leg in, so both feet were in the footwell. My hand reached out for the door, and pulled it shut. I pulled myself forward as if to speak to the driver, but I didn't know what to say. He put the car in gear and we moved off. I looked over my shoulder, through the window. No one was in the front yard, or on the upstairs gallery. Only the little brown dog who had followed me down the driveway was there, and she wasn't even waiting at the gate, but already walking back to the house, calmly, as if nothing important had happened.

When I finally got back home—all the way home: up the southern main road, past the oil fields, past the airport, through Port of Spain, and up to our house at the top of the hill—I remember that when I got out of the car—daytime, in the full glare of the afternoon sun—our dogs didn't recognize me. They barked as if I were an intruder: my mother and father had to push them back. Possibly my father took the dogs around to the back to tie them up, or he put them in the maid's room, which was just there off the carport. At some point, my mother and I were alone, there in the shade of the carport at the front of the house, and my mother put her arms tightly around me. I stood with my arms at my sides. She held me by the shoulders and gazed into my eyes, as if she thought that, by looking deeply into my eyes, she could see for herself what had happened. She shook me a little, holding me by the shoulders. I stared back at her, mute. Her eyes narrowed. She was saying, without words: Oh, so you're not going to talk to me, is that it? Is that how it's going to be?

And then she tried a different tactic: she loosened her grip and she said, in a soft voice, woman to woman, "How was it? It was bad?" And then I spoke, my first words since returning. I said, "Well, it's done now. That's the main thing, isn't it?" I remember that I spoke harshly, that I was full of bitterness. And my mother, her eyes narrowing further, hearing my tone, said, "Yes. It is. And you're lucky that you have parents who will do so much for you, make all these arrangements, and shell out money, and take you back. Eh? You feeling wrong-and-strong now, but over time, you will think about what you've done, and you will see that we were right." And I stared at her without responding, and eventually said, with restrained sarcasm, "Can I go now?" My mother stepped aside and I went slowly up the steps, the concrete steps that led from the carport up to the front door of the house. I was aware of her eyes inspecting my body as I went. I must have looked a fright. There must have been blood all over me: it was probably the smell of blood that had most terrified and confused the dogs. My stomach was still rounded from where the baby had been. My whole body was fatter, more flabby. My hair had grown; it would have been ragged, windswept, caked with sea grime. And whatever clothes I was wearing must have been darkened and salt-stained with seawater, from when I had gotten out of the boat and clambered through the waves up to the shore.

3

THE ACCOUNT I'VE JUST GIVEN—OF HOW I TRAVELED TO VENEZUela and stayed in a house with nuns and had a baby when I was sixteen—is a story I've never told to anyone before, at least not in the way I just did, recounting almost the entirety of what I remember. On the rare occasion when I have spoken about it, I've done so only in fragments: reluctant confessions uttered in a single breath and followed by an embarrassed silence. I had a baby when I was sixteen. I went to Venezuela. The baby was given up for adoption. She was a girl. I kept it a secret. For the last forty-odd years, the story has existed only in these disconnected pieces. It's only now, at this relatively late stage of my life, that I'm trying to properly put all these fragments together.

ON THE INTERNET FORUMS, I go by the username Dawn_in_London, or I use my married name, Dawn Wilson. But my real name is Bishop. If you've ever been to Trinidad, you'd know our name, from Bishop's Fruit Juices. It's a well-known brand. It was the first company my family owned, started up by my grandfather in the 1950s and still going strong today. I'm Dawn Bishop. Kenneth Bishop is my father; his older brother, Lloyd, is my uncle.

My uncle Lloyd lived down in the south of the island, as I've already said, but we lived near the capital, Port of Spain. I lived with my parents and two brothers in a house at the top of a hill, just off the north coast road. For nearly all the time that I was growing up, we had the whole hill to ourselves. In fact, it was my father who cut the road through the forest and built the house. He had these things done, I mean: he paid for them to be done. He bought the land from the government, and, over a period of months, heavy machinery rumbled up the hill—bulldozers and yellow caterpillar machines that tore down trees and dug out big clumps of red earth. Trucks came with ton-loads of gravel: I still remember the roar of that gravel being poured out, and how the surface of the big gray conical heap was like a mountain after rain; how tributaries formed along its sides as little stones slithered down; how whole sections of flanks broke and shifted; how dust floated above it and settled in the leaves of the trees. In the paths cut between the trees, men in black boots raked asphalt in black clumps; then they stood back, leaning on their rakes as the steamroller rumbled slowly past. They only cut down the smaller trees, the ones needed to clear space for the road: the mango trees, lime trees, portugals, breadfruit, pomme cythère. My parents told the men to leave the big saman trees where they were, and most of the flamboyants, and the two teak trees down at the bottom of the hill, by the golf course. And the silk-cotton tree: we wouldn't have cut it down anyway, but with their country-bookie superstition, the laborers wouldn't even go near it.

In any case, the house was in a nice spot. The view from the patio out back was of the surrounding hills, green and lush in the rainy season, and misty with low cloud, but it was the privacy my father liked, rather than the view. In the evenings, he liked to sit out on the patio with my uncle discussing company business, and to be able to talk without the risk of anyone overhearing. Some weekends, all my father's extended family would come up to Port of Spain from San Fernando, the town in south Trinidad where they lived. Then, other chairs would be found and dragged out to the patio, white plastic chairs, iron folding chairs, velvet-padded mahogany dining chairs, to add to the bamboo set that was already there. The grown-ups would settle themselves into a loose circle, and they'd be out on the patio talking and laughing late into the night. I would be among the little horde of children who roamed up and down the slope of the garden, or in and out of the house.

Those were the oil boom years—the 1970s and 1980s. Anyone familiar with the region will remember those glory days, or will have heard them spoken of. Money flowed like water, back in those days. They were the days of oil being thirty-five dollars a barrel, and in Trinidad, offshore rigs started popping up all along every coast: north, south, east, and west. They were the days of the new Bee-Wee jumbo jets, and weekly flights to Miami, New York, Toronto, and London. The days of the old waving gallery at Piarco Airport, where people came from all over the island on a Sunday afternoon, just for the thrill of seeing the big planes take off and land. It was the era of Peter Minshall—his "River" band, the legendary Mancrab and Washerwoman. Carnival, never a small affair, became bigger, grander:

Sparrow renamed himself The Mighty Sparrow; Kitchener became Lord Kitchener. The West Indies cricket team ruled the world; in downtown Port of Spain, men walked like kings.

It was during those decades, those oil boom years, that the Bishops' businesses really took off. It wasn't just that people had money in their pockets: what really made the difference to us was the availability of labor. The biggest problem for any business owner, my father and uncle said, those evenings out on the patio, was labor—finding people willing to get off their backsides and work. But during the oil boom, labor flowed in to Trinidad from all around the region. From all the little islands—Grenada, St. Lucia, Barbados, St. Kitts, St. Vincent; and even from big places: Jamaica, Guyana, Venezuela. Before, we used to have one car that my mother and father shared; now, new cars appeared in our driveway: a brand-new silver Nissan Royal saloon for my father, and a new white Toyota Corolla for my mother. On the patio, there was much discussion of buying a yacht, or a time-share in Florida, or of importing racehorses from Barbados.

But they were idle discussions: even I, the youngest, listening from the wings, could tell the grown-ups weren't serious about those things. When would they have time to go to Florida? "And what're you going to do there?" they said to each other. (Several people would speak at once, so it was impossible to say who exactly was saying what.) Play golf? But look the golf course right there! You could go down the hill right there, and look, you could play golf! And as for getting a yacht? Why for? To see the sea? But they could already drive twenty minutes, and look Maracas Bay right there. Right there! What's the point in buying a big yacht, just to show everybody how you richer than them? They didn't have time for golf, or to look after a boat, they agreed. When you own a business? It's only work, work, work. Work, work, work: all your time goes into the business, to make it grow.

OUR FAMILY DIDN'T START OFF wealthy, by the way, whatever people might like to say about us these days. And, yes, we look mostly fair-skinned, but it's rare for Trinidadians to be 100 percent of any one race, and our family is no different. My grandfather Frankie Bishop, who started the fruit business in the 1950s: he's the only one in our family who could confidently be said to be white-white, the son of a Portuguese mother and an Irish father, both immigrants to Trinidad in the late 1800s. But Frankie's wife, my grandmother on my father's side, was from Guyana—in photos, you can see she's mixed, white with something: actually she was part Amerindian, or what they would call "indígena" on the mainland. On my mother's side, we know about Spanish, French, and East Indian: who knows what else there is. In our family, we carry a range of skin tones. My middle brother, Ryan, has very pale skin and hazel eyes, and is prone to sunburn. I have quite fair skin, but I have dark hair and eyes; I have a few freckles, and my skin tans easily. My older brother, Warren, is the darkest of the three of us: when he goes abroad, people usually take him for South American, and they try to speak to him in Spanish.

So although we're more or less classed as white in Trinidad, we're just ordinary Trinidadians like everyone else. And society isn't segregated or anything—it's true that there are a couple of neighborhoods that are predominantly white, but there are also places around Trinidad and Tobago that are known for being mostly Indian, say, or mostly black. Everyone mixes up together, mostly quite comfortably—there's Chinese and Syrian too, in our rather weird and wonderful mix of cultures. Everyone is welcome at the various religious festivals, for example, whether Christmas, Diwali, Eid, anything: in Trinidad, wherever there's food, people will happily join any celebration.

Of course, it's not all peace and harmony; there's friction too, undeniably. But the point I want to make is that the Bishops were never colonial landowners or anything like that. My grandfather bought a few acres of land from the government and he planted citrus trees—oranges, limes, grapefruits, portugals, shaddock. It was just him and his wife, in the early days, and they picked the fruit themselves and squeezed and bottled it. When they had children, the children helped, and gradually they went into other fruit: mango, guava, soursop, coconut. It took decades, generations, for the business to expand into all the other areas that the Bishops are now known for: tinned fruit, bottled water; then transport, and construction, general import/export.

We weren't unique in being successful in business, by the way. Many other families in Trinidad have done the same—started businesses and worked hard and done well—not only white people. As far as the Bishops are concerned, what my grandfather Frankie always said, and what my father and uncle said after Frankie died, and what my brother Warren says now, is this: anyone in Trinidad who was willing to work hard could have bought a patch of land and planted some trees, as Frankie did. Anyone who wanted to could have made a living out of what was already growing on this island. You only have to take one look at this place, as Frankie said, to see fruit on every tree, fruit littered all over the ground.

FRUIT! IN OUR HOUSEHOLD, WHEN we were growing up in Trinidad, one thing we always had plenty of, was fruit. The fruit farm was down south, close to my uncle's house, about an hour and a half's drive from where we lived, but of course my father was up and down the southern main road nearly every day, and the farm laborers came up to Port of Spain often too, for one thing or another, and they always threw a few sacks of fruit into the pickup truck with them.

They'd arrive at the top of the hill, and they'd turn the truck around just outside the gate, and then honk the horn. Actually, there was never any need to honk, since the dogs would already be at the gate barking like mad. My bedroom was directly over the carport, and looked out toward the front of the house: from my window, I could see the road that led down the hill. When the workmen came, I tended to stay inside and watch the scene from my window. My brothers would be busy getting control of the dogs, and when it was safe, one of the farm laborers would get out of the truck, unload a sack from the tray at the back, hoist it over one shoulder like a bank robber with a sack of money, and, when directed by my mother, pass through the gate to bring it in. Depending on which laborer it was, the sack was either left in the carport, or brought around the back to the patio, and then placed just inside the glass sliding door to the kitchen.

The whole transaction required only a few minutes, a little more if the men were there to collect their pay, but it always felt tense to me. The driver of the pickup truck usually left the engine running while the sack was being carried inside the house, and while they were waiting, the three or four fellas lounging in the tray at the back always studied the house, and nudged each other and laughed in low voices. Sometimes, for fun, they threw stones at the gate, or barked at the dogs. Even after the men had waved goodbye and driven away down the hill again, it took the dogs a long time to settle down: they kept running up and down the driveway, sniffing the path the man had taken with the sack; all around the garden, sniffing and searching, always returning to the gate and looking down the road, their ears pricked up, hackles raised, as if expecting the men to return.

After the men left, I would come out to inspect what had been delivered: portugals, most often, but also mango, plum, sorrel, five-finger, pomerac, chenet. The sack of fruit was usually in this spot that I've mentioned, on the threshold between the kitchen and the patio outside, where people could easily just dip a hand into the sack to take a fruit whenever they felt like it. As they walked from the kitchen out to the patio, usually, they would already be tearing the peel off with their fingers, or biting into the soft flesh of the fruit. There was a bucket on the patio by the black wrought-iron railings at the far end, for the seeds and peelings and whatever else had gone uneaten, and, from time to time, one of us, or sometimes the maid or the gardener, would carry the bucket down the slope to the bottom of the garden, and throw the contents over to the empty land on the other side of the fence.

But I was talking about those conversations that the adults used to have out on the patio in the evenings, and how they had no time for time-shares in Florida, or boats to sail on the weekend. In the end, the only luxury they bought during those oil boom years was a bit of land in Tobago, and they built a beach house there for all the family to use. We went there during holidays and long weekends, and sometimes on a whim, whenever the grown-ups started complaining about how running a business in Trinidad would give them all heart attacks. When we were over there, the grown-ups still talked about the business late into the night, but during the day, they swam in the sea, or they cooked fish on the grill, or they worked on the house, building and extending and repairing. It was just a simple house in the early days, built out of roughly laid concrete and bricks—there was no electricity or anything like that: we had to carry candles from room to room in the evenings. But I loved Tobago. We all loved it. As children, we spent our days on the beach: there was a little cove a couple of minutes' walk along a sandy path through the palm trees, or you could take the short cut, by climbing down the rocks.

Over the years, of course, the house has been modernized: now it has air-conditioning and a proper kitchen, a pool, everything, and it has enough space to sleep eighteen people comfortably. My own children have been there many times. For me, Tobago still feels like paradise. Even now, all these years later, whenever I'm facing any worry or stress in my life, or someone close to me is facing worry or stress, it's always Tobago I think of. I still remember all those days on the beach: in the waves, and then on the sand; and then back in the water again and then back on the sand, hour after hour, day after day. It was a perfect childhood. Whatever else has happened since, I still feel lucky to have had those days.

4

I'M FIFTY-EIGHT NOW. I LIVE IN ENGLAND: I'VE LIVED HERE FOR most of my life. After I had the baby in Venezuela, I went to a boarding school in Kent for two years for my A-levels, and then to Scotland for medical school. I met someone there: Robert, English, also a doctor. We married, moved to London, bought a house, had children. I made a life for myself, in other words. By any objective measure, it was a good life.

I have two sons. Finlay, thirty, also a doctor, lives nearby, in south London. My younger one is Oscar, now twenty-eight—he went to the U.S. for his PhD, and he's doing a postdoc. My husband and I separated a few years before the pandemic, although it took a while for the divorce to be finalized. I'm back in London now, living alone for the first time, and working an office job. I have a scattering of health complaints, normal for my age—nothing too terrible yet, by the grace of God, and my only medication is an occasional sedative to help me get to sleep. I lost a lot of weight after the divorce, just from stress, I suppose. Before, I'd always been a little heavy around the hips, but now I'm quite thin—possibly a bit too thin. And I wear my hair short now, since it makes it easier to dye. If I didn't color it every four weeks in "Iced chestnut brown number 4," it'd be completely gray.

I BOUGHT MY SMALL THREE-BED terraced house with money from the divorce. My new neighborhood is a little shabbier than my previous one: I don't know if there's any point in mentioning names. Put it this way: when I was married, I used to live in a place where everyone had Audis and Range Rovers, and front lawns that were mown in those faint stripes, like you see on Wimbledon tennis courts. And the street itself was beautiful: two rows of handsome, redbrick houses, shaded by old beech trees. I miss those beech trees! For all the years we lived in that house, each autumn, I stood the boys outside our gate for a photo, every time in the same place, the reds and golds of the beech trees behind them, and the sunlight turning their hair gold.

I still have all those photos. The first is in 1999, when we bought the house, and Finlay was seven, Oscar, five. In that photo, they're both smiling, gap-toothed and delighted, Oscar tiny and knock-kneed, looking up admiringly at Finlay; Finlay looking at the camera, but with his arm around his little brother. In later photos, as they get to secondary school, the smiles look a bit rigid. Finlay, at thirteen, several inches taller than his brother, looks smug in his new secondary school tie and blazer. Two years later, Oscar has caught up with him in height, and the two of them have a new wariness about them, as if at any moment they might turn and wrestle each other to the ground. The year after that, Oscar's the one looking smug—taller, filled out, and on all the sports teams—and Finlay's looking sullen.

The autumn after that, I couldn't get the two of them out at the same time, so I got them individually. In Oscar's photo, he's in his red football sweatshirt: a handsome fifteen-year-old, with a lovely blond head of hair, my father's dark eyebrows, and the broad shoulders that all the Bishop men have, and my husband's (ex-husband's) six-foot height. He stands with his hands in his pockets, smiling confidently, knowing exactly how the photo will look, and how it will be treasured, and surely feeling that he deserves no less. Finlay, in his photo, looks happy enough, though thinner and more serious than Oscar, and as if he's already burdened by responsibility, even though he was only seventeen that year. Those were the last pictures of them I got in that particular spot. My husband and I were going through a rough patch, and photos were the last thing on anyone's mind.

I may as well just say the names of the neighborhoods. The previous house, on the street with the beech trees, was in a place called Wandsworth, in south London. The new house is a few tube stops away, a little farther east, in Brockley.

The style is what they call "terraced" in England: it means the type of houses that are joined at the sides, so that you have to go through the house to get to the garden at the back. Terraced houses here all have pretty much the same layout, and my new house in Brockley is no different: you come through the front door and into a narrow hallway; ahead of you is a narrow flight of stairs; to the right is a doorway to a sort of small sitting room that's called the "front room." If you stay on the ground floor and go along the narrow corridor past the stairs, you get to a nice open-plan room at the back, which is kitchen, dining room, and living room all in one, and which has a door out to my small garden. The bedrooms are all upstairs, and the bathroom.

The boys helped me paint the new house when I first moved in—that was during the summer of 2018, before Oscar headed off to the U.S. to start his PhD. I've been here nearly four years now, but some of that time has been blotted out by the pandemic, and I still haven't got it quite sorted out yet. It feels a bit cramped in here, to be honest, with all the furniture I brought from the Wandsworth house. Finlay and Oscar said I should go ahead and get rid of all our old stuff—start over, clean slate, etc.—but I'm not in any rush to clear these things out. I think it's nice for the boys to be able to sit or lounge around on the same sofas from our old den in Wandsworth, and to have their Christmas dinner at the same table as always, and to be able to sleep in bedrooms that feel a little familiar, with their old science projects and posters in boxes on the shelves, and their school jumpers in the wardrobes. To have a home to come back to. But of course, they're still young, they think these things don't matter—they don't fully understand yet what they've lost.

My new neighborhood isn't so bad. The street is all terraced houses, each with a very small front yard, just big enough for the rubbish bins that the council gives each of us, really. I have a few flowerpots out front, planted with red and pink geraniums. In my previous life, my ex-husband did the gardening and he had something much more delicate planted in the front garden—slightly odd-looking blue flowers that grew on long, thin stalks, I can't remember what they were called. But I'm only a beginner, so I have to start with something easy. I've been advised that geraniums are very hardy.

On this street the houses are all painted different colors, which sounds like it should be cheerful, but somehow it's not. We do have some small silver birches planted here and there along the pavements, but they're young yet, and mostly what I see when I step outside my front door are the rubbish bins. The local council gives each household three or four huge plastic bins in different colors—blue, brown, black, green, for different things—and because the houses are all squeezed so closely together, and no one has much of a front garden, when I step outside my front door to the street, it's mostly these rubbish bins that catch the eye.

But my neighbors are perfectly nice. In the house to my left, actually, is an elderly lady from Guyana. We spoke very briefly, once, when she gave me a parcel she'd taken in from the postman for me. I said, "Guyana! I'm from Trinidad!" Her eyes lit up, and I wondered if we were going to be friends, but in the two years since then, I've hardly seen her come out of her house.

In the house to my right is a fellow who's maybe late thirties, single, professional, though I'm not sure what job he does. He has a dog, a gentle Staffordshire bull terrier called Millie, who spends most days alone in the back garden: I pat her over the fence sometimes. The next house down is a Polish family. The dad must be in the building trade, with a big white van parked outside their house; the mother has long white-blond hair (bleached), and skintight clothes and nail extensions. Farther along is an older Jamaican man who's often outside in his slippers, going over his car with a chamois. (He's a good guy, Jamaican from Jamaica. He calls me "the white lady" or "the white Trini lady." Caribbean people are very matter-of-fact about race: there's none of the British anxiety about naming skin colors.) And across the street is another old man, Greek Cypriot, who comes out several times a day to walk his dog, an old German shepherd with weakened hind legs. We all say hello to each other when we see one another on the street, and we talk about things like rubbish collection and parking.

I am glad, of course, to have my independence again, now that the kids are all grown-up, but there's an element of empty-nest syndrome too. I guess it's good there's a name for how we feel when the kids grow up and leave home; but on the other hand, it feels a bit trivializing. There's an implication that you should be able to revert to the person you were twenty or twenty-five years previously, and carry on from there. It's really not like that. Raising children, it's like, say you have two glasses of milk? And you pour the milk from one glass into the other one. Then one glass is empty and the other is full. That's the transaction. The children feed off the parents: as they grow, the parents diminish. When they leave, it's almost like they take some of you with them. And you still know where they are and what they're doing and how they feel, almost as if you had a telepathic connection.

Take today, for example. It's Friday, quarter to ten in the morning, the end of October. I have the day off, and I'm here in the big Tesco in south London. A part of me is thinking about things like, whether to use this cheaper brand of canned coconut milk, or whether there's time to go to the Brixton market for something better; whether to get a tub of chocolates for trick-or-treaters. Thoughts of possibly carving a pumpkin; maybe making soup with the pumpkin flesh; freezing batches of soup—Do I still have my old Tupperware?—and so on. And as I sort of amble along, all those thoughts bump along together with thoughts of the kids: where they are right now, what they're doing, what's at stake for them; what I can do to help them, or not do.

Finlay's at the hospital right now—only about a mile away from where I am now. I never worked at that hospital myself, but my ex-husband did, so I know it well. Finlay's in the north wing, on the side facing the park, probably on the fourth floor, which gets good natural light. He'll be in oncology today. He likes oncology: it's well funded in the NHS, not like obstetrics or pediatrics. They have plenty of imaging—staff and machines—and fast test turnarounds. Now, coming up to ten o'clock, he'll be with the surgical team in front of a whiteboard in the ops room, discussing bowels, livers, brains; clamps, pumps, masks, CO_2 monitors. He'll be pushing to get the complex cases, because that's what you have to do as a trainee: get a broad range of surgeries and cases under your belt. And it's important for him especially now: he had a patient die in surgery last year, and then the family lodged an official complaint. His confidence is a bit shaken. He needs to keep operating, and keep having successes, to build himself back up.

I qualified in medicine too, back in the day, but I couldn't have done surgery. All the cutting into live tissue, the stress when a patient dies, and when a complaint comes in, and then an investigation. I worry about Finlay. And he's single. Single, at thirty years old! In my time, you'd never find a thirty-year-old man in surgical training being single, but maybe times have changed, or maybe it's something about the way England works that's gone over my head. Or maybe it's just him: I wonder sometimes whether he thinks that relationships just aren't worth it, families aren't worth it. I carry on long conversations in my head, trying to persuade him to get his act together, get a move on. Other times I think: Dawn, give it up, it's too late, it's out of your hands. But it's hard to let these things go.

As for my other son, Oscar—the one in Pennsylvania, doing the postdoc—he does have a girlfriend at the moment, but then that's Oscar. Oscar was never as academic as Finlay, but he was better at sports, and he's more easygoing generally, less wrought-up. Oscar thought nothing of going over to the U.S. for his PhD, without knowing anyone, or knowing where he would live—a person like that is bound to have an easier time in life. But even though he's so far away, and I do miss him, it's been easier to let him go. He and I were best friends when he was small, and the natural separation between us came when he was a teenager: that was when I mourned the loss of our closeness, really. After that, it was easier.

Oscar calls now and again on WhatsApp or Skype, but I don't hound him if I haven't heard. He sends me photos. He takes a little snap of his street, early in the morning when he's setting out for his run, or, you know, his lunchtime sandwich from the deli, that sort of thing. I send one-liners back to him in reply. I say "Wow!" or "Lovely!" or just send an emoji of a smiley face. I get glimpses of his life from these photos: the trip to Cape Cod with the group from his lab, the Halloween party at a friend's house, the Fourth of July biology department barbecue. And I've seen a lot of photos of his desk in the lab. It looks like an ordinary desk: two big screens covered with graphs and data, and empty coffee cups and paper napkins with the logo of the coffee shop they all go to; and sometimes there are his lab things, Styrofoam trays filled with a grid of tiny vials, and scattered pages of printouts of papers, the papers marked up with yellow highlighter pen. Behind the computer screens there's the corner of a window, and the leaves of the maple tree outside.

This past winter, he sent me a photo of a snowman in the backyard of the place he's renting with his girlfriend. The photo is taken from inside the house, through what must be their kitchen window. There's the edge of a red-and-white-checked curtain, and the little green leaves of their herb plants growing in pots on the windowsill. I feel I can imagine the scene when the photo was taken, the two of them come in from having built the snowman, laughing, cheeks flushed from the cold, brushing snow from each other's shoulders and hair. I imagine how they might have stood with their arms around each other as they looked out the window at the falling snow. I do miss Oscar; I won't pretend I don't. But it's also true that the thought of him living this life, what I imagine to be a blissful, peaceful life, with joy and fulfillment ahead, brings me a deep sense of peace, like watering a plant for twenty years and then seeing a flower bloom.

I think about the girl I had in Venezuela, as well. "Think" isn't exactly the right word; it's not exactly thinking that I do. She just drifts in and out of my thoughts, the way that a breeze might pass through a room. Driving back from Tesco, just now, for example, after I finished my shopping. While I was waiting at a traffic light, I saw a girl and her mother walking along the pavement just along that stretch opposite the playground. It looked like maybe they had been to an appointment, and the mother was walking the girl back to school. The girl was in her PE uniform, navy blue jogging trousers and a white T-shirt, a messy blond ponytail hanging down her back. She might have been around eleven or twelve, her hips just slightly rounded, just at the beginning of all that was to come, but still young enough to want to hold her mother's hand. As I watched, they gently swung their joined hands back and forth between them, and leaned in to each other and pressed their shoulders together. While I waited for the light to turn, my hands resting on the steering wheel, I watched her shape, her movements; and as I watched, I fitted them, I suppose, to the child I imagined.

But my own daughter would be much older than this child I saw earlier, of course: she would be coming up to forty-two. And her hair will be dark, like mine. All the women in our family have dark hair. It might be curly, or just slightly wavy: probably not dead straight. Good cheekbones, good eyelashes. And she'll have our waist and hips. All the women in my family have the same: the narrow waist, wide hips, big thighs. Me, my mother, my mother's mother, my aunts: she's bound to have our same body.

Over the years, I've come across a few photos in magazines and newspapers that I've cut out and kept, because they look the way I imagine her to look. I have them in different ages. One is a lovely young woman in her twenties, with beautiful long hair—curly, loose, dark, parted on the side. Perfect skin—fair skin, a little fairer than mine. Shaped eyebrows; no makeup. She looks like she's on her way somewhere—you can just see the straps of a handbag on her shoulder. A natural photo, not staged, an expression of well-being, ease, gentleness.

And I have another one of a girl of about six years old. The girl is seen only from behind, sitting on an outdoor swing. Dark hair, again, and tied in a ponytail, the curls unruly. Dressed in a T-shirt and some sort of jersey trousers. You can't see that much, really, from behind, except that she seems cheerful. I cut out the photo because it was from an article about orphanages in South America—Colombia, Venezuela, Brazil. But of course, I don't even know if she's still in Venezuela, or if she might have been adopted by someone in a different country. I don't know anything at all about how her life has turned out.

THERE'S NOTHING MORE TO TELL of that little anecdote from earlier today, by the way. I didn't follow the mother and daughter, or try to speak to them. When the light turned green, I drove the rest of the way home, and parked my car on my street. But as I set my shopping bags down on my front step, and rummaged in my bag for my keys, I thought that my daughter, too, might be standing in front of her front door at this very moment, wherever she is in the world, rummaging in her bag for her keys: she might also be pushing open a door, and stepping inside the place where she lives. As I passed through the dark corridor to the kitchen at the back of the house—thinking about what I would cook later, and which rooms I would tackle first, and how I would set the table for my friend who was coming to dinner later—the thought of her walked with me.

I like to imagine her still in Venezuela. At forty-two, she might have her own children; she might come home around this time every morning, after dropping her children to school. She might be carrying grocery bags now, just as I was, with heavy shopping bumping against her knees, plastic bag handles cutting into her hands. As I moved around my own kitchen, putting away parsley, onions, milk, I felt almost as if she were in the room with me. I'm dreaming, I guess. And yet the scene is so clear in my imagination. A friend has come with her; the friend now is pulling up a chair, chattering gaily in Spanish. She wets a cloth at the sink, wipes her kitchen table clean. Her movements are brisk, practiced. Breeze comes through the open windows; outside, in the forest, brightly colored birds warble and trill in the tall trees. The friend has to raise her voice to make herself heard above the forest cacophony. The women share food, talk, laugh.

BUT, TO RETURN TO MY own life. It was a Friday, as I've said, and I had the day off from work: a day for life-admin, as it's called these days. My groceries, my cooking and cleaning. And I was getting the place ready for a friend who was coming over to dinner later. I got out the nice tablecloth and napkins and put them on the ironing board. I squeezed limes for my lime cheesecake, and I measured out ingredients to make biscuits for the crust. (I make my own biscuits; the digestives here are too bland.) As I was doing that, I was also keeping my eye on the clock, because I wanted to call my brother Warren in Trinidad. For the last few weeks, I'd been turning over the idea in my mind of taking Finlay to Tobago for a few days of sunshine, to help him relax. I wanted to speak to Warren, to check that the beach house would be free. Warren isn't the kind of person to do emails or text messages. He's busy-busy: a now-for-now kind of person. The best time to catch him is first thing in the morning, just after he's left Port of Spain to head down south, when he can talk on Bluetooth in the car.

By the time I got the crust made, and the cheesecake into the fridge, it was twenty past midday—twenty past seven in the morning in Trinidad, the tail end of when I might catch Warren. I wiped my hands on the cloth and dialed the number.

"Aye," he said, when he answered. He sounded relaxed.

"Hey," I said. "You're in the car?"

"I'm just reaching San Fernando now," he said. "What's happening? Everything okay?"

"Yes, fine, fine," I said. "Everything okay."

"Tell me," he said. (That's Warren for you.) "What's up? You need something?"

"No no, I don't need anything," I said. "It's just . . ." I knew I may as well just come out with it. Once Warren reaches work, he wants to just get out of the car and go. Our father was exactly the same. "I'm thinking of bringing Finlay down," I said. "Just to Tobago, the beach house. Let him take some sun."

"Coming down? Great, man! Long time we haven't seen you all. Tell Oscar to come too. When?"

"I don't know yet," I said. "But it would only be me and Finlay. If we even come. He says he can't get the time off, but I'm trying to persuade him. You know, after all the stress. First the pandemic, and now he has work things going on. It would be nice for him to take a break. But I wanted to run it by you."

"Dawn!" he said. I heard the sound of the car door slamming, and then another person's voice, one of the workers trying to talk to him. I waited.

"Dawn!" he said again, when he came back. "You don't have to call me and ask me these things, you know. Just come! Get on the plane and come! What, you need help with the plane ticket?"

"No, no," I protested about the plane ticket. "Well, I haven't looked at flights yet. I don't know what they'll be like."

I don't know if Warren heard. It sounded like he was talking to the other person again.

"Sorry," he said when he came back. "Sorry, look, I better go. I'm at the office now. But call Mummy. Tell them your dates, and her and Suzanne will fix up. Anytime is good. You don't have to ask these things, you know. You could just show up."

After we hung up, I sat there with my phone. It was too early to call my mother or Warren's wife, Suzanne, and in any case, I didn't have concrete dates to ask about. But while I was leaning on the kitchen counter, scrolling through some of my old WhatsApp messages, my phone pinged with a message from my mother.

"Come anytime," she wrote. "Just tell me the dates and we'll get the tickets."

Another message arrived: a photo of the sunrise, taken from the front of our house.

I wrote a message back. "Thanks. I don't know if we can come yet. Just wanted to check beach house was free."

She wrote: "Hope you can. If Finlay can't get time off, why don't you come alone?"

I didn't know what to reply. I wasn't going to come alone. While I was sitting there thinking, another message appeared: "Can u talk?"

I wrote back: "Can't talk now. Cooking."

I did have a lot to do. I still had to finish getting ready for my friend Niall who was coming over later, and I was planning to do a big batch of stew chicken and rice for Finlay, to portion up for him to freeze. I wanted to get that done and cooled down, and out of the way before I started cooking for Niall.

Since living in England, I've learned a few dishes from cookbooks, and I have a few reliable basics that I used to make when we had people around for dinner when I was married. A nice beef stew, or a nice chicken-and-apricot tagine, or a seafood linguini, that kind of thing—not especially impressive, but the sort of food that satisfies everyone. I'm not very good with desserts, though. For Finlay's and Oscar's birthdays, when they were growing up, I used to make chocolate cakes from a Betty Crocker mix—reliable cakes, and very easy, and everyone liked them.

But cooking Trinidadian food is different. Even just an everyday dish, like what I was doing now for Finlay. It's just a stew. The only thing special about it is how you season it, and then you have to burn brown sugar in oil in the bottom of the saucepan before you put in the chicken. But it feels to me like real cooking—like I know who I am and I know what I'm doing. Which is a strange way to feel, considering that most of my experience of cooking in Trinidad was just watching other women cook when I was a child, sitting on the back step outside the kitchen. Houses don't have a back step here in England, which is a real shame. It's the ideal place for children to sit. You're out of the way of all the hot oil and sharp knives, but you hear all kinds of gossip not meant for children's ears: who's horning who; who's infertile, or impotent; who's been to visit obeah because of too many miscarriages; who's never gotten over a father's early death.

It's quite basic here in my new kitchen: it's what we would call "compact," which means that if you're standing cooking at the stove, you only have to turn to the left and take one step to reach the sink, or turn to the right and take one step to reach the fridge. When anyone comes over—Niall or Finlay, usually—they sit at the dining table while I'm here in the kitchen, and it works fine, quite sociable. Even if they're a little farther away, on the sofa or armchair at the far end of the room, it's still near enough to carry on a conversation.

My mother was more sorry than I was, about my losing the big kitchen we used to have in the Wandsworth house. I remember she came up to visit me in London soon after my husband and I had moved in to that house—this would have been when Finlay and Oscar were seven and five. She was so impressed. She was a working woman, she had always worked in the family businesses, but Trinidad is a very old-fashioned sort of place too, and I know my mother saw me as having married well—as having done well, after my "trouble." She was pleased to see me in command of a large kitchen, with its glossy white cupboard-fronts, the cool marble countertops, the three ovens, the big stove with eight rings.

"Eight rings!" my mother exclaimed, at the time. She hadn't even come properly into the house yet, I remember. I think she was still in her coat, her hair still mussed up from the long flight. Rob, my husband, had taken her suitcase up to her room, and my mother had been walking around the downstairs, pointing and marveling, while Finlay and Oscar watched, delighted. "Eight stove rings! So you could be making stew chicken on one ring, rice boiling on the next one, that one for roti, the next one making callaloo, another one boiled corn . . . and you still have space left over!"

I could already hear, then, what she would tell her friends when she went back to Trinidad: that Dawn was doing so well up in London; that Dawn had a big house, a comfortable house. She would have had difficulty explaining about the garden. She might have said, gardens in England, they don't go around the whole house—they just go behind, long and thin, like a bowling alley. But the kitchen! (I imagine my mother's friends gathered around, everyone leaning in close to better hear all this news from England.) Two sinks! Three ovens! And the stovetop has eight rings! Later on during that same trip, my mother took photos of the kitchen with her camera, so that she could prove it to her friends when she went home.

This isn't to make her sound backward or simple. In Trinidad, we lived comfortably: we had a nice house with electricity and appliances, a maid, a gardener. Not everyone lived like that, mind you; we were town people, and I suppose we were wealthy even by town standards. Back then, there would still have been plenty of country people who managed in the old-fashioned way, with kerosene lamps at night, and outdoor utilities, as they called it, meaning a sort of makeshift toilet, and a place to wash. And my mother would well remember the days when women had to cook over a fire—not a gas fire in a kitchen: a coal fire, in a coal pot, with whatever pieces of iron they could find, crisscrossed over the top of the coal pot to make a grill. And in those days, you would still see women with their skirts hitched up, up to their knees in the river, doing washing. They had to spend hours like that, bent over, the water turning white and frothy around them; and when they straightened up, they moved slowly, one hand pressed against their backs, and hobbled to the bank and sat there in the shade, and rested. Those were the olden days. But even I remember the amazement at the washing machine when it first arrived, when I was about five or six, and that it all worked by pressing buttons. And I remember how my father joked with my brothers that women now would get lazy, and that they would have to find ways to fill their time, now that the machines were going to be doing all their work for them.

My father passed away a couple of years ago, but my mother is still going: she's eighty-seven now, and still living in Trinidad. Small and gray and frail, still going to Santa Cruz green market every Saturday, and early Mass at Assumption RC Church every Sunday. When she was the age I am now, she was already a grandmother. My two older brothers were married with children by then, and my parents' house, the house on the hill, was like their daycare center. My mother used to have toddlers running in and out of the kitchen all day, and babies on rugs or bouncy chairs out on the patio under the shade of the awning. She talks about those days with the greatest fondness. It brought her the greatest joy, she said, to be able to do that: to help her children, and to spend time with her grandchildren, to know them and love them—with none of the worry, she liked to say, and all the joy. But, on reflection, I'm not sure whether that's something that should be talked about. Maybe some things are better left unsaid.

5

I MENTIONED THE INTERNET FORUMS—THEY TEND TO CALL themselves "online communities" nowadays. They have names like "ancestry" or "reunited" or "adoption" in the titles. I'm on at least a dozen of them. Bio mom seeking bio daughter; region Latin America and Caribbean; decade 1980–1990. I've set up a separate Hotmail address, and all the alerts go there so that I don't have to log in to each site individually to check for messages. To be honest, sometimes I forget to check the Hotmail for months. Mostly, it just fills up with spam. An email like the one I read tonight, after Niall left, doesn't arrive very often.

But let me go back a few steps. If it's one thing I'm learning in life, it's that I have to try to pay attention to exactly what happened, so that I can set things down in a way that might make sense.

Niall is Irish, a little older than me, and divorced, although his breakup is more recent than mine. (His name is pronounced "Nile," like the river.) We met earlier this year, at the leasing agency where I work. He came in looking for a place to rent, and I took him around to view properties, and then did his references and contracts for the house he's in now. He's a good-looking guy. He used to be a hockey player at school, and he's still pretty trim, which really isn't that common at our age. A decent amount of hair, still dark on top, graying at the sides, but he keeps it short and fixes it in place with gel, which makes it look thinner than it really is. He made a good living in construction, working all over the world, and he runs his business from the UK now, although he still travels quite a lot. He's actually been to Trinidad once, bidding for a contract—that was one of the things that got us talking when we first met. It's a nice friendship. Nothing heavy. We see each other every couple of weeks, and we just take it as it comes.

This evening when he came over for dinner, the weather was nice enough to sit out, and we had a drink in my garden before we came inside. It's more of a backyard than a garden—only twenty feet long and completely paved over by the previous owner. I have a few potted plants in clusters, and I have a little dark-green wrought-iron table with two chairs, and a garden parasol that I got secondhand from eBay. And I'd set it up nicely for the evening, with a matching tablecloth, and cushions for the chairs. It was as nice as I could make it, despite it being overlooked by the neighbors. At one stage, the Guyanese lady who lives in the house on the left came out in her dressing gown to take her washing down from the line. She didn't say anything to us, but with the gardens so narrow, and just the lowish fence between us, you can't help but feel that you're being observed, or overheard. And the dog in the house on the right-hand side kept whining, and jumping onto the roof of her kennel and scratching at the fence. But we made the best of it. At this stage of life, you're beginning to realize that it's the motto you have to live by.

Niall and I stick to cheerful, easy topics when we meet—what we've watched on TV, funny things we've seen on the internet. We talk about the kids a lot, and the families we grew up in ourselves, and how much we both want grandchildren. We try to avoid talking about our exes, but their names come up nearly every time we meet. Niall calls his ex-wife "herself," and I've taken to calling Rob "himself," and that feels like a way to avoid the issue. Still, it's one hell of a strange thing, to cook dinner for a man who's not Rob, and to share a bottle of wine with him, and then—all the rest. I still haven't gotten used to it. I sense Niall feels the same.

This evening, it must have been around ten P.M. by the time I waved him goodbye from the front step. I drew the bolt to lock up for the night, and then I paused in front of the hall mirror to switch the lamp off. Sometimes it feels like a shock to see myself in the mirror: it took me a moment, now, to steady myself. But my face is my ordinary face; it's the life I'm living that's the shock. I walked through the corridor to the living room at the back of the house, and stopped in the doorway. I've been here long enough; I should be used to it by now, I don't know why I'm not. I checked the sliding door to the garden was locked, and I pulled the curtains snug. In the house next door, I heard the dog moving around: the clicking of her toenails on the laminate floor, and the faint jangle of her toy.

I scraped the leftovers from the pots into smaller bowls, and wrapped them in cling film and put them in the fridge. There's lots of space in my fridge now; it's not jam-packed like in the family days. And I washed up the few plates by hand, rather than bother with the dishwasher. I set the plates and pots and glasses in the rack to dry, and I squeezed out a cloth and wiped all the counters, and the part of the dining table where we'd eaten. I pushed the fruit bowl and the jug of flowers back to their usual place against the wall. Then I rested my hands on the counter while I checked whether anything else needed doing. The clock on the oven said it was twenty past ten. (Trinidad was five hours behind London: twenty past five in Trinidad on a Friday evening. Right now, in households across Port of Spain, men would be jumping in the shower, or changing into fresh clean clothes, slapping their cheeks with cologne. All around the country, women would be holding dresses up against their bodies, turning this way and that in front of their mirrors as they decided what to wear.)

I picked up the iPad from the counter and went to sit on the couch. I brought up CNN on the TV—not really to watch, just to have something on. I put the blanket over my knees, and folded the iPad open on my lap and rested my fingers on the keyboard. I knew I should look up flights to Tobago, check prices for different dates. But when the Google page came up, my fingers hesitated, and then I typed in my ex-husband's name, Robert Wilson. I clicked on his NHS profile page. The photo is from at least ten years ago: he's in his gray suit, in front of a shelf of leatherbound journals. We were still together when that photo was taken, all still living in the Wandsworth house.

Then I looked up Rob's new girlfriend: she's a medic too, a dermatologist, around the same age as me. In one of the photos, she stands behind a lectern in a tailored suit, and pearl earrings. I would guess she's had a little Botox. She's petite, with sort of blond hair, but really natural-looking, with really good highlights.

Then I typed into Google: "Girl November 1980 Venezuela." I clicked on "images" and scrolled through the pictures that came up. Smiling women, mostly. Beautiful women, models in swimwear, or actresses, TV presenters. I clicked on the ones who looked a little bit like me, and every now and again I right-clicked on a photo and saved it to my desktop.

She'll be forty-two this year. A lot of decisions are behind you at forty-two; whatever life you've chosen for yourself is speeding by. (These musings took over as I scrolled through photos online, with CNN on the TV screen over the fireplace, showing something about children in a classroom in South Africa.) She might be in a great job, upwardly mobile. Right now, this moment, she might be filled with the spirit of celebration, at what her forty-two years have brought her so far. Maybe somewhere like New York City. Out with friends at a cool bar. Just as I had looked at my face in the mirror a few moments ago, she might be doing the same: leaning in close to the mirror in the restroom of a trendy bar, touching up her makeup. Her hair might be still longish—past her shoulders. I think she wears it loose, using a setting spray to keep the curls in place. She smooths her dress down over her hips, and turns, happily, to admire herself from one side, and then the other.

On the TV screen, the CNN segment about African schools ended, and then the "Thirty seconds of calm" came on. They've been doing this since the pandemic, trying to ease everyone's anxiety. An image came up of a lake at sunset. Then a boat moving briskly across the surface of the lake. Then an aerial shot of the lake, showing a handful of boats all moving in different directions. Then the newsreader lady came on with the news at the top of the hour, the same stuff that had been scrolling across the bottom of the screen on an infinite loop since I'd been sitting there. Eleven o'clock. Really and truly, I'm too old to be wasting my time on earth like this, I thought. I'm fifty-eight years old, and every day when I look at Facebook, I read about someone else my age dying of cancer, and here I am whiling away my time on earth. Dawn! I said to myself. Put the iPad aside, or at least do something useful. Look up flights to Tobago. Look up what plants can live in north-facing gardens. Anything productive, rather than sit here and daydream.

I opened another browser and went to Hotmail, and logged in to the email account I use for the adoption forums. My Hotmail inbox had two full screens' worth of unread emails. My eye caught one with the subject line: "My name is Monica Sartori. I was adopted in Venezuela in 1982."

I picked up the remote and switched off the TV. I clasped my hands together, and for a while I sat like that, looking at those bold black words on the iPad screen. Then I touched my finger to the mousepad and clicked. A brief, polite email, in English, with an attachment. What I'd just read was actually the first line of her email. Her name was Monica Sartori. She had been adopted in Venezuela in 1982 by her parents, who'd lived in Caracas during the period 1979 to 1984. She was Italian; she lived in Verona, in the north.

I clicked on the attachment. A photo appeared of a woman in her thirties: a studio headshot. It had the slightly too-smooth, plasticky look that you get with artificial lighting, and a background in swirly dark blue. She looked about the right age—maybe late thirties. Fair, smooth skin, with a certain amount of melanin: the skin was a possible match. Her hair was shoulder-length, dark, curly; much curlier than mine. The eyebrows looked S-shaped, but that could have been the way they were plucked; my eyebrows are arched. Her cheeks looked a little wider or maybe plumper than they should: the women in my family have quite defined cheekbones. The nose and mouth were similar to mine: a little bit of a flare in the nostrils, a full lower lip. She was nice-looking, lightly made up, smiling.

Obviously, I registered on these websites myself. Obviously, I want and hope and expect to find possible matches. But as I studied her photo on the screen, I was aware of different parts of my body going haywire. My chest went hot, then my hands, then my forehead and cheeks. I had to focus to make myself inhale and exhale.

It might turn out not to be her, of course—but, on the other hand, it might be. In a matter of weeks, or months, we might come face-to-face. The possibility was already taking shape in my mind, what it would look like, feel like. How we would sit across a table from each other. I pictured a plain, small square table in a bare room. This girl would sit next to her other mother, her adoptive mother. The girl called Monica Sartori would be smiling, but uncertain, wary. The adoptive mother wouldn't smile. I could already feel hot patches all over my body, as if we were already in the room all together and they were waiting for me to begin giving an account of myself.

I found her LinkedIn profile. She was a chemist with a pharmaceutical company in northern Italy. She'd been to secondary school and university in Italy. She had a different photo on her LinkedIn profile, but I could tell it was the same person. In the new one, she was standing in front of a bright pink wall, the color of the pharmaceutical company's logo. She wore a light-colored silky top, and a dark blazer, and dark-rimmed glasses. Her lips were painted in a dark red lipstick, and she smiled widely, but without showing her teeth. Her hair was styled differently in this photo—the curls straightened out so her hair looked quite a bit longer than the first photo, and styled into soft waves. The company was in Verona. I don't know how long I spent on all this, reading and rereading her email, and looking up her address, and zooming in on different parts of her face.

I took my hands off the keyboard and folded them over my stomach. I raised my eyes from the screen. The curtains were drawn snug. My own feet, in wool socks, poked out from the other end of the wool blanket. The TV screen was quiet, a sheet of dull black plastic, with vague reflections. Next door, I could hear the dog whining and scratching occasionally at the door, wanting to go out.

I'm just going to come out and say that I took half a sedative pill. That was at about eleven thirty, and by midnight, I felt the Xanax getting to work: my mind slowing down, everything going foggy. I don't want to say too much about all that: I'm perfectly aware that any middle-aged woman talking about her "palpitations" is only inviting mockery upon herself. I only mention it by way of explaining why I didn't reply to Monica Sartori straightaway. I lay down in bed at some point, with the bedside light on.

I don't think I was properly asleep. I heard the Guyanese lady next door moving around quietly in her house, and speaking to someone on Skype. Then, the sounds of neighbors waking up, front doors being opened and pulled shut, cars starting. The rumble of the rubbish truck coming along the road, and the men calling out to each other as they emptied the bins, and then the truck rumbling on.

6

THERE'S A STORY I CUT OUT FROM A NEWSPAPER SOME YEARS AGO. Back in the 1970s, in a crowded marketplace somewhere in China—I don't remember the exact place—a mother had turned her attention away from her two-year-old son. She might have been chatting with a grocer, or buying some fish; the transaction took a short amount of time—a few minutes, I suppose. When she turned to look for her son, he wasn't there. A search was carried out, with help from the community and the authorities, but the boy wasn't found.

The mother carried on alone. Over the next months and years, she went from village to village. She went to marketplaces carrying a sign written on cardboard. She handwrote posters and stuck them up on walls and bus stops and telegraph poles. Years passed; it was widely assumed that the boy was dead. The woman separated from the child's father. She began to put advertisements in newspapers. (How she supported herself, I don't remember—perhaps she lived off alms.) People must have thought her deranged. She had had more than one heart attack. Despite all this, she carried on.

The boy found the mother through one of her newspaper

advertisements: he recognized his own face in the photo she had given to the newspaper, even though the picture was of him as a toddler. He had a memory of being lost in a marketplace. The sequence of events was unclear, but he ended up being raised by a family out in the countryside in a different region, far from the place where he had got lost. The mother and son arranged to meet, and although over thirty years had passed, they knew each other on first sight.

The newspaper printed this story, together with photos of the reunion. I couldn't say for sure that I saw the resemblance in their faces but I saw it in their manner, in the way they embraced each other. The mother, small and wizened and gray-haired, tears glistening on her cheeks; the son no longer a toddler but fully grown, even a little past his prime. In the picture, they stand side by side, their arms around each other, with no awkwardness at all, but at perfect ease, as if they'd never even been separated.

The son said that he had had a happy childhood, that he had been well treated. He had been told by his adoptive family that he had been taken in as an orphan. However, he said, he had always had a memory that seemed disconnected from everything else. In the memory, he was very young, and he was in a busy, crowded place, somewhere outdoors—somewhere far from the village where he eventually grew up with his adopted family. The ground was very close, and he remembered paving slabs and water or some other liquid in the gaps between the paving slabs.

The family who took him in were decent people, a schoolteacher and a nurse, though he was sometimes aware of a certain anxiety. The memory of being very small and being close to the paving slabs did not fit anywhere in the life he had eventually grown up in. It was difficult to explain to anyone, he said, but when he became an adult, he began to try to work out where he had really come from. When he finally found his mother through the newspaper advertisement, he said that what he felt was relief. All these years, he said in the article, it was as if I knew I was lost, and that my mother was looking for me.

There are so many stories like this one nowadays—you can search for them on the internet and read them by the dozen. People leave comments underneath the articles. ("Brings tears to my eyes! That mother! She never gave up!" Or just rows of heart emojis.) Stories like this should give you hope; they do give some of us hope. But on the forums, it's understood that, for those of us who are in the trenches, so to speak, our responses are more complicated. The story of the woman and her son in China takes a few minutes to read; the story is, somehow, of a fundamentally different nature to the forty years that have passed since I was in Venezuela. And that story is notable for having an ending: on the forums, one thing people often talk about is that many of us will never find the person we're looking for. What we're living through aren't even stories that can be told—they're just assortments of facts and feelings that amount to nothing very much, except for what we choose to make of them ourselves.

I'd like to be able to say that I've been looking for my daughter all these long forty-plus years, but the truth is that many years passed before I made even my first, small move in that direction. I had promised my parents I would keep it a secret, you see—that we would never speak of it again. We had made a pact, as my father called it, on that first terrible night when my mother and father and I gathered in our living room and decided what to do. Just the three of us were present: my brothers were away at college by then. It was a relief, in a sense, not to have them there as witnesses, but I felt very alone that night. Later, I wondered whether my father had even really used the word "pact," or whether I'd just imagined it. It's a word that, even now, conjures up images in my mind of blood, fire, howling winds. I know it's ridiculous. I think the association between the word "pact" and those images must have come from those low-budget movies that used to show on TV sometimes on Saturday afternoons, the ones aimed at adolescents just as I was then, high in melodrama. In any case, whatever it was that my father actually said, it was this sense of having made a dark promise, and this fear, that stayed with me for many years.

The mistake, as my mother and father called it, occurred during Carnival of 1980, when I was sixteen. Carnival in Trinidad and Tobago takes place on the Monday and Tuesday immediately before Ash Wednesday. Ash Wednesday, a holy day in the Christian calendar, arrives exactly forty-six days before Easter Sunday; and Easter Sunday, in its turn, is worked out according to the appearance of a particular full moon. All of this is to say that you can google it and find out the date of every Carnival for all of eternity, and so I can record here, with absolute certainty, that the mistake took place on Monday, February 18, 1980, at about eleven P.M. I wish to state, unequivocally, that I have no one to blame but myself. Other key facts, which by no means diminish my own utter stupidity: yes, obviously, a man was involved; yes, he was a white tourist; yes, he was a good bit older than me; no, we never found him again.

I know that many places around the world celebrate Carnivals, but in Trinidad and Tobago, we consider ours the best. In fact, we put things like modesty and small-island reality aside, and we just come out and brag, in our grandstanding, grandiose way, and say that T&T Carnival is the original and the best. It was started by the slaves: the slaves were freed; and they celebrated and made music and danced in the streets. You may have heard of steelpan: steelpan is ours, it comes from us. Nowadays in Trinidad, one part of Carnival consists of round after round of steelpan band competitions—heats in multiple categories, from villages the length and breadth of the country, starting from January, on and on through February, first-round heats, second-round heats, quarterfinals, semifinals, culminating in a fire-and-brimstone clash at the Saturday night Panorama in Queen's Park Savannah in Port of Spain. The calypso and extempo singing competitions carry on in the same way, all the way up to Dimanche Gras on the Sunday night. And then there are all the mas bands, the Kings and Queens, the band sections, kiddies' Carnival, the ole-time mas characters, the Moko Jumbies, the stick-fighters, the Dame Lorraines, the Jab Molassies, j'ouvert . . . it goes on and on. And that's not even counting all the fetes in the weeks and months leading up to Carnival, each with its own character and name; and then the cooldown beach-venue events the weekend following Ash Wednesday. Carnival is huge. It's always been huge, and every year it gets bigger.

My family never used to jump up. It was called "jumping up" back in those days—to join a Carnival band, and put on the band's costume, and then parade through the streets on Carnival Monday and Tuesday. In those days it was seen as uncouth:

not something for respectable people. I don't just mean white people. A few of my schoolteachers, all shades of brown, played mas, but they played in respectable sections of certain bands, in respectable clothing, and it would have been a scandal if their pictures had appeared in the full-color spreads in the newspaper, of women getting on wassy, behaving badly. All the dancing at Carnival time—what is called "dancing"—involves grinding up against each other—often, a man behind a woman, him holding her hips, and grinding into her backside. For many years, this was Carnival: four days of men and women drinking continuously; packed crowds; heat; glass bottles swinging; half-naked people, lathered in sweat, carrying on in this manner in broad daylight.

This is why, I suppose, my parents always saw Carnival as something to escape from, back when we were children. We got one of the workers to come and stay in our house to mind the dogs, and we packed up my father's car and either went down to San Fernando, to stay at my uncle's house, or we took the ferry across to stay at the beach house in Tobago. All that drunkenness and throwing glass bottles and wining up and bad behavior that went on—that wasn't for us.

At some stage, though, a change crept in. Part of it was almost certainly to do with a particular artist who arrived on the scene around that time. Everyone in Trinidad will know who I mean: Peter Minshall, of course. I remember seeing his first King—this would have been in 1976, with the band he named Paradise Lost, after Milton's poem. I remember the excitement that night as we all drew closer to the TV, and marveled at what we were seeing. A man who seemed to be painted in gold, covered head to toe in glittering, shining gold that clung to his skin, but you could see that he was still a man, with the shape and muscles and movements of a man. And behind him, or attached to him, a sort of golden shadow—in his same shape, but much larger than him, and looming behind him just like a shadow, but gold and shimmering, and moving as he moved. Alone on the dark Savannah stage, this golden creation, half-man, half-shadow, swayed and moved, for what must have been no more than a few minutes. Over the following days—then weeks, then years, then decades—at home, at school, downtown, at church, on the Savannah, all around the country, people couldn't stop talking about Minshall.

He brought out band after band, year after year; newspaper columns overflowed. "Carnival of the Sea." "Jungle Fever." "Rat Race." "Papillon." "River" was the one that changed everything. The Queen was Washerwoman: honest, simple, pure, dressed all in white; Mancrab was the King, fearsome, metallic, half-man, half-beast: he symbolized evil, technology, greed. A forty-eight-hour battle between good and evil played out on the streets. The masqueraders' costumes, initially pure white, were then stained with dyes of different colors, so that the spectacle of these multicolored thousands dancing was briefly pleasurable, glorious. But the River People continued in their frenzy of pollution, squirting paints and dyes all over each other, until there was a chaos of color, a frenzy of color, all colors running and bleeding together to make an ugly purplish brown; they were all stained in it. Mancrab's final triumph over Washerwoman was to cross the Savannah stage again, holding her limp dead body aloft in his claws.

I was up in England then, and I had to experience "River" through the retelling, but it was clear that the spectacle, and the partaking in the spectacle, had shaken everyone. We didn't know what it was, only that it seemed to be speaking to us in our own language. Carnival changed during those Minshall years, is what I'm trying to say. It changed artistically, it became more theatrical, loaded with ironies and sharp, ugly truths—and a social change came with it too: Carnival became more appealing, and acceptable, to the middle classes.

This is just my personal theory, of course. I'm sure others would disagree with me. After all, it's only now, in my middle age, that I'm trying to put these pieces together, to retrospectively make an order out of these things. And I'm mindful that it's easy for a bit of nostalgia to creep in—we all fall victim to it when we've lived away from home for too long. Really, the only facts that are certain are these: firstly, that when I was growing up, my family used to avoid Carnival; secondly, that when I was sixteen, I was allowed to go to a Carnival fete, and at this Carnival fete, I made the foolish mistake that would come to define the course of my life. What happened during those in-between years, how I got from A to B, is one of the mysteries that I've spent so many hours since then trying to solve.

I was the only girl in my family. There was my mother, of course, but she was so busy. In the kitchen, she worked fast: Chop-chop-chop! Stir-stir, done! Plates out with a clatter, and then the call: "Food!" When we came down to the kitchen to help ourselves, she might fire off a few quick questions: What you have to do? Geography? English essay? Get it done, eh? And then it was handbag on shoulder, keys in hand, and out the door and into the car, straight off to the next job, whatever it was. When I try to think of her as she was then, at that stage of our lives, I remember her mostly as I saw her from behind, always setting off to wherever she was going next. Her trousers were always tight around her bottom and thighs but loose at the waist, so that she had to wear belts to hold them up. Wherever she went, men's eyes were drawn to those wide hips. When she was out of the house, she tended to walk with her eyes down—it conveyed modesty, maybe, or somehow counteracted the message of temptation she must have seemed to be sending. ("Sssss! White-lady! White-ting! Ssss! You ever go with black-man?" That sort of thing was constant—for her, and, later, for me.) But what I remember is that womanly walk through the kitchen, bag on her shoulder, keys in hand. The slight jiggle of her bottom in her tight-fitting pants, the dark patches of sweat on her blouse in the spaces between her bra straps, the car keys jangling in one hand.

I don't know if her name was officially on any of the paperwork, but she did a lot for the family businesses. She did all the bookkeeping, all the banking; every Friday was payroll for the workers down south. And there were all the older people in the family to look after—my father's uncle, for example, who had to be taken to see various specialists about his heart and, later, his prostate. The elderly aunties had to be driven to confession at church, seamstress fittings, hairdresser's appointments. And my mother still drove to her own mother's house in Cascade nearly every day, to help with something or other, or just to drop in and see her.

So, aside from my mother, who existed as a blur in the background, I was in a family of men. My father was the head of the household. When he came home from work, we all stopped what we were doing and came out to greet him. In those days, the patio furniture was a set of four wrought-iron chairs and a low table, all painted white, though slightly rusted, and while my father went upstairs to shower and get changed, we tidied up and organized the chairs, to be ready for when he reappeared. Then, out there on the patio as the last rays of sunset cast themselves over the hills, he kicked his slippers off and put his feet up on the low table, and he held forth about the day he had had, and we all gathered around to listen.

My father was a good-looking fellow. I was aware of it on some level when I was a child, but it's only through looking at old photos that I can really appreciate it. He wasn't that tall, about five feet nine, but he was trim and fairly muscular, with broad shoulders, and, with God's blessings, a full head of hair.

Those evenings, my father always had the best seat, with his back to the French doors so that he faced directly outward, looking over the hills. The coffee table was drawn up close enough to him so that he could rest his feet on it, and he set his plate of food on his lap while he ate. Immediately to his right was another small table, for his drink: ice water first, and then, after the food was eaten and the plate taken away, rum and Coke (the short glass; a half-inch of rum, then Coke up to halfway, and then two ice cubes). My mother sat on the chair to his left, closest to the French doors (which led back inside to the kitchen and living room). My brothers sat on the two remaining white metal chairs, and if I wanted an official seat, I brought one of the plastic ones stacked up by the wall.

I loved these gatherings. I loved hearing them talk and make jokes. I talked a bit too, and I also made jokes, but they were all older than me, more mature—they knew more, had more to say. But I don't want to give the impression, by saying that I didn't have a proper chair, or that I had to bring my father his dinner, that I was a sort of servant, or oppressed or anything like that. I had my place: I belonged, and I was happy. I was the baby of the family; and what was special about me, besides being a girl, was that I was the brightest of the lot. In those days, that was enough—more than enough.

My brothers were older than me. The two of them went to the same boys' secondary school, had the same friends, played football with the same people, went to the same swimming club on Tuesday and Thursday nights. They complained about having to share a bedroom, and said it was unfair that I, the youngest, had my own room. But the truth is that I was jealous of them. I often came to the doorway of their room (I wasn't allowed beyond the threshold) just to watch them. And sometimes, if they were out of the house, I used to tiptoe in and look at their things. Rooms were very bare back then, none of the mountains of paraphernalia teenagers have nowadays. Two beds, two bedside tables with one drawer each; a set of fitted cupboards along one wall, a long oval mirror hung lengthwise on the wall in between the beds. Bottles of cologne and aftershave on their bedside tables; shoes scattered around—the shoes seemed absurdly huge compared to my own small ones.

When they came back from having been out with their friends, sweaty and boisterous, dusty or muddy from having been on the playing field all day, I longed to be close to them. I came to the kitchen and watched admiringly as they slurped tall glasses of water. They took dishes from the fridge and piled plates high with food, then stood in the middle of the kitchen in their bare feet, gnawing at chicken drumsticks, or pork ribs. I watched, envious and admiring, staying close by to catch all the news and jokes and gossip. Whose garden the football had ended up in; which vicious dogs they had had to get past; the tricks they devised; how someone had run, his legs a blur, like the characters on *Scooby-Doo,* to escape from the dog. That they had all gone to so-and-so's house and raided his kitchen, eaten the man out of house and home; they had finished out two loaves of bread making sandwiches; so-and-so had found a tub of ice cream in the freezer and eaten the whole thing; so-and-so had just had juice—he had walked around with the juice box in his hand, drinking from the box and saying, "Fellas, I drinking this, because if the people get mad, at least we could always get more juice! Pay them back in juice! Eh, Bishops?" Sometimes, when they said these things, my eyes would go to my mother or father, to see how this was received, but there was never any trouble, only chuckling and shaking of heads.

Warren went up to Florida when I was twelve, to do a year in an American high school before applying to college; Ryan followed him soon after. Then, my mother decided that she may as well let the driver take me to school in the mornings and pick me up in the afternoons, rather than waste time in traffic herself. The same driver took me wherever I wanted to go—to ballet, or to a friend's house—and I suppose my parents must have felt that I should be happy to have the same independence they'd allowed my brothers at that age. But the house felt very empty. My mother was always busy, as usual, and with my brothers gone, my father sometimes stayed down in San Fernando for dinner with my uncle, and only got back to our house in Port of Spain late, at ten or eleven o'clock at night.

Where I'm trying to arrive at with all this is Angie. Angie and I aren't in touch now—we were only friends for the couple of years that her family lived in Trinidad, in the house next to ours at the top of the hill. Her father was a head honcho with Shell: they were the sort of family who moved around every few years. They had been in Texas before they came to Trinidad on a contract, and they went to Norway after they left, but for the two years that she lived next door, Angie and I were best friends. Before she arrived, I'd had schoolfriends, yes, and sleepovers and parties and all those things—but it was different having a friend right next door, and being able to go in and out of each other's houses with such ease. And she was white, as I was, and from an affluent family—we had that in common too. For those two years she lived in Trinidad, it felt like we would be best friends forever. She wasn't wild, exactly, but she was European, with a relaxed attitude to things, and I suspect that my parents later regretted that they had let me be friends with her at all.

The other factor—a perfectly obvious one, but the last one to occur to me—was that I was no longer a child. As years had passed—as my brothers sat their A-levels and then went off to Miami; came back for summers, went back to Miami—I didn't remain a flat-chested ten-year-old girl, like a doll. I grew; my body grew. I knew it not so much from looking in the mirror, but from how conversations paused when I arrived in the kitchen where the women were always gathered during family get-togethers, and how the women's eyes studied me as I poured a glass of water, or helped myself to a portugal from the sack by the door. I heard their murmured comments as I slipped away, blushing. ("See that bust? And the hips! Childbearing hips!") The inescapable fact was that, by the time I was sixteen, I wanted the attention of boys. I wanted sex. It happened to all my friends, all the girls who lived in the neighborhood at the bottom of the hill who I used to play with when I was at primary school. As we got older, we eyed each other coolly when we crossed paths, sizing each other up now as competitors, rather than as friends.

There's no doubt I should have known better. Every year of my life before that, I had overheard the whispered conversations in friends' kitchens, where women gathered and gossip was shared. It was a standing joke that it—"it"—always happened at Carnival. Even in church on Ash Wednesday, people would be surveying the girls in the congregation to predict which ones would be in trouble. By Easter, six weeks later, people would be naming names, even placing little bets. And over the next few months, girls would quietly disappear from public view; only to reappear around Christmas, thickened and aged, with weak excuses that no one believed.

1980: THE YEAR OF PETER Minshall's "Danse Macabre." The King was a classic Carnival character, a Midnight Robber, but reimagined, and resized to a twenty-foot height, and awed everyone when he took to the grandstand. He was white and silver, eerie, deathly, half-friend, half-foe, with skeletal wings like a giant bat, or maybe the reaching, elongated arms of a spider. He had a skull where his face should be—and more skulls at his groin—and a long silver beard like a man from the forest. I didn't watch the Kings and Queens with my family, as I had in previous years. I was probably at Angie's house—it was where I usually was in those days, with no one else at home.

I was definitely with Angie the following night, Carnival Monday. We were at an over-18s fete on the north coast that

Angie's brother got us into. There were a lot of foreigners there. Some of them were island-hopping; they had moored the boats right there, near to the restaurant and open-air bar where the fete was taking place. Angie, who was more experienced than me in these matters, was locked mouth to mouth with someone she had just met. I wanted to keep up. I did ask the name of the man I selected: he gave his name as Nick, or maybe Mick. He said he was from Scotland. I only ever saw him in dim lighting, but I'd guess he was in his midtwenties, slim, but with a firm chest and arms. He still had smears of white paint on his face, and glitter on his neck, and he was wearing a black headpiece of a Minshall band section, a black hat encrusted with silver skulls. He smelled good; his mouth tasted of beer, in a nice way. We kissed very willingly; I remember trying to position us so that Angie could see.

I took Nick or Mick's hand, and led him down to the beach. At first, I only wanted for Angie to see me leading him away, and for her to be impressed. As to what happened next—well, I'm hardly the first. It was exciting for being daring, discovering new ground. I wasn't a total idiot: I asked if he had a condom, but he said not to worry, that he would just pull out. He sounded confident, like he had done it before, and like it was a fail-safe method. It didn't take long. It was painful at first, then boring, then embarrassing. Afterward, he said, "Thank you," and I, feeling as if I should say something snappy, replied, "No, thank *you*!"

Soon afterward, though, as we were walking back along the beach to the club, I began to feel light-headed—not because of anything physically wrong, but because of the knowledge sinking in, of what I had so casually done. On the faintly moonlit beach—the dark waves breaking behind us, and strobe lights from the bar up ahead—I felt as if I could already hear the whispered exchanges that would take place in school corridors, or teachers' staff rooms, or in ordinary kitchens of houses all around Trinidad, where women gathered to discuss the latest news. I felt hot with shame, as if the women were right there watching me: how they would be shaking their heads with knowingness, having seen all this before, and maybe lived through it themselves. "Foolish child," they would say. I could hear the words as clearly as if they were already being spoken. "Look what the foolish girl gone and do! Now, let we wait and see if she get ketch." Get ketch, as in get caught, get caught out. And as we now know, I did get ketch. Oh Lord, how I get ketch.

IN MODERN TIMES, MODERN COUNTRIES, girls have a lot of options. But in Trinidad, in 1980, as a white girl from a well-known, well-respected Catholic family, I had none. Even something as simple as a pregnancy test was beyond my reach. I tried Long Circular Mall, but the pregnancy tests were all behind the counter of the pharmacy, and the pharmacist was a lady we knew. I tried walking downtown after school one day, to a pharmacy on Frederick Street, but the pregnancy tests were behind the counter there too. I took something up to the cashier, a box of Band-Aids or some toothpaste, something like that, and for a few frightening moments, my eyes rested on the pale blue boxes stacked on the shelf behind the lady. But I couldn't bring myself to ask for them; I was in my school uniform, after all. I seem to remember the lady looking at me sympathetically: I realized later that she must have known.

All I could do was try to hide it. That part was easy. My parents were busy with company business anyway; at school, exams were upon us, and everyone was busy studying. I tried to study, but I was consumed by exhaustion. Weeks passed in that way, in a fog of stumbling through the days at school, and then collapsing into my bed, and waking up when it was dark, disoriented and nauseated.

THE MISTAKE HAPPENED IN FEBRUARY, and it was the end of May when, after school finished one afternoon, I walked up to the corner by the museum where I usually met our driver, and saw that my mother had come to meet me instead. I got into the car. We set off for home: past the museum, past Memorial Square, then around the Savannah. I set my schoolbag on my lap, and held it against my stomach. I was aware of her studying this. We came off the Savannah by the Hollows as usual. Through Boissière, then a right turn by the country club, toward Maraval. When the traffic slowed us down, she dropped her hands from the steering wheel to her lap, and glanced at me. I didn't dare look at her directly, but I knew she was looking at my stomach. Out of the corner of my eye, I saw that she wrapped her fingers tightly around the steering wheel, and fixed her eyes on the road ahead.

I don't know if she'd planned what to do, or if she only decided on the way home, once she was sure. After we drove past the golf course, instead of turning left to go up the hill, she carried on along the dirt road that ran alongside the edge of the golf course. Slowly, bumpily, we traveled, past tall overgrown bush on one side, and the tidily mown contours of the golf course on the other, until she came to the two teak trees at the end, where there was a flattened-out space in the bush, just wide enough to turn around. She switched off the car, and turned to face me, her arms folded.

"Tell me who," she said. "Tell me his name."

At first, I tried very hard not to cry. I felt I should try to maintain some dignity at least by not crying. But the harder I tried, the worse I failed. And it was so shameful. She had assumed that some schoolboy had pinned me down; she'd been envisioning a certain course of actions based on this assumption. I don't remember exactly what I said. I suppose I outlined the circumstances, in as few words as I could. In my recollection now, I see my mother almost as if she were some kind of spirit, some Carnival character, something amorphous, white-hot, incandescent with fury.

I don't remember the details very well of how the time passed until my father got home. I remember lying on my bed, and feeling truly sick. And I remember coming downstairs to the living room, and seeing that my mother had closed all the doors and windows, and drawn the curtains over the windows. My father sat in the leather armchair that faced the silent television, his hands clasped at his waist; my mother was near to him, on the sofa, with her back to the wall. I sat on the small armchair, so that I was on my father's left side, facing my mother across the coffee table. I was shaking when I sat down, and it only got worse from there.

It's only a blur. I remember the white-tiled floor and that all the ceiling lights were on, and that it seemed unnaturally bright. I remember the new way my father looked at me, with knowingness and contempt. He asked what kind of girl I was, if I was trying to stitch up some fella, trying to get him in trouble. Mostly, my mother and father talked to each other; I cried, as quietly as I could, wiping my eyes first on one sleeve of my school blouse, and when that was sodden, on the other sleeve; and when that was sodden too, on the front of my blouse, a scratchy polyester that irritated the skin around my eyes, so that as the hours wore on, my eyes were so puffy that I was hardly able to see. The discussion went on and on—about me, about what to do with me. Send her to San Fernando? Send her to England? The States? Barbados? Jamaica? They must have talked about the tourist too; that must have taken up a lot of time—all wasted time.

"You want to be an adult," my father said eventually, his voice heavy with anger and contempt. "You've behaved like an adult, so I'll treat you like an adult. You tell me. What do you want to do?"

It was a trick question. What did I want to do? I wanted to do whatever they told me to do. I think I must have said I was sorry. Maybe that I wanted to have a normal life. That I wanted to continue at school; I wanted my life to carry on. I didn't want to become one of those girls—there were so few of them who lived openly with their babies, but those few were all shrouded in shame: dropped by their friends; frowned at when they dared to come to church; stared at in horror when they came out in public with the baby in a pram, to do ordinary things like buy diapers, or food. But, as I say, I really don't remember. I was so tired. I could hardly see. I think I said I didn't want anyone to know. I didn't want my brothers to know. At some stage my mother started crying too. I remember it as being awful for me; it only occurred to me much later that it must have been awful for them too.

"We will make a pact," my father said, finally: this is the part that is lodged in my memory. "We will make a pact never to speak of it again. It will be like it never happened."

"Yes," I said. "Yes. Yes. I'm sorry. I'm sorry. Thank you. I'm sorry. I love you both." This is what I imagine or remember saying; and that the words my father had spoken were like a blessing, or a balm. And it must have been then, when it seemed like there was the possibility of redemption, that I came close to my father and knelt at his feet, and reached to take his hand.

7

I READ THE EMAIL FROM MONICA SARTORI ON FRIDAY, OCTOber 28, 2022, but it had been sitting in my inbox unread since Monday the 24th. It was quite possible that, during these intervening days, she'd been hitting refresh on her phone every few minutes. I hope my reply was fast enough: by now, she could easily have got cold feet. She might block me, deregister from the sites.

I've spent enough hours reading the online forums to know that this process is hard on all of us: the birth families, the adoptive families, the adoptees, everyone. On the forums, the birth families and the adoptive families usually keep their posts factual: they list dates and locations, names; they write out the full addresses and phone numbers of contacts in government departments who've been able to help them, in case they're useful to anyone else who might be looking in the same area. The posters who ramble—who write long incoherent posts all in capital letters, or without any punctuation at all—tend to be the birth mothers, or the adoptees.

"Adoptees" is an awkward word, and one which doesn't

translate well into other languages. The adoptees are the children. Some of the children have had difficult lives—struggles with relationships, addictions, stints in prison, homelessness. The ones who've been in therapy are the ones who speak most easily about feelings of abandonment. It hasn't been easy reading for me.

But on the other hand, it seems that a great many adoptees are happy and settled in their lives, and they don't have any interest in this process at all—on the contrary, they feel that to embark upon a search would be a betrayal of the people who raised them. I've taken so much comfort in that: in envisioning her happy and safe with a loving family, growing, thriving all these years, wherever in the world she might be.

The possibility has occurred to me that the person who'd written the email wasn't even really Monica Sartori herself, but someone related to her—her sister, or cousin, or spouse, or her own grown-up child, even. After all, sometimes it's the people around the adoptees who are more curious, or who feel the loss more acutely. And I've also read of cases of people hiring intermediaries to carry out the search on their behalf, to save them having to go on the emotional rollercoaster that this search inevitably brings. There was no knowing, really, who had written the email, and who might read my reply, and what course this new journey might take. None of us know what we're letting ourselves in for.

At some point during that night, I went upstairs to the loft landing, and sat on the carpeted floor and took my green box file from the bookshelf, the one with the maps. I spread out a map of Caracas, and tried to find the places Monica Sartori had mentioned. I traced the tip of my finger along the roads. The places she'd mentioned didn't have any meaning for me.

I took out another map, one of the whole of Venezuela, and spread it flat on the carpet. Several places were circled in blue ballpoint; again, none of them seemed to bear any relevance to the names Monica Sartori had mentioned. At some point, I looked up and saw that there was daylight coming through the skylight, where before there had been only my own reflection against the dark. The fog of the Xanax was beginning to clear, but I hadn't really slept, and now, at daybreak, I already felt drained.

It crossed my mind to call in sick to work, and to just go down to my room and get into bed for a few hours, but I've been strict with myself about keeping up a routine since living alone. So I folded the maps closed and put them back in the box, and slid the box back onto the shelf. Then I did my exercises in my bedroom, as usual, as if I'd just gotten out of bed on an ordinary day: ten touching toes, ten circling arms like a windmill, ten side-to-side squats. It's not much, but it's a routine, and it's how I start the day. Shower, get dressed, makeup, coffee, and then out the door, and into the car to go to work. Keep moving, keep busy, focus on what's in front of you—it's the only way.

I WORK IN TOOTING. IT'S a twenty-five-minute drive from my house usually, a bit quicker without traffic. I turned the window down and drove with the freezing cold air blowing in to keep me alert. I've done this drive hundreds of times, but sometimes—

times like today—you worry that you might go blank and make a mistake. You might drift into the wrong lane by accident, or confuse the brake for the clutch, or stall the car at a traffic light and then somehow manage to forget how to switch it back on again.

Saturday morning—the roads were quiet. A few joggers; a couple of other people out walking their dogs. A truck outside the little Sainsbury's near Clapham Common, fellows in thick gloves and bright orange jackets pushing trolleys stacked with goods from the truck into the store.

The office is on what they call the High Street: it's the main shopping street of the neighborhood, maybe half a mile long in this case. The buildings that line the street are Victorian terrace-style, for the most part, with the ground levels converted into shops, and the upper floors used as flats. It's a busy high street, mostly little shops, with the odd chain store here and there. Hairdressers and barbershops, nail bars, charity shops; fishmongers, butchers, secondhand bookshops, one post office; a couple of gyms. Our office is sandwiched between a cheap café and a fast-food counter that sells fried chicken and chips.

I parked around the corner from the office, and walked past other houses—all redbrick terraced houses, nice houses—up to the high street. Only the cheap café was open: through the fogged-up glass, I glimpsed dark shapes of old men at the tables inside, hunched over big plates of hot food.

Our office is glass-walled too, hung with property advertisements in little Perspex frames. I was the first one in; I dug in my handbag for my keys, and unlocked the glass door and then locked it behind me. It's not a big office, just one main room, open plan, and two doors at the back that lead to a kitchenette and a windowless room with a toilet and a sink. The office is very gray: the owners think it makes the place look sophisticated. So we have a gray office carpet (cheap); six rectangular, gray office desks, arranged like a classroom, three along one side of the room, three along the other side of the room, so that as you come in the door, you stand where a teacher would stand at the front of a classroom. I've persuaded them to put in a bit of comfortable seating by the door to give the appearance of welcome, so now we have a gray sofa and an artificial plant, and we have one of those water dispensers with conical paper cups. I've put some cushions on the sofa and there's a small IKEA table with some magazines, but aside from that, the only decoration in the room is the wallpaper along the back wall, a custom-made print of a street map of London, in black and white. My desk is closest to the front in the left-hand column of desks as you come in the door.

The owners are two brothers, Jamie and Mark Palmer. They have the two desks at the back, with two computer screens each, instead of the one that the rest of us have. Then there are two other sales people: Krisztina, a nineteen-year-old with blond hair extensions and fake nails—she looks a bit ditzy, but she's actually very good at leasings, very energetic and ambitious, even a little cutthroat; she's also bilingual, English and Polish. Then there's a younger guy whose full name is Anthony, but goes by Ant. He does residential sales, along with the brothers. His desk is cluttered with empty cans of Red Bull, and when he's not working, he's on the football news sites, or online poker. Then there's Diana, Lady Di, as we call her, who's the granny of the office, in her sixties, missing a molar on her upper right side. Ant and Lady Di are smokers. If they're not at their desks, they'll usually be somewhere around the corner, leaning on the front wall of someone's garden, and puffing away there.

I've been working in the leasings agency for about a year now. I'll be honest: it's not what I would have foreseen myself doing at the age of fifty-eight. I trained in medicine: all through my twenties, I made sacrifices so that I could qualify, and work. I'm a Bishop: I have a certain work ethic. All the women in my family in Trinidad had worked, and I'd expected to do the same. I chose general practice because I thought I could make it fit in around having a family here in England.

Nowadays, there'd be a label for what happened to my dreams of a medical career, something along the lines of "epic fail." As soon as I got married? One bump down the ladder. Pregnant with Finlay? Another bump. There wasn't much in the way of maternity leave back in those days, so I had to resign the job I did have, and after that I could only come back part-time, or to do short-term locum work. Bump, bump, bump, all the way down. I'm sure there's a meme for it on the internet somewhere.

After Rob and I divorced, I briefly considered trying to re-register as a GP, but I didn't feel I was sharp enough to pick it all up again, after all these years, and I worried I wouldn't be able to keep up the pace GPs have to move at nowadays. And it turns out that there aren't many jobs that'll take a woman at the age of fifty-eight, without any previous experience. So this little job at the estate agency is fine, for now. The salary just about covers my outgoings: my household bills, groceries, the cost of running the car. I don't have a mortgage, luckily, but on the other hand, I don't have a pension either. Rob and I went for what's called a "clean break," in financial terms, and he gave me a lump sum. I've put a few chunks into little investment accounts that the bank recommended, but most of it is just in savings, and I'm trying not to touch it.

But even if I didn't need the money, it's good to keep busy with something. On this particular Saturday especially, it was good to have somewhere to be—to be able to keep my hands busy, with typing and filing and answering the phone and handing people clipboards to write their details down on the office forms. And even little bits of small talk around the office—about the football match the guys were looking forward to later that afternoon, or that Lady Di was taking her grandchildren to Alton Towers during the half term—all those things are sustaining in their own gentle way.

I didn't tell them about Niall. If they knew he and I had been seeing each other, there'd be no end to the teasing. So my offering, instead, was about Finlay. I said that Finlay was busy at work, as always—that he'd had to do another string of three nights in a row, and that the last time I'd seen him, a few weeks ago, he'd looked like death. (Lady Di: "It's terrible, what they make them do!") (Ant: "Fucking Tories.") I was exaggerating about Finlay looking like death, of course, but it was true that he hasn't been looking good. He's lost weight, and his eczema is flaring up on his hands and face, and I'm sure it was on his elbows and the backs of his knees as well. I said to Lady Di and Ant and Krisztina that Finlay was coming over to mine later that day, and that I was going to cook him a nice steak, fatten him up. And when the Saturday workday was done at two o'clock, it was good to gather up the mugs from everyone's desks, to wash up in the kitchenette, and to leave everything tidy; good to finally push open the glass door back to the pavement, to the cold, bright afternoon.

I walked down the high street, instead of going around the corner to my car. It was a busy Saturday afternoon, plenty of footfall for the local shops. Actually, on Tooting High Street, it's almost like being back in Trinidad. Little shops with the smell of incense wafting out to the pavement. Long narrow stores that blare out Caribbean music from big speakers at the front of the store and sell all kinds of familiar things: Maggi seasonings, Cream of Wheat, ground provisions—yam, dasheen, eddoes. One shopkeeper, an old Asian man in loose clothing and slippers, rested his eyes on me and studied me unashamedly as I went by.

I didn't spend long on the high street. I got two plantains and then went and sat in my car. I checked my emails on my phone. Nothing yet from Monica Sartori. On the pavement, just beside me, two women walked past pushing prams. Both beautiful, young women, with long blond hair, looking like they'd just been to the gym, in their workout gear. A door opened, the front door of the house I was parked by, and a woman in a dressing gown came down the path with a big black rubbish bag. Out of the corner of my eye, I saw her study me, and I started tapping at my phone just to look like I was doing something. She tossed the rubbish bag in the big plastic bin and let the lid slam shut, and walked back up the path to her house.

This time of day on a Saturday used to be a quiet hour in my previous life. The boys would be back from their Saturday morning activities; they'd have had lunch, and then gone out again to see their friends. I'd be in the kitchen—the big glossy Wandsworth kitchen—clearing up from lunch, getting on with washing school uniforms and sports kits. If Rob was home, his garden boots would be missing from their spot by the glass sliding door, and his regular shoes would be there instead. Sometimes if I looked out, I could see him stooped over the flowerbeds, working away with his trowel.

I'd started writing a message to Rob, while the woman was throwing her rubbish out. He and I are still on reasonably good terms. We talk about the boys, or occasionally about friends we used to share. Now I wrote, on WhatsApp: "Hi, hope all well. Am seeing Finlay later. Let me know if anything I should know re complaint?" I didn't really need to check with him about the complaint. It was more of a slightly passive-aggressive nudge. (As in: "I hope you're helping Finlay? What exactly are you doing to help Finlay?")

I read through old messages for a few minutes, and checked my emails again. Nothing from Monica Sartori. Then I saw that Rob was typing, and I sat with the phone in my hand and waited. The sun had gone down; it felt colder than it had been a moment ago.

"Spoke to F this week. Sounds like all under control. He knows he can ask me if he needs anything specific. Will be more than happy. Hope all well with you."

It still feels unusual to get such a quick reply from him, but he has much more free time now than he used to. It was only in the early days, the hard days when I was at home alone with babies, that he had to work the crazy hours. Now everything is good for him. He bought a sports car, joined the golf club. I hear he's been vacationing in the South of France with his girlfriend, the consultant dermatologist with the expensive blond highlights and pearls. She was probably with him now. I put the phone in my bag and started the car, and set off for home.

IT'S ONE OF THE THINGS I worried about the most, when Rob and I first decided to separate: how he would carry on with Finlay and Oscar. Whether he would cut them off to spite me, or whether he would try to turn them against me. In the end, he was good about it, decent. (I should add that I didn't squeeze him in the divorce settlement for this very reason: I didn't want him to have any provocation to turn vindictive.) But while we were going through our separation, it was very much on my mind. But over the nearly three decades we were married, Rob and I always disagreed about the boys, how much to do for them, how much help to give them.

His attitude to raising children was to say, "They'll be fine." When we were married, literally every time I tried to talk to him about something to do with the boys, Rob would shrug his shoulders and say, "They'll be fine." If I really pushed it, the next thing he would say was, and I can repeat it verbatim, because I've heard it so much, "All that matters is that they're happy. If they're happy, everything else will follow." To me, that's madness. Why will everything else follow? What possible basis could there be to assume that everything else will follow? In Trinidad, people who said things like that would only ever be mocked: the "God will provide" people. The people who expect manna to fall down from heaven.

Rob and I fought and fought, all while the children were little, over one thing after another. I had to fight him to get what the boys needed. I'm talking about basic things. To be outside. To get sunshine. To get proper food. To have friends to play with. To get exercise. I took all those things for granted in Trinidad, but they don't happen naturally here in England. And Rob didn't see that they were important. He said things like, "Oh, you know, fish fingers were good enough for me"; or, "So what if they spend all weekend inside watching TV." Over time, he became an adversary: I wasn't prepared for that.

By the time Finlay got to around ten years old, and it was time to think about secondary schools, I said to Rob, I'm not putting up with this anymore: I want them to go to the good school. I said, if we can't afford it, my family will help. Rob came out with his usual nonsense. Truly, I've spent hours and hours of my life listening to people in England talk about this: how society should be equal; how inequality was morally wrong; private schools were morally wrong; private school parents were morally wrong and also selfish, and also they were "fucking Tories." It would inevitably lead, I knew, to the miners' strikes in the 1980s, and Margaret-Thatcher-milk-snatcher.

The incident I'm recounting was sometime during the summer; we were in the Wandsworth house by then. We'd had people over for a barbecue, and Rob and I were talking in the evening after the guests had gone home, and the boys were in bed. We had been discussing it while we cleared up in the kitchen, and we carried on discussing as we went upstairs to our room. Rob had started taking off his clothes and had gone into the en suite. I had followed him in, and we carried on talking, the conversation getting more heated. I stood in the doorway. Rob folded the toilet lid and sat down. I picture him now as he always sat, like a consultant anesthetist in a meeting, legs crossed, hands clasped over his knees, dignified and restrained even in his underwear. I said to Rob, I've had enough of this. I said, look here. I said, do I look like I care about other people's children? I tapped a forefinger to my chest: hello, I care about *my* children. I want the best for *my* children. And I said (and I meant it this time, because I'd had enough of this bullshit by this stage), either they go to the good school, or I'm taking them home to Trinidad to put them in St. Mary's College.

He knew I was serious. He had seen St. Mary's; he had met my brothers and their friends, all St. Mary's boys; he'd even met the old St. Mary's College principal one evening on our patio in Trinidad. I know he'd been astonished at what he saw: how tightly knit the network, how extreme the wealth, how remarkable the concentration of power, even on what he must have assumed was a puny little joke of an island. That day in the en suite, after the barbecue, he finally gave in about the private schools. And the surprising thing was that as soon as he gave in, a change came over him: a mixture of relief and pride and excitement. And over the following years, we never argued about that particular issue again. I think now that he secretly wanted to send Finlay and Oscar to the best schools, to give them the best things. Rob had done well in life, he was earning well, he could afford it, but the way he had grown up—with this fear, or grudge, or I don't know what—he couldn't contemplate it on his own.

Then there's the whole thing about teenagers doing drugs, here in England: it's common here, it's accepted, expected, even. I had heard about the phenomenon in my own days practicing medicine, but I couldn't quite compute how it would be possible. In fact, I didn't believe it was a real thing until it came up in conversations with other parents—mothers, in those days—at the boys' schools. All these women—all educated, successful people!—talked about drugs, about their teenage children using drugs, as if it were perfectly normal. They didn't just mean marijuana. They meant coke, ecstasy—I don't know what else. They laughed about it. Truly, these people are mad.

I spoke to Finlay and Oscar about it alone. I sat them down on the steps in the hallway one afternoon when they'd come in from school. I don't remember the year, but if I had to guess, I would say they must have been about fourteen and twelve, because they were both at secondary school, and it was just before they outgrew this kind of bossiness from me. They were too big to both fit on one step, so Finlay sat on one step, and Oscar sat a few steps above.

I said, I want to tell you something. (They sat there, wide-eyed, because they knew this particular voice, this hello-the-boss-lady-taking-over-here voice.) I said, listen to me. I said, serious business. Drugs? If you see someone taking drugs? Run like hell. I said, I am from Trinidad! All the drugs your friends are taking? They come from by us! I said, these people don't realize! They're crazy! And I said, if I catch either of you doing drugs? Any kind of drug, I don't care what the name of it is. I said, you mark my words! We're not even going to stop to pack a bag! We're just taking passports and going straight to Heathrow. (I pointed at the door, as if we were about to depart for Heathrow this very minute.) And we're getting on the first plane to Trinidad. And I'll put you straight to work on the buffalo farm down south. And you can work with the laborers out in the hotsun from five in the morning until five in the evening, and believe you me, once you've been doing that for a month, you'll come to your senses. But if we need to stay longer, we'll stay. We'll stay for a year, two years, however long. Watch me.

Well, thank you, Heavenly Father—it worked. Almighty Father in heaven, amen. It worked because I was serious, and they knew I was serious: that's the trick, which is not really a trick. You have to really mean it. As you speak, as you stand over them, pointing at the door, you have to truly be preparing yourself to get the passports, to drive to the airport, to slap down your credit card and buy tickets, whatever the cost. I heard them joking about it later between the two of them—Careful Mum doesn't send you to the buffalo farm!—but I only smiled at that to myself. They could say whatever they liked about me, as long as they behaved themselves.

And I didn't even bother trying to talk to the other mothers here about it. What could I say? "You're letting your children do drugs? You're laughing about it? Like, you people are crazy or something?" No, they don't want that here. They don't want opinions, discussion, any kind of challenge. Not in my experience. I've given up trying to make it make sense.

THE JAMAICAN FELLA WAS OUT washing his car when I got home. We waved hello to each other across the street. As I pushed open the gate to my front yard, I noticed a little twitch from the curtain in the Guyanese lady's house next door. I paused on my front path, pretending to take a long time finding my keys. She must have been looking at me from behind the curtain. Sometime during the night, last night, while I was up on the loft landing with my maps, I heard her talking to someone. They were on Skype: I heard the little electronic bing-

bing-bing ringing song that it makes, and then a man's voice. Maybe someone back home. Guyana's on the same time zone as Trinidad, five hours behind England. The times would make sense.

I found my keys and then as I walked the few steps to my door, I smiled in the direction of her window. There was no movement, but I had the feeling that she was there, a few steps back, watching me through the curtain. I stood still, my handbag over my shoulder, my keys in my hand, and smiled again, more deliberately, so she would know it was meant for her. Still nothing. I carried on to my front door, fitted my key in the lock, went in. So strange to live on opposite sides of a wall, and never speak—both of us from the Caribbean, who know another way to live.

I miss the company of other women. Now, all these years later, now that I live alone in London, I often think back to how it used to be in Trinidad, how women used to gather and talk. Of course, women here get together and chat too, but I'm thinking of how it used to be at home when I was a child, I suppose in the more old-fashioned days, when the kitchen was the place for the particular kind of conversation I'm thinking of. All ages of women could be there together: the younger ones doing the cooking, the slightly older ones directing or modifying, the oldest ones sitting down somewhere comfortable, positioned so as not to be in the way, but close enough to hear all the gossip.

As I'm trying to piece my own story together, I can't help but hear how it would come out, told in one of those kitchens. "Remember Dawn, who got pregnant at sixteen, and then look how her life turned out! Let that be a lesson to the others!" The other women would nod in full agreement, and *mm-hmm* and chime in, because, after all, there's nothing new under the sun, and once you start on a story, all these women already know how it goes. Maybe this is why I sometimes find myself talking as if I were talking to those women in the kitchen. The night my parents sat me down and Venezuela was agreed, has become, in my mind, "that terrible night." It was a terrible night. I really wept that night. But it was so long ago; I can look back now and feel sympathy for my younger self, and tenderness, and I can see it the way the women in the kitchen might see it, which is to see not only one foolish sixteen-year-old girl who got herself in trouble—I know, I know—but all the foolish sixteen-year-old girls. There are so many of us, and each of us had our own "terrible night," and each thought we were the only one ever to suffer through it. And while the suffering was real, the perspective on it changed over the years, so that, to call it, in the melodramatic words of a daytime soap opera, "a terrible night," was to both tell the truth of what had been felt, and to be gently teasing too, to mock or expose the foolishness of youth. It was comforting. It made it possible to laugh at yourself a little bit, and God knows we needed to be able to laugh sometimes, after all that crying.

8

I'D NEVER BEEN TO VENEZUELA BEFORE THAT TIME I DESCRIBED, and I've never been again since. It hasn't been a very easy place to visit. Their economic crisis must have started at around the same time as ours in Trinidad, in the mid-1980s: the years that came immediately after were a bad time for the whole region. It was a time of the IMF descending and strangling everybody, rioting, coup attempts—that kind of madness. We had a coup attempt in Trinidad and Tobago in July 1990; Venezuela had one in February 1992, and then another in November of the same year—that pretty much summarizes how things were in the region, during that period after the oil crash.

Then, over the next couple of decades, at least up to the time of the pandemic, it seemed as if things in Venezuela, particularly, went from bad to worse. Crime, gangs, kidnappings. Hyperinflation, food shortages, electricity blackouts. In recent years—say from 2013 up to 2016—I've saved the news articles and features whenever they made headlines: pictures of empty shelves in the grocery shops in Caracas, or pictures of doctors trying to do surgeries by the light of their mobile phones. Diabetics who couldn't get their insulin; or children left at churches because their families couldn't feed them. And dramatic pictures of great crowds of people walking over the mountain roads to cross over into Colombia or Brazil, trying to get out of Venezuela.

Trinidad and Tobago has had more than its share of problems, of course, but even we were shocked by the extent of what was happening in Venezuela. You have to understand that back in the good days, Venezuela used to be the richest country in all of Central and South America. If we thought we were rich in Trinidad and Tobago in the 1970s and 1980s—well, Venezuela was on another level. They had serious oil in Venezuela. Serious. When you heard people talking about Trinidad, you heard figures in the millions: how many millions of barrels of oil. For Venezuela, the figures were in the billions. In the good days, Venezuela may as well have been dripping in gold and jewels, they were so rich. They had infrastructure, they had healthcare, they had schools, universities, high-rises, electricity, multilane highways—everything. They had everything.

All I knew of Venezuela, really, when I was growing up, was the shopping malls: it used to be said that the shopping malls in Caracas were even bigger and better than the ones in Miami. People used to fly over to Caracas with empty suitcases, and come back with them full. Mostly with clothes. I remember being jealous of girls at my school, or girls who lived in the neighborhood at the bottom of the hill: the ones who, every Sunday at church, wore beautiful, fashionable clothes that had come from Venezuela. My family was frugal with things like that; my parents were reluctant to advertise their wealth.

Some people went to work in the oil fields over there. By "people," I mean men. They disappeared for a few years, and when they came back, they came back rich, and dressing differently to Trinidadian men: smarter, with pants with creases down the front, and leather belts; they even combed their hair differently. And they could speak Spanish—that also set them apart. They would be the only ones who could speak to the Venezuelan tourists we occasionally ran into around the place. The Venezuelans didn't bother with our little islands very much, but very occasionally, you would see a family somewhere like Tobago or Barbados. They were always well dressed, the women with plenty of jewelry, and puffed-up blow-dried hair; at the airport, you would see the whole family all with matching suitcases. And even though they looked like any ordinary person from the Caribbean might look, with brown skin and dark hair, and the same indigenous eyes that so many Caribbean people have, they carried themselves differently. They didn't mingle with other Caribbean people; they had an aloofness that made them seem foreign, even though they were, in a sense, just like us.

And my grandfather and uncle and father used to go over to Venezuela regularly, throughout the 1960s and 1970s. I don't know for sure, but I'd presume they went to the capital, Caracas: it would have been the most likely place to get materials—machinery, packaging, parts; advertising materials; T-shirts and baseball caps with the company logo for the workers to wear. They must have traveled by plane, but I don't recollect ever going to the airport to see them off. I only remember my father's absence: that the rhythms of the house were different, that the evenings were empty without him; and then the sense of relief and restoration of normality when he was back. I have one clear memory from that time: my father standing in the doorway of his office room downstairs, with Venezuelan currency, paper notes in gray, blue, purple, and green, spread in his hands like a magician's pack of cards, and my brothers and me crowding around him.

But by the time I was in secondary school, my father's trips to Venezuela had stopped. Maybe there was some sort of change to the trade agreements between the two countries. Or maybe it was just that they had all the machinery they needed. I don't know. I never thought to question it at the time.

THE NIGHT OF THE PACT would have been at the end of May, just as my O-levels were finishing. The summer was supposed to have been filled with all kinds of good things—beach trips, river limes, fetes, pool parties, shopping—but, of course, all that slipped away once the mistake came to light. My brothers came home from Miami for their summer vacation. I don't know exactly how the information was transmitted to them, only that it was, because the happy, lighthearted, festive atmosphere they brought with them from America turned sour. The house, briefly filled with their laughter and chatter and good cheer, turned quiet.

My brothers were too old to share a bedroom by that stage—Warren would have been twenty-one by then, and Ryan nineteen or twenty—and that summer, if I remember rightly, Ryan had the bedroom across the corridor from me, and Warren had made some space for himself in the room next to mine, which was more of a storage room. He did it for his own comfort and privacy, but the effect on me was to feel that I was under assault from two sides. I stayed in my room whenever they were at home. I could hardly meet their eyes, when I encountered them around the house.

I'd always been a little fearful of Ryan. When I was at primary school—say around age eight or nine, so he would have been eleven or twelve—he used to do this thing where he'd flick his fingers against my ear. At first I giggled, thinking he meant it playfully, but he used to kind of smirk, and then come back flicking harder, all around my face and body: sometimes I had to fight him off. And when we were at the beach house in Tobago, he always used to tell me that the manta rays that swam out by the rocks were stingrays, and that I'd get electrocuted if I set so much as a toe in the sea. He wouldn't remember any of that now—he's not like that anymore. But that summer, when I was pregnant and hiding in my room, I started pulling a chair in front of my door during the night. I couldn't have articulated to anyone exactly what I was afraid of, except that it was Ryan I was barricading the door against.

That difficult summer, the rift with Warren was harder to bear. When we were small, Warren was always kind to me. When we got into the car on Sundays to drive down to San Fernando to visit my uncle and his family, my parents in front, and my brothers and me in the back, Warren often let me sit on his knees so that I could lean my head out his window, which was nicer than being in the middle where your hair got blown about like mad. And if there was a big mango chow being made, he used to sometimes let me have the seed, or one side of the seed. I adored Warren. When he got his driving license that summer before he went away to college, he used to jangle the keys and say, "Dawn! We have wheels, man! Let's go! You and me!" When we went out, Warren drove, and I sat in the passenger seat in the front, music blaring from the car stereo. We just went wherever—to drop by a friend to lime for a while, or to the grocery to pick up something for our mother, or around the Savannah for a roast corn, anything like that. Before my mistake, Warren had been kind to me in that way: he had welcomed me into his grown-up life, and given me a taste of the freedom that might be in store for me when I was his age.

That year, 1980, when Ryan and Warren came home from college, I remember hiding in my room behind the door I'd tried to barricade shut; anxiety whenever I heard footsteps pass along the corridor just outside; relief at the sound of the thud-thud going down the stairs. And it was only when the two of them went out, off to see their friends, or to drive down to Maracas, or to play football with friends on the recreation ground down the hill, that I crept out of my room and did what I had to do—used the bathroom, or got some food, or sat out on the patio to take the breeze on my own for a little while. But even the dogs were uncertain around me. They sniffed long and curiously at my palms, and then, instead of sprawling comfortably near my feet, they retreated to some distance away and lay down, looking troubled. Occasionally, they lifted their heads and sniffed in my direction again, as if they couldn't quite work out who I was.

It must have been a relief for everyone when I went to stay by Auntie Pam in Cascade for the remaining months, until it was time for me to make the trip to Venezuela. Auntie Pam was actually my grandmother, my mother's mother, but everyone called her Auntie Pam. She lived on a quiet road just behind the botanical gardens, off the Savannah, and her garden bordered the playground of a little primary school. During term time, she would often be outside watering her plants in the back, and chatting to the children who clustered on the other side of the fence. I knew her well; I was comfortable at her house. She had a small wooden house, one of the old-style ones with wooden louvers in the windows, and a pitched roof in red-painted galvanize. It was a nice house: sturdy, gracious, and because of the louvers, it was a breezy house, cool. Auntie Pam had been widowed young; for all the time I knew her, she lived alone. She worked as a seamstress, mainly. She had a front room where she did fittings for her clients, and sometimes I had to help her clear space on the patio, if, say, she was doing a set of bridesmaids' dresses, and a whole group of people would be coming. The floors were all of some smooth, dark wood; she had them polished every few weeks, and when I was small I loved the smell of the polish, and how the floors gleamed.

Auntie Pam had already been informed of my troubles by the time I arrived with my bag of things. I remember her standing on her front porch, at the top of the short flight of wooden steps, her arms folded, her face stern, as she watched my mother and me open the gate and come up the path. When I reached the top of the steps I stopped, waiting for some sort of greeting, but there was none, just the angry expression and the coldness, from both her and from my mother. I turned and walked through the house to my usual room and I tried to get myself arranged.

I can still picture the room easily now. It was on the left side of the house, looking out to a narrow strip of garden, with the next house just beyond the fence. It was a dark, cool room, shaded by the other house, and a mango tree in that narrow strip. Leaves from the mango tree often blew in through the louvers. Inside the room, there was a single bed, pushed into the corner, and a desk beneath the window, but most of the room was taken up with Auntie Pam's sewing things. Satin bridesmaids' dresses hung from a rail inside the cupboard. Bolts of fabric were propped up in the corner. An ironing board was set up in the middle of the room. Bits of sewing paraphernalia filled every drawer in the chest of drawers: neatly folded offcuts of fabric, lengths of ribbon, spools of different colored threads.

At some stage later, after my mother had left, Auntie Pam pushed open the door and came in. She must have paused in the doorway for a long time. I don't remember, and I didn't look at her. I think I must have been crying, but probably quietly, so as not to provoke her. People must have been getting very tired of me with all my crying: I was getting tired of myself. I only wanted the whole ordeal to be over: to get to Venezuela and have the baby, and get back to my life.

I think I must have been sitting on the edge of the bed with my face in my hands, and what I remember is that Auntie Pam came and sat beside me on the bed, and put her arms around me and hugged me. She's gone now, Auntie Pam, but I still remember that moment very well, and I'm still grateful to her for her kindness.

Auntie Pam put me to work during those months. Not in a mean way, just that she gave me enough to keep me busy. I did a lot of cleaning. I remember working through her entire linen cupboard, taking each thing out, sheets, blankets, tablecloths, pillowcases, towels, bath mats, everything, and putting them through the washing machine and then the dryer, and then ironing everything that could be ironed. Even to this day, sometimes, when I'm doing my own ironing, the linen cupboard in Auntie Pam's house drifts back to me, clear and present as if I were right there in the flesh, with the smell of the floor polish and the memory of those dark gleaming floors. It was a recessed cupboard in the corridor between the kitchen and the bathroom; the cupboard doors were slatted, to allow for air; handmade in pine, painted a gloss white. An old suitcase was stored in there, in the darkness of the top shelf. The floor polisher, about the size of a large vacuum cleaner, was at the bottom. A cardboard box with the tins of floor polish or wax, and the blackened cloths stuffed in beside them.

And I learned to sew while I was there. I remember making a woman's blouse out of a pale yellow fabric, and that my collar was a bit lopsided, and my sleeves were really quite dreadful. My mother, when she came to visit, held up the blouse and said, "Hmm!" sternly, as if unimpressed. Auntie Pam said something to my mother like, "What, you think you were never a beginner?" And I looked away because I knew I wasn't allowed to gloat at Auntie Pam taking my side.

My mother stopped by every few days. She was already in the habit of dropping in quite often, even when I wasn't staying there. She and Auntie Pam sat out on the front porch with their cold drinks and talked for a while. Sometimes I sat with them, if I felt I was welcome; otherwise, I went out to the backyard and walked in the cool grass, or sat on the back step and watched the birds in the trees.

There are two other incidents from my time at Auntie Pam's house that I can't quite position in time, but that have stuck with me. The first might be early in my time there, so perhaps June, I'm guessing. My mother and Auntie Pam were on the front porch. Her porch was a little raised off the ground, maybe three or four feet, and with a ledge all around with potted plants. I remember it as a cool, shady place, green and leafy. And she had bamboo chairs that I'd always liked: the frames bent into big lacquered curves. I used to love running my fingers along those smooth glossy curves. She'd made the cushions herself: brown, with a tropical bush pattern, in green and pink.

But about this moment that I'm trying to return to: I can't remember now if I was actually sitting there with them, or if I was listening from somewhere out of sight. They were talking about where I was going in Venezuela. My mother said that they were going to drop me deep in the jungle: to drop me out of a plane and let me find my way out again. She didn't mean it seriously. It was a sort of joke—a harsh, stern joke, like a clip on the ear. And then after the joke was made, the follow-up, the no-but-seriously: "To stay with nuns, nuh. Who else but nuns would take in girls like her?"

Then a different memory. I'm guessing this was later, because I recall a feeling of being more comfortable with Auntie Pam and with my situation, so the awkwardness and shame of those first early days must have worn off. I think it must have been just the two of us there, out on her front porch. The recollection is of the light being dark and shadowy—dusk time, before anyone had got up to switch on the electric lights. Auntie Pam saying, "I'm surprised at your father, sending you to Venezuela." The way she said it, it was like she wasn't talking to me; as if she were just saying her own thoughts aloud, or talking to someone who wasn't there. She could have meant many things by it: that she was surprised at my father's cruelty, sending me on a dangerous journey, all alone; or that she was surprised my father hadn't found another solution—to let me stay in Trinidad, or even send me to England to have the baby. All I remember is that there was something enigmatic about the way she said it, that it was half an invitation to ask more, and half a trap. But I didn't ask more; and nothing more came. The neighborhood barking took over, or one of us got up to switch on the light, and then she went inside to watch the news. We went our separate ways in the house, and the moment, such as it was, was lost.

9

FINLAY HAS THE SPARE KEY TO THE NEW HOUSE IN BROCKLEY, but he still rings the bell when he arrives at the door. I always have to hide a little double take when I open the door, because every time I see him, it's like I'm seeing many people at once—all the men in my life, concentrated into this one body on my doorstep. Finlay has Rob's same body: slim, not especially muscular; a good height on him. But his hair is like my father's: good hair, dark, thick, quite lustrous. I'm not sure which side the eyes come from: clear bright eyes, big European eyes; dark brown like mine; no need for glasses yet. His nose is from Rob's side, an unremarkable nose, symmetrical, with a straight bridge: maybe a little longer than average, but a perfectly good nose.

As I hugged him hello, just inside the doorway, I was thinking that sometime soon, I had better stop this polite-polite English-holding-back thing I was doing, and just find someone nice for him. He's a handsome young man. Hardworking, well qualified. There had to still be nice girls around the place, somewhere. (For a moment, the other thing on my mind receded, and I wished it had never arisen.) But you have to focus on the here and now: Finlay was here, grown-up, thirty years old, and still needed sorting out. I didn't care if people called me interfering or old-fashioned, whatever. I don't care about all of this "modern life" nonsense they keep trying to tell me. People haven't changed. Everyone needs somebody. A companion to walk through life with. I can't go to my grave and leave Finlay here with no one. And under my hands, he felt thin. Even thinner than last time. The same smell as usual, laundry detergent and hospital antibacterial soap.

I stepped back to make space for him to take off his coat. My new entrance hallway is much smaller than the old one—it's more of a corridor, about three feet wide—but I've organized it so it's like our old house. In fact, the hall table is the very one from the Wandsworth house—pine, with two little rickety drawers and a built-in shoe rack below. And it's adorned with the same framed photos of the boys, and the same Moroccan brass bowls that we've had forever, and the same little lamp with the faded green tasseled shade. Finlay rested one hand on the edge of the table for balance while he slipped his shoes off. I watched his eyes move from one photo to the next, taking each one in, and then to the mirror, where he glanced at his own reflection, and lifted a hand to smooth his hair.

"You don't really need to take off your shoes, you know," I said.

"No, no," he said. He bent to gather up his shoes and set them on the rack under the table. "Habit, you know. And why bring dirt in? I take mine off at home too."

"Well, you're so clean," I said. I meant it fondly. Doctors who work in surgery are always clean.

"Did you cook?" he said, as he followed me toward the kitchen. "I could have eaten the same macaroni pie and stew chicken you made the other day. I didn't want you to be rushing out shopping."

"No, no," I said. "I just got some steak from the butcher. Easy-easy. And the fella in Tooting had plantain, so I got some for you."

I had the curtains open in the living room, with the view of my bricked-over garden with its table and potted plants—always a little dispiriting, I think, when Finlay must always think of the garden we used to have. It was officially autumn: the end of October, the clocks due to go back that night. The day before, when Niall had come over, it had been mild enough to sit out in the garden. Today it had turned cold. I had the heating on, and if the fireplace in this house weren't bricked in, I would have lit a fire. But even so, the place looked cozy, with the two side lamps on in the living room on the left, and the table set in the dining area on the right. And even though they've insisted I should get rid of the Wandsworth furniture, I always see Finlay relax when he walks in here and sees the familiar things—the same corner sofa from the den in Wandsworth, the same cream rug from the den, with the black line pattern; the same oak dining table and chairs that used to be in our kitchen. I went to get the drinks, and Finlay picked up the remote control from the coffee table, and pointed it at the TV.

"Cricket?" I said. I was in the kitchen getting glasses out of the cupboard. "Who's playing?"

"T20," he said. "India, South Africa. In Australia. The replay."

He scrolled through the channels until he found it. When he brought it up—the helmeted batsman standing calmly in front of his wicket, eyes narrowed against the sun—Finlay stood back, one hand on his hip, and muttered something to himself.

"We could eat by the TV," I said. "Actually, I'm not eating. I just made for you."

"I don't need to watch it," he said. "I'll just keep it on. Just to see the score. You know."

I did know. If it's one thing you learn growing up in the West Indies it's that people want to know the score. And Finlay hasn't got a TV in his place—he's renting a studio flat near the hospital. That's the only reason I have all the sports channels on my TV package: so the boys can get the games they want to watch when they come over here.

"I have beer," I said. "Beer, wine, Fanta, Coke. And apple juice. You're on tomorrow morning? You could have one beer if you want?"

"Tomorrow evening," he said. "They changed the rota again."

"Again! You're working another night? Didn't you already do two this week?"

He pulled out a chair at the table where his place was set, and I set the beer in front of him while he explained about a kidney that was supposed to have been done on Friday, and had had to be rescheduled for Monday; something complicated about lab results from a blood test that hadn't come through because someone had put the wrong color label on the package. The story involved the consultant and another surgeon, and the admin staff and several nurses. I started frying his steak while he talked. I already knew the names of all the key players: the efficient office lady, the lazy office lady, the new clueless girl, the nurses, with their varying degrees of willingness and competence; the other trainees and their propensity to suck up to the consultant; as well as the unspoken hierarchy between all the trainees, based on things like how many appendixes they had taken out, or how many complex Cesareans they'd seen, or what tools they'd used to get inside a patient's skull. It's not for the fainthearted, some of it. But I like hearing about it. I enjoyed practicing medicine for the time that I was able. I was good at it too.

"Not eating?" he asked, when I brought his food over to him.

"Nah," I said. "I already ate. And I only eat once a day now. Slow metabolism."

He sat in his usual spot—the spot that always used to be his when this table was in the old house, with his back to the wall. I pulled out the chair at the head of the table and sat.

He pressed the back of the fork against the steak and studied the juice that ran out. Then he cut through the middle and studied the color of the inside of the meat. He takes it well-done: no oozing blood. Satisfied, he cut a small bit off and put it in his mouth and began to chew.

For a few minutes, I watched him eat. I've always made a point of sitting with them for meals. My grandmother used to do that with me and my brothers, whenever we were at her house in Cascade—I think that must be where I got it from.

Usually, I talk about this and that: the goings-on in our network of friends and family, what I'd been up to—just the little ordinary, day-to-day things. But now, as I watched Finlay work through his steak, I wasn't sure where my mind was. Monica Sartori was now present in my mind as a kind of alertness, or anxiety. I had Finlay in front of me, with those red patches on his knuckles and in between his fingers, and the winter hadn't even started. And so thin! Jesus Lord Father, I was thinking. Not in a religious way, you understand, it was more of a general motherly despair. Jesus Lord Father! Help me with this child!

He must have felt me studying him. "Don't ask me about the complaint," he said. "I don't want to talk about all that right now."

"I wasn't going to," I said. My eyes drifted to the TV, and then back to him. Silence fell again, and then he must have seen something on my face, and he raised his eyes, as if to say, What?

"I wasn't going to tell you," I said. "But I guess, why not. Another person has been in touch. A girl. I mean, a woman. From the websites. As a possible, you know. Match."

"Oh!" He put his knife and fork down, and sat up straight.

The atmosphere changed and I wished I hadn't said anything. It's only weakness on my part, anxiety about it, anxiety about him, that made me open my mouth. But it's not good for him. It never brings anything good.

"Okay," he said. "When you say 'possible,' what do you mean?"

"Well, the right age," I said. "Presumed age."

"Right, sure. So"—he paused, calculating, or pretending to calculate—"how old is that, forty? Fortysomething?"

"Forty-two."

"Okay, well that's a good start," he said. "Have you told Oscar?"

"No, no," I said. "This only just happened. I only saw her email last night, and I replied to her this morning. This is new-new. I wasn't even going to mention it. No point getting people excited, you know."

"Sure. Makes sense."

He was watching me closely, and I tried to take on the right manner. Steady and controlled, hopeful but in a measured way. With a hint of detachment, as if I were talking about something at a much greater remove, of academic interest. I said she was in Italy, a town in the north, and that she was a professional person, a biochemist with a pharmaceutical company.

I could see all the questions in his mind, an explosion of questions arriving all at once, and so I carried on talking in the same calm way, answering them, as far as I knew. The town was Verona. Yes, I know, we had been there ourselves. Funny, wasn't it, to think that we might have practically rubbed shoulders with her, so to speak. I said she'd sent a photo, and I got up as I spoke, and opened up the iPad, and said, I'll show you, let me just log in and find it again. I explained the circumstances she'd outlined. That her parents, her adoptive parents, an Italian couple, had been living in Caracas at the time, and she had been adopted there in 1982.

"Hmm," he said. "I mean. Sounds plausible. Right? Are you excited?"

"Too early to get excited," I said. "You know how it is. She could be anybody."

"Right," he said. "Sure. Right." He was holding out his hand for the iPad, so he could look at her photo.

He pushed his chair back to make space, and he held the iPad with one hand, and hovered his other hand over the screen. I watched him study the image that came up. He touched his thumb and middle finger to the screen and zoomed in. He might have been analyzing cells under a microscope: the eyebrows, the hairline, the chin, the shoulders. He zoomed out again, held the iPad away from him and considered the picture again; and then he shifted in his seat to face toward me, and he looked at the picture on the screen and then lifted his eyes to look at me; back down to the screen; back up at me.

He screwed up his mouth a fraction, as if saying, Hmm.

"You can't tell anything from the photos really," I said.

He set the iPad on the table, propped up so the screen was visible. He slid back in his seat and then put his hands in his pockets. His expression had changed. He seemed to be looking toward the wall. His plate was still in front of him with the remains of his dinner, the dark oil and juices from the fried plantain, and a few bits of gristle from the steak. I looked at the screen, where the woman named Monica Sartori smiled in our general direction. Beyond, in the living room, the umpire stood impassive with his hands behind his back, in his white shirt and sun hat and sunglasses, and a white streak of sunscreen on his nose.

"Ah well," I said. "That's what's going on."

Finlay nodded slowly. His expression had turned dark.

There's a whole history to all this, you understand. This isn't the first girl I've found, or who's found me. I wish I'd been able to hide how it's made me feel, over the years, but I haven't always been able to. I think he sees her—the invisible "her"—as a threat, or a kind of aggressor, someone who he needs to defend me against. That's part of why I shouldn't have said anything to him. But the truth is, that having shared the secret, I felt a little lighter, and I felt guilty to have made Finlay share the weight of it with me just so I didn't have to do it alone.

I got up and picked up his plate, and began clearing away. "Anyway. What about you? Any major developments on the—you know, the thing?"

The "thing" was the complaint. He doesn't like to be grilled about it, but we had to get away from the subject we'd been on, since there was nothing more to say, and it was inevitable that this subject would come up eventually.

Finlay sighed, and he leaned forward and started rubbing his hands over his face like I was stressing him out. The complaint is nothing terrible—just one of those things you have to learn to live with when you practice medicine: the fear of things escalating, and ending up in front of the medical board, and, ultimately, being struck off the register. It's all managed very slightly better than it used to be, but even so, doctors of all levels of experience find it stressful, and Finlay's always been a worrier.

He gave me an update anyway—holding his head in his hands while I cleared the table. He said he'd had a phone call with his medical association's support line, and there was a date set for an internal meeting with management. He loosened up as he went. He doesn't like to talk about it, but it's better for him—better not to hide things and let them mount up.

"Well, Warren said the beach house is free," I said, when there was a pause. "He said if we want to come, just come."

Finlay uncovered his face and looked at me through his hands.

"I know you said you can't go," I said, hastily. "I'm just passing on the information anyway, so you have it."

"I just cannot get the time off," he said. "I already told you."

"I know. I understand. Forget it. Some other time."

His mood had turned.

"You know, running off to Trinidad isn't necessarily the answer to every problem," Finlay said, suddenly.

"Sure. I know. I didn't say it was."

"Trinidad isn't exactly paradise or anything," he said. "All the crime, all the car crashes."

"And mosquitoes!" I added. I said it as a joke, to try to lighten the mood.

"Right."

"And flooding," I said. "They're having plenty rain now." And then I went on, trying to get him to warm to the joke. "Earthquakes! Floods! Plagues of locusts!"

But he was still looking angry, so I changed tack and said, "But don't you like it in Tobago? The beach house, man. We're so lucky to have it. Don't you think?"

"Sure," he said. "I mean—it's fine. It's not paradise. It's just a house by a beach."

"And a pool," I added, interrupting him. "We have the pool now too."

He sighed again. "It's nice. But it's not the solution to every problem. With you, it's like, any problem? Go back to Trinidad! That's your only solution to things. Go back to Trinidad. You know, if that's your solution, fine, go ahead. But it's not—just stop pressuring me."

"I'm not pressuring you," I said. "I'm only saying." I hesitated, and then took the plunge. "It's a thing you have to learn, Finlay. How to handle stress. You're a hard worker. Any time you have a problem, you think what you have to do is just work harder. Everything with you is just work, work, work. But you can't do like that. You'll burn out. You have to rest. That's all I'm trying to tell you."

Miraculously, it seemed to go in. He lowered his shoulders, and there might even have been a little nod, of him accepting the truth of what I'd just said.

"You're having a stressful time at work," I said. "First, the pandemic. And now this whole complaint business," I said. "Look at how baggy your clothes are. You're losing weight. Take a few days' rest in the sun. That's all I'm saying. A little vitamin D."

He looked down at his hands, at the red patches between his fingers. I had to stop myself from saying all the things I used to say when he was younger. ("Cream, Finlay! You have to use the moisturizing cream! Morning and night!")

That was the end of the conversation for that evening. He settled down on the sofa and watched the rest of the cricket. I washed up, and then I came and sat with him, my hands clasped in my lap, my eyes on the TV screen but not really paying attention. When the match finished, he yawned and looked at his watch, and not long after that, we were back in the hallway by the pine table and the mirror on the wall, and he was resting his hand on the table, and putting on his shoes to leave.

10

ALTOGETHER, OVER TEN YEARS PASSED BEFORE I SPOKE ABOUT THE baby. It seems hard to account for all those years now. From the age of seventeen to twenty-six, my life carried on, I suppose, like a normal life. I did all the sorts of things that other people of my age did: I got through my A-levels, went on to medical school. I pulled all-nighters before my big exams. I had friendships, afternoons in the pub, boyfriends, even. Movies. Shopping. Picnics. It sounds carefree; it wasn't quite that. But I suppose I was sticking to a sort of conviction that I had a right to these things: privately, I felt a mixture of relief and guilt, to have escaped the life of prams and dirty diapers and milk bottles and plastic toys. When I thought about the baby, I imagined her growing well—being cared for by someone adult and capable. It seemed quite logical that she was being looked after by someone else, since I wasn't good enough to look after her myself. But I wasn't able to express that at the time: it's only through so many hours reading the adoption forums that I'm able to recognize, and put into words, that that's what I felt.

Somewhere along the line, though, I started having a bad dream, of a person with no hands. I couldn't see the person clearly, and I didn't have a sense of them being male or female, or big or small, only that they were watching me from somewhere nearby, and their hands were missing. It was like the hands had been cut off, but there was no blood or anything like that, just stumps. It doesn't sound that scary, but it was a terrible dream. And I was always alone when I woke up: that was almost worse than the dream itself. I'd wake up to the room all silent and black, and I'd listen out for the sounds of my mother and father down the corridor, or my brothers in the room across the hall, and gradually I'd remember I was in England, alone.

DURING THOSE TEN OR SO years, I went down to Trinidad regularly—at least once a year, sometimes twice. I'm sure people knew about me: I wasn't so naïve as to think that it could have stayed a complete secret. It was humiliating, at first: wherever I went, I was aware of people's eyes fixing on me, studying, taking note. Even in the departure lounge at Heathrow, for example, there was nearly always someone I knew on the same flight down from London, and then I had to try to pretend to sleep for most of the ten-hour flight to avoid the interrogation. Then, when I was home, of course, I ran into people I knew everywhere. Jogging around the Savannah at five o'clock in the afternoon, I was aware of people studying me through their car windows as they drove by. (I knew what the conversation in those cars would be: "Who's that white girl again? She look like a Bishop! That must be the one who . . .") It was impossible to hide. In the aisles of Tru Valu grocery in Maraval; at the UWI traffic lights on my way down to San Fernando to see my cousins; every Sunday morning at Assumption Church: standing in our usual pew, then going up for Communion, then after church, while everyone milled around chatting in the car park—everywhere I went, I knew, I was being whispered about and scrutinized.

But if people knew about me, there was also a social convention to allow me to keep up my pretense of a secret. At many of these places I've described, wherever I ran into someone I knew, there'd be the usual conversation—always casual and cheery questions, to which I gave casual and cheery answers, even as the questioner's eyes flicked all around my body, searching for telltale clues. Oh, Dawn! You've been away! Where you've been? (I'm in England, I'd reply.) Oh, England! Where, London? (Yes, London.) Oh, what you're doing up there? You're studying? What you're studying? (I duly replied to all these questions.) Oh, medicine! Well, you were always bright! And how long you're down for? Oh, only two weeks? So short? You're going to come back after you qualify? Oh, you don't know yet? You'll wait and see? And all the while, the eyes would be flicking about, taking note.

In retrospect, these little interrogations with their hidden subtexts didn't last as long as I'd feared: in fact, after I'd got through the first few visits home, the feeling of being closely observed wore off. It's possible that I just got used to it, or that people got used to me. But it's also true that, around that time, the early 1980s, bigger changes were happening in the country, and people's attention was elsewhere. That was at the beginning of the oncoming oil crash, just at the point when prices were beginning to slide. Whenever I was down, the talk was of retrenchments and recession; how to apply for a green card; get the hell out of here. (The blasted oil cartels; blasted Saudi Arabia and the U.S.; how Venezuela could stand up to them; or Castro could stand up.) The side effect of this nervousness was that a lot of people my age were applying to universities abroad, or trying, in whatever way they could, to "get out." When I was in Trinidad during the holidays, I was one of many people of my age who were studying abroad, and had come home—for Christmas, or for the summer, or for Carnival, or for Easter, whenever. It was easy to blend in, is what I'm saying, with all of this going on in the background.

Economically, a bad time was coming, that was clear. Every morning, first thing, people checked the front page of the newspaper for the price per barrel; every evening on the seven o'clock news, the first thing the newsreader announced was the price it had reached so far that day. Some people said the volatility was only temporary, and that, in any case, Trinidad had other things besides crude oil: we had ammonia, fertilizer, methanol; we had steel, cement, refineries. Others said that the petroleum industry could be built back up over time—after all, the oil was still in the ground, and the natural gas and the pitch lake, and that would count for something in the long term. Other people again said that we would have to turn to tourism. Nobody believed that would ever work for us, though: having to be like the little islands, groveling for tourists' money.

All this was discussed all across the country, in countless homes and rum shops and maxi taxis and street corners: month after month, this went on. Then, word came that the government would have to devalue the TT dollar, and that made it more or less official. The good times were over: the crash was real.

I was in medical school in the UK by that stage, with a good few years to go before I was fully qualified. Ryan had dropped out of his degree in the U.S.: he'd come home for a short period, and then gone away again to the Cave Hill campus in Barbados to start his law degree. Of the three of us children, only Warren was living in Trinidad at the time. I'd always thought that Warren was the most likely to go into the family businesses anyway, but he said to me later that it was only during the worst of the oil crash time, the late part of 1985, when he finally made his decision. He'd had no choice: he couldn't just sit down and watch his family's companies disappear—everything he'd watched his father work all his life for, just go down the drain. It was he who told my father to shut down the less profitable businesses and focus on the two or three companies that were still making money. Juice was making money; food packaging was making money. The branding business—it was a new business, just a little company printing signage for advertising billboards—that one got shut down. The transport business, they scaled back to Trinidad only.

They had to lay off some people: Warren did it. There was no HR or anything like that in those days: Warren would have just gone to the workers, wherever they were, in the factory, or in the fields, and said, Look, man, we winding up. He gave them good severance pay. Out on the patio, retelling the story of it, in later years, he said, it wasn't kindhearted, you know. (I'm paraphrasing, but this was the gist of it.) He said, it wasn't, oh, I am a Christian, I'm handing out charity. He said, no. When you run a business? Every decision is a business decision. It cost me less to give them a little payout, rather than have them come back a month later and slash my tires, or burn down the trees on my farm. Better to pay them off. And if in a few months' time, or a year's time, things improve? Well, then you might be able to rehire them again.

But that was later, when there was time to sit out on the patio and old-talk and reminisce. In those tough early days of the oil crash, I hardly saw Warren when I was down. He left the house before five A.M. to drive down south to the farms; he was back late, close to midnight.

I was struck, in those days, by how much Warren looked like a man. Not just in a physical sense—he would have been in his late twenties—but a man in the Trinidadian sense of the word. It's something to do with a sense of authority, and a sort of fearlessness that some men grow into. It helps to have worked outdoors with other men; to know how to swing a cutlass. When Warren arrived back at the house in the evenings, his shoes were caked with mud, and he smelled foul. His shirt-sleeves were smeared with grime, from having used them to wipe sweat off his face. The dogs approached him cautiously, and he let them sniff for a few moments, but when he was done, they knew it, and drew back. As for us, we made way for him. Food and drink were brought to him, replenished, cleared away. When he opened his mouth, the rest of us hushed and let him speak.

EVERYONE KNOWS THE TIMELINE OF those years, so much has been written about the boom-and-bust of that period. Prices peaked in mid-1985, and over the course of a terrible, jittery year, they went down . . . down . . . and down again. When the crash hit, it was like an earthquake, with so many aftershocks reverberating throughout the region. Foreign companies began pulling out. Laborers who were suddenly unemployed piled up rubber tires in the middle of the highway and set them on fire in protest. Everywhere you looked, in those days, there was smoke rising up from these fires, and everywhere you went, the smell of burning.

Trinidad and Tobago had to devalue its currency in late 1986; a second devaluation came two years later in 1988; the IMF came the year after that, 1989. And not quite a year later, Trinidadians got a real shock: an attempted coup d'état in the capital, Port of Spain, on the afternoon of Friday, July 27, 1990.

I was in England when it happened, but my parents rang me within the hour, and over the following days, it came on international news: the BBC radio first, and then CNN. A group known as the "Jamaat al Muslimeen" were behind it, led by a man who went by the name Abu Bakr. His real name was something else: he was a black man, a convert to Islam. He was well known in Trinidad: he had a certain following.

The Jamaat invaded the Red House, where ministers were debating in parliament, and took the ministers hostage; at the same time they took over the broadcasting station, and took hostages there too; and they bombed the central police station in Port of Spain. Then at seven o'clock, Abu Bakr came on the evening news, him in his white robes, with fellas with balaclavas and machine guns standing behind him, announcing that he had taken over the country.

In the end, it was a failed coup—it lasted six days, and order was eventually restored—but there's no doubt that it was a turning point for Trinidad and Tobago. And as I've said, Venezuela had several coup attempts not long later, so all this was symptomatic of the anger and unrest that had taken over the entire region.

But I'm getting carried away. What I really wanted to get to was the trip that Robert and I made down to Trinidad the year of the coup. We were already engaged then—it was a sort of engagement, meet-the-family trip. We were supposed to have gone down in the summer, but as soon as the coup happened, of course, we had to cancel our flights. We ended up going down, instead, at Christmas. Rob, by the way, is English-English: white English, from a place called Derby (pronounced "darby"). We got engaged while we were both still in medical school. It was what people did back then—everyone paired up quite early. No one wanted to be left on the shelf.

In any case, what I remember is that once Rob and I landed at the airport in Trinidad, the reality hit, how very different it was to England. This was back in the days of the old airport building—such a meager, ramshackle thing, back then. I hadn't paid it much attention before, but now, arriving with Rob, I noticed that the paint peeled off the walls, the fluorescent lights flickered. The tourist board posters, in the room that was grandly labeled "Arrivals Hall," with their photos of Carnival and hummingbirds and bottles of Carib beer, were faded from age. Everything struck me then as amateur and ridiculous. And as for Rob—I think it must have been a shock for him to be the only white man; a shock to be surrounded by so many black faces. As we waited by the conveyor belts for our suitcases to arrive, standing side by side with our arms folded, I was aware of his discomfort. But maybe it's a reflection of the fact that we really didn't know each other all that well, because I couldn't think of anything suitable to say, and I suppose neither could he, and as we walked out toward the exit barriers to meet my waiting family, I think we both felt slightly embarrassed.

Even the nighttime drive from the airport back to Port of Spain, which I've always loved, seemed different. The swamp had a worse stink than usual. And there were so many dead dogs on the highway! I saw him take in all those little huts by the side of the road, the silhouettes of children sitting on the back steps of the houses, while, behind them, women in loose, ragged dresses moved around inside. The music and noise from the rum parlors, the men who sat at tables there drinking and playing cards. These things seemed to indicate something that I'd concealed about Trinidad, although I couldn't have articulated exactly what it was. Everything that I loved—the familiar outlines of the big trees, the warm, open air, the generous scattering of stars above us—all those things, I felt, went unnoticed.

As we came into Port of Spain, though, the place looked more respectable: better roads; bigger, nicer houses; restaurants; hotels. I saw him take note of the Hilton, and that he seemed to mentally tuck it away as a landmark. It was Christmastime, and usually on the drive back from the airport, we would have commented on the buildings and trees that had been decorated with lights: President's House, Manghal's restaurant on the eastern side; the champagne tree on the corner by the museum—not really a champagne tree, but lit so as to make the outline of a champagne glass. But all that went unremarked upon: all anyone could talk about on that trip was the coup. How it had happened, where everyone had been when the news broke out, what they thought when the fella who called himself Abu Bakr came on TV announcing that he had taken over the country.

As we came around the Savannah, my father, who was driving, took a detour downtown. Only a few months had passed since the attempted coup; no reconstruction had as yet begun. All along Queen Street and Charlotte Street, shops I used to know were caved in, everything blackened and melted by fire. My father drove slowly, the car tires crunching over broken glass, narrating the story of what had happened in those places. Brick walls and red stop signs and even tree branches were all pockmarked by bullets. From Charlotte Street, onto Queen Street: all along here, he said, as we drove slowly along—all along here, there was looting, and fires. We drove past the broadcasting station on Marli Street—three dead in there, he said. Past the Red House, our version of a Houses of Parliament, where so many government ministers had been held hostage for six days. "Twenty-two," my father told us, pointing one finger toward the blackened building. "Twenty-two dead in there."

I WAS TWENTY-SIX ON THAT trip, so Ryan and Warren must have been around thirty. We look so young in the photos I have in the album. I still had long hair then, dark brown, with a bit of curl. For most of that trip, I wore the kind of clothes you can only wear when you're young: tight, denim short-pants, rolled up to make them even shorter, and snug T-shirts or sleeveless vest-tops. I looked so good. I've always thought of my hips and thighs as a bit on the big side, but my waist has always been small, and the proportions on the young woman who I used to be are quite eye-catching, if I do say so myself.

We all look young in those photos. Warren with his smooth,

full cheeks, just the beginning of his real adult shape thickening out. He was married by then: with the first two children running around, and Suzanne, his wife, pregnant with the third.

Suzanne is my age, from south. A light-skinned Indian girl, dazzlingly pretty when she was young. She actually did a few beauty pageants when she was in her teens, and there was talk of her being Miss Trinidad and Tobago at one of the Miss World competitions. Her father was the CEO at the bank, and on all the boards. Warren and Suzanne have made a good couple: they have four children now, and they're still together and happy, after all these years. Suzanne is practical and sensible, more than a match for Warren and his I-wear-the-trousers sort of thing that I'm sure he likes to pull.

My middle brother, Ryan, is in the photos from that trip in 1990 as well. He had finished his law degree by then, but he was still living in Barbados, and married, to a white Bajan woman called Samantha, also a lawyer. (Samantha was pregnant too: in one of the photos, she and Suzanne stand back-to-back, to show off their respective bumps.) But where Suzanne was always sensible and matter-of-fact, I seem to remember that Samantha was one of those porcelain-pregnant women: dainty, ostentatiously protective of her bump, and full of her own importance. I remember Ryan being bad-tempered on that trip. At the time, I took it personally: I thought he didn't like having me around, and that he didn't like having to come all the way from Barbados with his pregnant wife to make a fuss about me and my new fiancé.

Ryan and I have never got on that well, as I've mentioned. During all those years, the pact had been maintained at home, and I had never spoken to my brothers about what had happened. But still, there were occasionally uncomfortable moments, when I could tell the memory of my mistake passed through their mind—what I had done, the age I had done it, the shame we were all now tinged with because of it. But I'm only guessing. It's possible that what I interpreted as bad-temperedness or a dislike of me personally was something else—worry, or stress, something that might have been nothing to do with me.

Everyone had come to the house to welcome me and Rob home, and we gathered on the patio in the evening, as always. Warren had cleaned up after work, and changed into clean shorts and T-shirt. You could see my father in Warren, in the broadness of the chest and shoulders, and in the strong, muscular calves. Even their way of talking was similar—loud and somehow persuasive, by virtue of its being direct, and down-to-earth. Warren had a light-brown color all over him, a healthy, toasted color, compared to the pale skin that Rob and I had from being in England. My other brother, Ryan, had always been paler-skinned than Warren, and he was still very fair-skinned as an adult, with his air-conditioned office life. That evening, he was wearing trousers and a button-down shirt, and lace-up shoes. He sat very neatly and calmly, with his legs crossed, and if I remember rightly, he may even have refused my mother's offer of beer, and taken a glass of 7 Up instead.

Now that I've had two sons, I realize that there must have always been a little friction between Warren and Ryan. When they were younger, Ryan always used to be the more academic one: he had studied law, while Warren had only done sports science, which wasn't really a proper degree. But now, Warren had taken over the businesses: it would have brought him closer to my father; it might have made Ryan resentful. In any case, when we were all together, as on that first evening, it was Warren who spoke the most, but glancing frequently at Ryan, as if to see what his reaction was. He said things like, "You see me? I am just a humble businessman!" And he would laugh, as if inviting people to laugh with him. "Me? I have no brains like Mr. Law-Man there. Me? The only thing for me? Was to work with my hands. But let me tell you something! I drive up and down this whole place every day. Every day, from six o'clock in the morning, I'm out on the road, working, sweating. I don't know about books, but I know what I know, because I see things with my two eyes." And he would put two fingers to his two eyes, for extra emphasis. And everyone would be nodding along, in full agreement with everything he said.

Rob was a little nervous, but he tried hard and he did well. My family, for their part, tried hard to make him feel welcome. He liked the rum—that was good. There was a lot of talk about the coup. And I can't quite remember how the conversation took the turn that it did—I think Rob must have made a comment, designed to be neutral and polite, something along the lines of, "Well, it looks like you've pulled through the recession," or something like that. He meant that the Bishops seemed to be doing okay. And I think that Warren said something modest in response: "Oh, we're staying alive." If I had to try to replay the conversation, Warren would reply more fulsomely: he'd say, "We're staying alive," and he'd raise his shoulders in a sort of long shrug, as if to indicate something like uncertainty, or modesty. "By the grace of God, we're still alive. The businesses I mean. Not us. Well, us too, ha ha! We're alive. For the moment."

And I think Rob must have spoken next, and again he said something that was meant to be generic and broadly cheerful, like, "Well, you must be doing something right."

Whatever it was, there was a momentary lull. Drinks were lifted and sipped. Rob must have sensed that he had strayed into the wrong territory, and he sat with a polite half smile on his face, looking out at the night sky, waiting for someone else to change the subject. I also sensed a tension, but I didn't know what it was about. My father looked steadily at me, one arm bent behind his head, in a way that made me think he was avoiding looking elsewhere. Warren drank from his glass, but his attention was on my father. My mother gazed at nothing in particular. Suzanne and Samantha, the two wives, exchanged a look.

"Well, what you have to do is choose who you get into bed with," Ryan said, dryly. "That's the way it works in Trinidad these days. You have to get into bed with someone."

Ryan said those words: You have to get into bed with someone. I remember the deliberateness in his expression, and how he sat with his legs crossed, and his glass raised in his hand, and he said the words as if carelessly, but that others were bristling.

"Things are very complex here," Warren said, to Rob, in a tone as if explaining what Ryan had said. "It's a very complex place."

"Luckily, there are a number of options," Ryan said, in the same dry, didactic tone.

"Well, you can't survive alone, that's for sure," Warren said. "In life, and in business, it's the same. Who can survive all alone? You need alliances."

It was becoming tense; the wives tried to break it up. I think it was Suzanne, Warren's wife, who spoke.

"Yes, it's late. Look, Dawn and Robert want to get in their bed," Suzanne said. Then she caught herself, and put her hand to her mouth. "Not together," she said, hastily. "I mean—they do want to get in bed together, but . . ."

It did break up the tense mood: everyone laughed at that, and there was a little joking about how we had been put to sleep in separate rooms.

"You have to wait until the ring is on the finger," Warren said to Rob. They were all being jokey, messing around, taking the opportunity to laugh after the uncomfortable moment. "You're in my father's house now, young man. I hope you know how to behave."

And then Ryan said—and this is where I've been trying to get to, all this time—Ryan said, "Well, Dawn has learned her lesson. She'll be firm with the man if she needs to be. Tell him to hold his horses."

It was so casual. He just dropped it in, like it was nothing. Everyone laughed, probably, and my guess is that I must have laughed too, loudly, trying to hide my shock. I don't recall that Rob heard, or if he did, it must have gone over his head. We all cleared up, and then went up to bed—me to my old bedroom, and Rob to the room across the corridor, the one that my brothers used to sleep in when we were all children, and we all lived together under the same roof. Nothing further was said about it at all, that night, or anytime during the trip, or in the intervening years. But for me, that moment on the patio marked a subtle shift: for the first time, it occurred to me that my family might have talked about it—about me—between themselves while I wasn't there. That they might not have kept to the pact as strictly as I had, in other words. I began to wonder if the loyalty and trust I had felt toward my family might instead have been a sort of gullibility, or a childish innocence.

FINLAY WAS BORN IN 1992, two years after that trip to Trinidad, in a cool gray London hospital room, with a midwife and doctors this time, and machines, and medicines. His was a difficult birth. Rob was there for most of it, but he seemed to me like one of the doctors, studying readings, snapping at the nurses, standing beside the other doctors with his arms folded, looking between my parted legs. That makes him sound dreadful; he wasn't dreadful. It's just that hospital consultants tend to feel that the world revolves around them, and in a way, it does. Also, it was on that day that Rob found out about the child I'd had in Venezuela. I saw him pick up my notes from the end of the bed. No one stopped him. It must have been a shock to read that this was, in fact, my second baby, and not my first. He silently slid the clipboard back into the pocket at the foot of the bed. He walked a few steps away, toward the window. There, he stood for a long time, his hands in his pockets, looking out at the Houses of Parliament across the Thames.

But it was only during the very early stages of that labor that I had any spare attention to notice what Robert was doing. Once things really got going, I was on my own. And I had the strangest experience during that labor: flashbacks, I guess. There must be a physiological explanation for this sort of thing.

But really vivid. It was all in front of my eyes, clearly—or even more than that: it was as if my body were literally there, in the room in Venezuela, and I were living through it all again. I saw the burglar-proofing that was over the windows. (Later, I was able to draw out the pattern with a pencil and paper, from this renewed memory.) The newspaper that the other girls had laid over the floor to catch the blood, the faintly dusty smell of it, the soft crackle that the nuns' footsteps made. As I lay on my back, I saw the Celotex ceiling panels, the fluorescent striplight; the clock on the wall, slightly askew; the wooden crucifix over the window. And yet, while my body was remembering being in Venezuela, it was also, physically, in London, in the cool gray room. What was wrong about London was that no one was praying. I felt the lack of that. I wanted the words. I tried to speak them, or, rather, they tried to speak themselves, in fragments.

The pain was just like the first time. It starts as an ache in the small of your back, and wraps itself around your abdomen—gradually, like a warmth spreading. Then comes a tightening, or squeezing, more merciless than the warmth: more like the action of a steel clamp. The clamp tightens; the pain increases. You kind of count your way through it until you can't count any more, and you want to die, and maybe your eyes flicker open for a moment to look for a gun or something to shoot yourself with; no gun, no escape; and then the pain keeps on going, and then the room drops away to a kind of darkness, or nothingness. During those moments of peak pain, incandescent pain, it felt as if I weren't with my body at all. Trying to describe it now, I might say: imagine the bottom of the seabed. Or imagine drifting in millions of dust particles out in space. Or being tucked safe inside a cave deep in the mountains. Back I came to the hospital room: objects hardening into their physical shapes; sounds returning; voices; meaning. Then the warmth in the small of my back; the wrapping of the steel claws; the increasing pain; the desire to die; the dropping away; the dark. The bright hospital room, the cold steel instruments, the buzz of machines—the spreading warmth, the evil tightening, the dark. On and on it went, relentless. At times, in the dark, I felt as if I sensed the presence of others. I couldn't see any faces: it was as if we were gathered around a fire, and I saw their shadows on the wall.

In London, in that hospital with the view of the Thames, the baby, Finlay, was placed in my arms: 7 lb., 2 oz., swaddled so that only his face was visible. I was on one of those big mobile hospital beds. I only vaguely recall being pushed into the wide elevator by the hospital porter. I must have looked a sorry sight: pale, unwashed, with bloodshot eyes, and greasy, tangled hair. People must have pressed themselves against the walls to make space for me; they must have stared, or tried not to stare.

The porter wheeled me to a different floor. I don't have a clear memory of it, just that it seemed a gray, dreary sort of place, like a waiting room. Women were wheeled in looking stunned. Sometimes they got out of bed and went down the hall to find a nurse, and then they walked slowly and raggedly, wheeling their babies with them. At night, the lights on the ward were dimmed so that we could try to sleep, but I doubt anyone slept. Babies cried all through the night. Women cried too, behind their paper curtains.

What I remember about that first night in the hospital with

Finlay. The night seemed endless. The semidark. The paper curtains of my cubicle. A dazed feeling: drugs wearing off, maybe. The memory of the labor still present in my body, the violence of it, my body's unexpected betrayal of itself. And the result: the new infant body in the plastic cot at my bedside; the rise and fall of his chest as he breathed.

I should have been exhausted. I hadn't slept for many days, or eaten. I had the feeling of my body being busy attending to its wounds, like an army of invisible workers setting to work after a battle. It wasn't so much a repair as a remaking. I was aware of a new wakefulness taking hold of my body; a new way of being; a vigilance.

And that first night, there was a moment that was different to the others. I remember it as a pause, a momentary hesitation, a glimpse of the road that lay ahead: days, months, years, as Finlay's custodian. My job was to keep him moving, inch by inch, breath by breath, along the tightrope of his new life. I wouldn't have been able to use those words then, of course; language hadn't come back to me yet. I just remember a feeling of dread as if facing something fearsome—once I took up the burden, I knew, I would never put it down again.

A moment of private observation, that's all: of a choice quietly made. When I closed my eyes to rest, I laid a hand on Finlay's chest so I could feel the rise and fall of his breathing.

At some point during the first night, standing in my dimly lit cubicle, I looked down at the floor and I remember not being able to comprehend where so much blood had come from: one large pool on the ground around my feet, and another smaller one just behind me, and other drops and smears where my feet had stepped. I remember that I felt strange, lightheaded; that I held the bed with one hand, and the edge of Finlay's cot with the other, trying to keep myself steady; and that the larger pool of liquid, dark and shimmering, spread and shifted until it touched the smaller one and seemed to engulf it.

11

THERE WAS A WOMAN WHO CAME TO THE HOUSE WHEN FINLAY was a baby, a sort of healthcare worker, by the name of Mrs. S. Mittle, who was sent by the hospital after I was discharged, to check how I was getting on at home. We were living in Clapham when Finlay was born, in a rented attic flat up three flights of stairs. The woman visited several times over the course of a few weeks, and she probably gave useful advice—I was struggling; Robert was back at work, and I was on my own—but only one thing that she said has stuck with me. She was Irish, this Mrs. Mittle, middle-aged, with short, graying hair and glasses with thick lenses that had the effect of magnifying her eyes. I remember the enlarged brown eyes behind the thick lenses, and that they were mesmerizing in their steadiness. It was clear from the way she walked into the flat, stepping over rubbish bags that hadn't been taken out, and clearing a space for herself at the little rickety table in the kitchen, that this Mrs. Mittle had seen everything and knew everything, and nothing could surprise her. She had my maternity notes with her, a thick folder containing all the forms I had filled in while I was pregnant, all the scans and blood test results and measurements taken. While she waited for Finlay to settle down, Mrs. Mittle opened the file and began to leaf through. "Now, it says here, this is your second baby?" Mrs. Mittle asked. "Where is the older child?"

This would have been three or four days after the birth: I was half-awake, unwashed; I was probably also half-clothed, struggling to get the baby to feed. I said that the child was gone; that I had given her away. I might also have said that the older child was twelve, or would have been twelve if she was still alive, or something like that: I only remember that I didn't have the energy to come up with a fabrication.

Mrs. Mittle must have been at least a little startled; she must have asked some further questions, and I must have replied. In any case, what I do remember is that Mrs. Mittle, looking back at the file, adjusted her glasses calmly, that she seemed to have to take a moment before getting back to the job at hand, and said, "I'm sorry." She didn't mean that she was sorry for asking; she meant that she was sorry I had had to give the baby away. Later, it occurred to me that Mrs. Mittle was the first person to have said that.

The nuns hadn't talked about how it would feel, nor had the other girls at the hostel. Or maybe they had, and I hadn't understood. The one thing that they had done, which somehow everyone had understood and accepted, was that as soon as the baby was born, they quickly took it away to another room. The first time I witnessed it was with the girl called Salomé, the one who had looked like a corpse on the bed when I crept in to see her. I remember she had long black hair; she was proud of her hair. She brushed it frequently, and kept it in a ponytail, which she liked to have over one shoulder. On that particular day, her hair had been plaited, whether by her or someone else I don't know, but when I came in, the plait was frayed and loose. One of the younger nuns was at the side of the room with the baby, holding it in her arms and smiling down at it while it cried. The baby was a boy, I remember that. Salomé's skin was an unnatural color, and her eyes were bloodshot. The newspaper on the floor was soaked a dark maroon color; the room smelled of rusted iron. When the baby cried, Salomé turned her head toward the baby, and an older nun quickly made the younger one turn around, and she said something to her. I watched as the two women's shoulders moved close to each other, and then the one who was holding the baby went out of the room.

The older nun, let's say her name really was Hermana Maria-Theresa, came to Salomé, carrying a plastic bowl she had filled with water at the sink, and she dipped the washcloth into the warm water and wrung it out, and she lifted Salomé's hand and began to wipe it clean. She cleaned that hand, and then the next; and then she dipped the cloth in the water and wrung it out, and gently began to clean Salomé's face; and as she cleaned, she spoke all the time, her voice soothing.

Maybe it was because I was having to guess the meaning of the words, I watched the Hermana's face closely, and I saw that she felt sorry for Salomé. At the time, I thought she only felt sorry because of the state Salomé was in, and because there was so much blood. But later—not immediately after the incident with Mrs. Mittle, but at some point after that, when the words had sunk in—when I recalled that moment with Hermana Maria-Theresa murmuring to Salomé and gently washing her hands with the cloth, I understood it differently.

THAT ATTIC FLAT IN CLAPHAM: we'd moved in just after we got married, and it was only ever meant to be temporary, but it was nearly eight years before we were able to save enough for a deposit for a house, and we finally moved to the nice house in Wandsworth. I hated the Clapham place. It was tiny, for a start: one bedroom, one bathroom. When Finlay was born, we put a cot in the corner of our bedroom, and then when Oscar came, we had to rearrange everything to fit a second cot, and a foldout sofa in the living room for when one of them was sick and I had to stay up all night. Then when they started school we had to find space for bigger beds, school uniforms, scooters, bicycles—those eight years in Clapham were spent in a constant shuffling around of furniture, folding things out for the night and folding them back up in the morning, trying to make things fit.

It didn't have proper windows: there was one dormer window in the living room, which gave a view toward Clapham Common if you were able to get up high enough to see; the rest were just skylights, so that you could only see a little rectangle of sky. And it was cold. That was the worst thing. Drafts came in through the floorboards, and through the open fireplace, and through gaps around the windows. When I was on maternity leave with Finlay, walking around half-clothed, with baby Finlay on my hip, I tried to fill in these gaps as much as I could, with newspaper or wads of cloth, but it didn't help that much. The cold still came in.

And Rob was infuriating about the heating: he insisted on having the heating on for an hour in the morning "before work" and for an hour in the evening "after work." They were the timings he had grown up with, timings that worked well for people who worked in offices, and who were out of the house all day. I couldn't make him understand that if I was at home with a baby all day, the house needed to be heated. I alternated between sitting on the sofa breastfeeding Finlay, covered in blankets and worrying I was going to smother him, and turning up the heating, and preparing for an argument with Rob.

Rob and I argued a lot in those days—about bills, about him not getting enough sleep, about me not getting to work enough hours, since I had qualified as a medic at the same time as him, and I wanted to keep up my career just as much as he did. And we argued about the way we were living, cooped up in a little flat, no garden, having to carry the pram up and down three flights of stairs, and Finlay having to go to nursery for ten hours a day so I could go back to work.

Those early days when I was newly qualified were tough, for all sorts of reasons. Clinically, I was overly conscientious, and slow. Patients sometimes asked to see "the real doctor," or asked, suspiciously, where I was from. Within a few months, I learned how to handle that aspect of things, though. I smiled warmly as soon as the patient came into my drab little consulting room, and gestured to the gray plastic chair where they should sit. I introduced myself (as "Dr. Wilson"), I said that, yes, my accent was from Trinidad, in the Caribbean. I preempted their next question, and just went on to say that yes, there were white people in Trinidad. "It's very multicultural," I said cheerfully. This usually broke the ice, and then I would say, warmly and reassuringly—and I said this so many times, I still remember the exact words—"But I did all my training here in the U.K. I'm fully qualified, but if I have any doubts at all, I'll confer with my colleague. I'm here to look after you."

I did my best to appear calm and confident, in other words, and I think I succeeded to at least some extent. I hung a stethoscope around my neck: that must have helped. Previously, I'd had a wardrobe full of nice, professional clothes, but none of them fit me, after having Finlay. In those days, I remember, I had one pair of black nylon pants that I wore to work every day, and then a blouse and a cardigan, which sometimes went unironed—and, actually, weren't always clean.

My schedule in those days was punishing. I'd be up with Finlay two or three times during the night; then up for the day properly at around five thirty. I'd feed him and then lay him on a towel on the bathroom floor while I showered, and move him from room to room with me as I tried to eat breakfast, or made the bed, or gathered up his things. Then there was the battle with the pram and the three flights of stairs, and then a twenty-minute walk across Clapham Common, to take him to nursery. (That was the nicest part of the day, those early-morning walks through the Common with just me and Finlay.) I was at the nursery gate religiously every morning by 7:55; it would be 8:10 before my hands were free, and I'd jog back across the Common, down the hill to get to the practice with just enough time to let the sweat dry off before I had to see my first patient at eight thirty.

Every time Rob and I had a moment together, at that tiny square kitchen table that Mrs. Mittle had spread out her papers on, I tried to persuade him to move to Trinidad. I said, "My parents will help us. We can have a nice house, a pool. We can both work." He laughed politely, as if it were a joke. It never got beyond that: polite laughter, brush-offs. He said vague things like, "Maybe in the future." Or, "Let's see how things go." Or, "But there's no comparison, really, is there?"

Those first few months in the Clapham flat, after Finlay was born, were hard months for me. What I remember are the nights, when baby Finlay and I were alone in the living room, bundled under a pile of duvets to try to keep warm, and the room dark, the outlines and shadowy shapes of the objects in the room in their nighttime slumber, and realizing that I was stuck here in England, at the beginning of a life that I hadn't properly anticipated.

Nursery was hard on Finlay, and what was hard on Finlay was hard on me too. He went in when he was only a few months old: after the first week in nursery, he got a cold, and then a fever. He had to stay home for three days; I had to miss work. A few weeks later, he got another cold: another couple of days at home; another couple of days off sick for me; another couple of days that the GP surgery where I worked had to call in a locum, and the practice manager murmured about me being slack and unreliable. An argument with Rob. A few weeks later, another cold. This one came on the weekend, and he was improved enough by Monday to go to nursery, but by midweek, he had an ear infection. Antibiotics. For a baby! Then the eczema started, and the slathering on of creams, morning, afternoon, and evening. People tried to tell me it was normal, that it was just what happened when children went into nursery and picked up bugs from other children there. But by that stage, I'd had enough. I got on a plane and I took him home. Robert didn't argue with me—probably he was glad to have the flat to himself, and to be able to get an uninterrupted night's sleep.

I was home for a month, that time. This would have been in June or July, when Finlay was a few months old. It was the beginning of the rainy season but still nice—hot and bright in the mornings and scattered showers in the afternoons. My mother took time off; Warren's wife, my sister-in-law Suzanne, took time off. We went first to Maracas, the beach that is a twenty-minute drive from our house on the hill, and he improved so quickly that after a few days, we took a flight over to Tobago, and stayed the next ten days at the beach house. Finlay says that anytime I have a problem, I want to go back home: it's true, and it's partly because of that trip to Tobago. Finlay doesn't remember, but I remember. Sunlight. Birds. Splashing in the warm seawater. Digging his little hands through the sand. Biting into soft fruit picked from trees in the garden: guavas, mangoes, bananas. And my mother watched him, so that I could sleep—that was the miracle for me, the chance to sleep for a few hours at a time.

After those healing weeks in Tobago at the beach house, we came back to Trinidad, back to my family's house on the hill. A lot of visitors came to see us then: some of my old schoolfriends who I was still in touch with, family friends, my cousins—everyone came to see Finlay, and to give him a cuddle and a kiss, and bring some sweet little clothes for him, or a little toy. And we went out and about a lot too. Around the Savannah for coconuts and snow cones; to the Emperor Valley Zoo to show him the blue-and-yellow macaws, and the alligator and the one lazy lion who'd been there forever in his same walled enclosure. He was too young to remember any of it, of course, but my mother and I enjoyed showing him things for the first time, and taking photos.

When we were at home, we spent most of our time in the living room downstairs, the same living room as always, with the white-tiled floor, just by the kitchen and the doors opening out to the patio. There were the same brown corduroy couches as always, the same lamps on the small tables in the corners of the room. My mother sat on her same place as usual, the left side of the sofa, with her back to the wall, so that she looked out toward the patio. We pushed the coffee table away to the side, and Finlay had his space on the floor in between us, on a rug, with soft blankets and cushions, and his changing mat, and all his squeaky toys.

We must have spent many hours like this during that month-long trip. My mother on one side, and me on the other, both of us watching Finlay lying on his back on the floor, kicking his chubby legs, grasping at the colorful zebras and lions of his mobile. We chatted, of course, and laughed at Finlay and spoke to him, and to each other; but the moments that are fixed in my memory are the ones when we both fell silent. It's possible, I think now, that we were both thinking the same thing: about the girl, who had once been this very age, who must have lain on a carpet somewhere with her own chubby legs, and her own colorful toys. She would have been twelve years old by then. I imagined her with smooth cheeks, her hair dark and curly like mine, tamed in two neat plaits.

And then this. It was in the car. My mother was driving—I think we must have been coming back from the grocery. Finlay had stayed at home with the maid, and just my mother and I were in the car together. There must have been some preamble, something that allowed me to ask the question I asked, but I don't remember the details, and in any case, it doesn't matter. Somehow, these words spoke themselves: I heard myself saying them. I asked, "I've been wondering. You remember Venezuela. Where is the child now, do you know?"

We were passing that busy stretch by Maraval police station just then, with people walking in ditches at the side of the road, or walking out into the street and crossing in front of the car. My mother dropped one hand to the gear stick, and shifted down into first gear. Then she glanced at me and said, "Who?"

"The baby. From Venezuela."

I watched the left side of my mother's face. A flush of red, like a faint rash, appeared on her neck. The car lurched forward, stopped, lurched again.

She shot me a sharp look. "I don't know. How would I know?"

"But you must have a connection," I said. "You must know something."

"Why you're asking me this?" She was suddenly agitated, voice loud and then louder. "What are you getting at?"

"I'm just asking where she is."

She mashed gas, and then abruptly braked and then pulled over. My hands reached out to the dashboard to stop me sliding forward.

My mother turned her head and glared at me. "You want to get out?"

"What?"

"You want to walk the rest of the way?" she said.

Cars whizzed past us on the road just beside us. Inside the cars, heads turned to look at what was going on.

"You *want* me to get out?" I asked.

She glared at me a few moments more. Her face was flushed red all over. Then she pulled out into the road again. We turned in by the golf course, and drove past the bungalows. She turned up the steep road, and she drove the car hard all the way up, the engine loud and angry around the blind corners. At the top, the road leveled off and we passed the other houses that had sprung up, and then Warren and Suzanne's new house, which was just next to ours. She reached for the fob and pointed it toward our gate. As it slid open, she folded back the visor and she leaned forward over the steering wheel, checking the front drive.

"Look all around," she said. Her voice was more steady. This was their new ritual; we had done this before, arriving back at this gate. "Check your side. Look in those bushes." We looked around carefully as the gate slid open, all around the bushes to both sides, and in the front yard and the empty carport.

It took some time to get inside the house, waiting for the gate to slide closed, and then looking all around again before we unlocked the car doors and stepped out. The flush had subsided to just a few patches. Her hair stuck to her forehead with sweat.

A little later, in the kitchen: the two of us drawn together by her agitation and my unanswered question. She was by the sink, I was near the door to the patio, the kitchen island was between us.

"Why are you asking this now?" she said. "And you have a

husband, and a baby, and everything is going good for you? Eh? Why you're doing this? What's wrong with you?"

It may not have been exactly that, but it was something like that. And while she talked, from time to time she put up her hands near her head and she flapped the hands, distressed, as if flapping away a swarm of bees. I felt badly to have brought on this distress; I felt something was happening that I didn't fully understand.

"But *do* you know something?" I asked. "Are you trying to hide something?"

"No!" she said. "No! I'm not!" She flapped the hands. She was defensive, distressed, honest. "No. No! Not at all."

There's nothing else to recount of that incident, or that trip. She went upstairs to her room: I heard her shutting the door. I went out to the patio, and then, with the dogs trotting ahead of me, down the slope of the garden. We stayed in that uneasy silence until Finlay cried to say that he had woken, and I went back into the house, through the white-tiled living room, up the carpeted stairs, to the corridor. My mother must have heard Finlay crying too. She was standing in the doorway of her bedroom, facing into the corridor. It looked as if she were on her way to pick him up herself, but perhaps she had stopped when she heard me coming up the stairs. Her hair was untidy; she stood with one hand on the doorframe as if for support. She watched me, I thought, as if she were seeing something new, or unexpected. I pushed open the door to my brothers' old bedroom. I reached into the cot where Finlay lay crying, and picked up my child.

12

I'D SEEN MONICA SARTORI'S FIRST EMAIL ON FRIDAY, OCTOBER 28; I'd sent her my reply within a few hours, early on Saturday the 29th, and then I set about trying to stay busy, to keep my mind off it. Saturday was taken up with work in the morning, and then Finlay's visit in the evening; I needed another half tablet that night to help me sleep. On Sunday afternoon, I messaged Niall asking if he was around. He reminded me that the clocks had gone back. He said he'd be back from the gym around five P.M., and he suggested I come over to his house to watch a movie. He's very decent that way. I know the friendship we have won't last forever. He'll move on, at some point, or maybe I'll move on, and I'll be sorry to lose him, when that time comes.

Niall has a three-bed terraced place not far from our office in Tooting. It's bigger than he needs, but he took the first place he saw in the window when he came into the leasings office. He was just breaking up with his wife at that time, and he just wanted to get out, and he didn't care where, and he didn't care how much it cost. The house is on quite a nice street, and he's got a big garden out the back, which he doesn't bother with at all: he has someone come and cut the grass in the summer, and he lets the owner come in through the side gate whenever she wants, to do the flowerbeds. It's not that he's the careless sort. It's only that, I suppose, this place is a sort of stopgap for him. (A stopgap on his way to where, is the question, but at least he's well-off enough that he doesn't have to make up his mind just yet.)

In the living room, where we settled ourselves down to watch the movie, he's got two dark brown leather sofas at right angles to each other, one against the long wall, facing a big flat-screen TV, the other with its back to the bay window. The sofas are brand-new, good-quality leather, from an upmarket department store. I got him the rug, and a few cushions and lamps. They're from IKEA, and at first he resisted, said it was depressing at his age to be in a house with crap from IKEA, but I said, no, just imagine you're twenty again. It's your second chance. Life beginning again. The rug and the lamps are still there, anyway, he hasn't got rid of them, so I guess he was partly convinced, at least.

We sat on the bigger sofa together, with the takeaway boxes and our drinks on the coffee table, red wine for me, beer for him. I put my phone in my handbag, and pushed it under the table, out of sight. Niall put the movie on, the new Batman.

"To think this story started off as a comic book," I said to Niall. "And look how much they've done with it. So many movies!"

"Good against evil," he said. "It never gets old."

Niall's phone rang when we were halfway through. He looked at his watch, and then looked at the screen of his phone.

"My son. He hasn't called for a while," Niall said.

I pressed pause on the remote. "Of course," I said. It's something that goes without saying: whenever the kids call, you make time.

"Yeah, I've got a visitor," he was saying, into the phone. "No, it's fine. All good. How are you?"

I gave him a thumbs-up and then made a motion as if to say, Go, go, and he nodded and got to his feet, holding the phone to his ear. I heard him walk slowly down the corridor, and into the kitchen at the back.

I sat where I was for a while, comfortable. The room was dimly lit, just the light from the corridor, and the big flat-screen on the wall, with an image of a flight of stairs and a dark blur that was Batman's cape. On the coffee table, the scattered boxes of takeaway, glass bottles, paper napkins. The bottle of wine was half empty.

I reached for my handbag and unzipped it, and slipped my hand in to find my phone. I was thinking I would look up the buses, or see if I still had the Uber app on my phone. But once the phone was in my hand, my forefinger just tapped automatically on my email and brought up my inbox, and there was an email from her at the top.

Only some of it was in English, the rest was in Italian, as far as I could make out. Broadly positive. She was happy I had replied. Here was her "autobiography," below, in Italian, because it was difficult to write it all in English. I scrolled through the autobiography. I saw "Caracas" more than once, and other place names I didn't recognize, and several dates, 1981, 1982, something like that.

Niall appeared in the living room, holding the phone to his ear. I could hear his son's voice through the mouthpiece. Niall gave a thumbs-up, like a question, and out of instinct I smiled and nodded and gave him a thumbs-up back. He went back to the kitchen, and I was alone again. But now I wanted to get home, to be with this email that I'd just read, or sort of read. I poured myself some more wine, I have no idea why—I'd decided I had to leave, so I don't know what I thought the wine was going to do for me.

Anyway, I left. Not very elegantly. I meant to slip away without disturbing Niall, and to message him when I was outside, something friendly, saying that I was heading home, and we could finish the movie another time. I wrote the message out on the pavement, under a streetlamp a few doors down from his house—it took me ages, several people looked out their windows at me. Getting home took ages too. I shouldn't have had so much to drink. I rarely drink, for this very reason. One wrong bus, and then another wrong bus. And then I walked into the side of a bus shelter, I have no idea how. Then somehow it was midnight and a BMW slowed down as it passed me, and the window wound itself down and the driver stared at me through the window. I nearly laughed at my own stupidity, at a fifty-eight-year-old woman, an old hardback woman like me, getting myself into such a situation. And when I finally did get home, I realized that I'd never sent the message to Niall, and that he'd left me several voicemails asking where I'd gone.

SOMETIME DURING THE NIGHT, BACK in my house in Brockley, I got pieces of Monica Sartori's autobiography figured out. Her adoptive father was some kind of engineer, and he had worked in Venezuela from 1979 to 1984. Her adoptive mother was a music teacher. Monica wrote out the full address where they used to live in Caracas, and the place where her adoptive father had worked. Also the address of the government office that issued her birth certificate, estimating her birthdate as January 1, 1981. Also the address of a Catholic church where she'd been baptized, in July 1981. And more along these lines: more dates, more addresses. Somewhere in the email, she wrote, in English: "Does this match with your information? I cannot wait to hear back from you as soon as possible!"

I had brought my green boxes and maps downstairs by this time, and I spread the maps out on the kitchen table. It took me a long time, bending low over the map to read the tiny lettering, and touching my forefinger to the paper, trying to find the places she'd mentioned. The places she named didn't mean anything to me.

I don't know if I was ever in Caracas. I don't think I was. Caracas is a big city: densely populated, brightly lit, with high-rise buildings and massive multilane highways; it's nothing like the tranquil, rural place I remember staying in with the nuns. Plus, there's a big hulking mountain looming over all of Caracas, just to the north: El Ávila, over nine thousand feet high. If you look at a photo, you'll see: it's distinctive, inescapable. If I'd been in Caracas, I would have a memory of it, surely.

I opened up the other green box file. There were several big brown paper envelopes inside, each one stuffed full. Resting on top of the stack of brown envelopes were bits of paper that I'd torn from magazines and newspapers. I took out a handful from the top. The table was covered: I sat on the rug on the floor instead. I laid the glossy pieces of paper on the carpet between my knees.

I sat there for a long time. I didn't know what to write to Monica Sartori. She'd asked for information, but I didn't have anything concrete to give her. All I had were these cuttings that I'd laid out around me.

This handful of pictures closest to me, for example, were all of nuns. In one of the pictures, three women in brown dresses stand side by side, smiling for the person taking the photo. They're outside, in the bright light of day, in some sort of garden, with big green leafy plants just behind them, and the covered walkway of a building a little way behind the plants. I don't recognize the nuns, or the place where they are. But I've had this picture a long time, and I take it out sometimes to look at it. The nuns are all happy. You can see the happiness in their faces, their smiles, the youthfulness of their skin and their carriage and their expressions, even though the one in the middle might be in her sixties, the one on the right maybe her forties. The one on the left looks like the youngest, perhaps not yet thirty, that would be my guess. But all happy women—women who look as if they already know you, or, if they were to see you appear in the garden, would call you over, welcome you without questioning, probably give you a hug, and give you something to do.

They're all in long brown shapeless dresses. I think the Hermanas in Venezuela, in the house where I stayed, some of them may have worn brown dresses, but I'm really not sure.

In another photo: a nun inside an old people's home, or possibly a hospital, tending to an old man. The nun is fair-skinned, old, with prominent veins in her hands, and fingers knobby and misshapen by old age. Her dress and veil are both white, and she wears a pale blue apron. In the picture, she's standing at the bedside of an old man, and holding a bottle of some liquid over his hand as if about to pour—maybe medicine, or maybe just water. Nothing about the nun herself triggers a memory for me, but I cut this picture out because of the room they're in. The room: dingy, but probably cleaned and disinfected as well as it can be. Seen in daylight, a tropical-spectrum light, maybe four o'clock in the afternoon. Two beds, side by side, each with a high bed-head in what looks like iron or maybe aluminum, and colored or painted olive green. On the wall behind the beds, a tiled wall, white square tiles, the kind that used to be standard bathroom tiles in Trinidad, six inches square, plain white, the grouting between the tiles darkened almost to black with grime and age. The top row of tiles just beneath the windows with a pattern of a simple dandelion-type flower, gray stalk, blue strokes for the "petals" of the dandelion. Between the beds, a metal locker, about four feet high by one foot wide and one foot deep, painted or sprayed a kingfisher blue, but now faded and rusted. That rusted metal locker is what caught my eye, that and the feeling or impression of scrubbed dinginess of the room. We had lockers like those in the factories down south, in Trinidad. The workers used to use the lockers to put their clothes away when they got changed. And as I try to imagine the nuns' office in the house in Venezuela, I imagine a locker like this might be somewhere in the room.

I have lots of pictures like these. I have nuns, I have houses, I have pictures of rooms with black-and-white floors. I take them out from time to time and spread them out and sit with them. Over time, some of the pictures begin to seem irrelevant, and I throw those ones away. The other ones, I keep. But the pictures of the nuns are my favorite. I've spent a lot of time just looking at them. If a baby were left in the care of any of these women, you know the baby would be well looked after—held, fed, changed, burped, cuddled, loved. Any baby would be safe, and happy, with them. In the first photo, for example: I look at these three women standing in their sunlit garden, all different ages, all together and happy, and I know that one would hold the baby, and the others would gather around, and they would treat the baby as a blessing and a gift.

EVENTUALLY, I MANAGED TO PUT together an email reply to Monica. Better to send something, however brief. I said that I was happy to hear from her, and I was writing back straight away, because I didn't want to keep her waiting. I said I would use Google Translate and read her autobiography properly the next day. I said, in the meanwhile, what are your thoughts about a DNA test? I said, I'm not saying it to rush you. But I've been through this before, and the sooner we know for sure, the better it will be for both of us. And I copied and pasted a link to the company I used last time. I took a selfie of my face, just as it was, without tidying my hair or putting on lipstick, and I attached it to the email. As a friendly gesture, I guess, because to talk about a DNA test so soon was a bit of a risky thing to do—she might think it cold, or unfriendly. It was coming up to three A.M.: the alcohol had worn off enough that I was able to type without too many mistakes, and I read and reread the email carefully, and when I was sure it was okay, I clicked send, and then checked in my sent items to make sure it had really gone.

I sat with the iPad warm in my lap for a little while. I was thinking about how much Xanax I still had, and whether I could afford to take another half tablet to help me sleep. It was then that I checked my phone again, and saw the missed calls from Niall, and realized that my message to him hadn't sent. I sent it then, and started typing out a long message apologizing, explaining what had happened.

After that, I sent an email to the older Mr. Palmer at the office: he's the sterner, more serious one, who looks after payroll and HR. I said I was sorry, but that I had a sore throat and a fever, and that under the circumstances, I'd stay home for a few days as a precaution, so as not to spread the germs around the office. Things have changed since Covid: all you have to do now is claim a sore throat, or a mild cough, and bam, you get to stay home. It was around two A.M.: a good time to send an email, if you wanted to claim to be too ill to come in to work.

I didn't have a sore throat or a fever, of course. I did have a bump coming up on my forehead from walking into the bus shelter on my way home from Niall's house. But the bruise wasn't the problem either, I just didn't want to go. The leasings agency felt irrelevant. This connection—possible connection—felt important.

"I'll take it as annual leave if it's easier," I wrote, in my email to Mr. Palmer.

He'd be furious. When he got to the office and read the

email, he'd stomp about, complaining about f-ing sore throats, and f-ing Covid, and the f-ing Tories, and how, in his day, he'd never missed a day of work, rain or shine, five feet of snow, etc., etc. He'd think of me now as unreliable. If the estate agency had to cut back on staff, I'd be the first to be let go. I should have cared more. I already knew what was ahead for me: a bleak hour of "leaving drinks" in the office; a card from the corner shop; an Amazon voucher for £30. And then having to start all over again: dressing in my smartest clothes, going into one estate agency after another along the high street, with my CV. I'd move on from Tooting. I'd try Dulwich next, or Beckenham. I'd have to offer to do all the unsociable hours. All the late evenings, all the Saturdays. Again.

The screen of my phone flashed. A message from my mother in Trinidad.

> Mummy: You're up late! You know your dates yet?
> Suzanne and I will come over to join you all.
> And maybe some of the kids.

I'd tapped on the screen and opened the WhatsApp message without really thinking. An annoying mistake to have made: now a blue tick would show, and she'd know that I was indeed up, and that I'd read her message. Two A.M. in London would be ten P.M. for her in Trinidad.

I wanted to type back that Finlay and I weren't coming. I didn't like to think of her getting all excited about seeing us, and making plans and getting carried away, and then for her to be disappointed. But I didn't want to get into a conversation with her now, and for her to ask why I was still up. If I messaged her back, then she'd straight away do a video call. She'd think that we may as well just talk normally rather than text, if I was up anyway. And my mother is very nosy. She wants to know everything about everything. (How is Finlay? How is Oscar? When last you saw Finlay? Finlay doesn't have a girlfriend yet? Why not? Why you can't find someone for him? Why you don't look into doing a refresher course to work as a doctor again? Why you can't sleep? It's most likely hormones—you checked your hormones?)

I didn't answer her just then. I'm not sure exactly how much time passed. Maybe it's the Xanax, but it's like time just disappears sometimes: I blink, and two hours have gone by. In any case, when I picked up my phone from where it had been lying facedown on the couch, two more messages had come in from my mother.

Mummy: You have particular dates in mind?
What about Thanksgiving, and then Oscar could come too?

Mummy: Let me know.

I tapped a message back as I walked along the corridor to check I'd locked the front door.

Dawn: We're not coming. I suggested it to Finlay
for a little break but he can't get time off.

Dawn: Sorry for false alarm.

I waited for a moment with the phone in my hand. I turned the double lock on the front door, and then stood by the hall table while I typed out another message.

Dawn: And I'm in touch with another possible girl.

Dawn: Hoping to do DNA test. So can't really travel.

I started typing something else, something angry and sarcastic. (Yes, this is number four. A complete waste of time, probably. Yes, I'm back here again!) But I saw that she was typing, so I deleted my words and waited. I switched off the hall lamp and went up the stairs in the dark, and took the phone with me to the bathroom while I brushed my teeth. I finished in the bathroom, and carried the phone with me to bed, and got into bed and lay down, and all the time, she seemed to be typing. It could be that she kept trying to return to her message, and that she kept being interrupted. She could be saying goodbye to Warren and Suzanne, and making sure that the house was locked up, and all the security cameras were on. Or she might be speaking to the lady who stays overnight with her, Mercedes, and getting her glass of water and saying good night. With all the time it took, I was bracing myself for a really long message, but when it finally arrived, it was just this:

Mummy: Can we talk?

I picked up the phone. I typed fast. My hand was shaking a little.

Dawn: No, going to bed.

Dawn: We've had 40 years to talk.

Dawn: NOW you want to talk???

I switched off the phone, and rested it on the bedside table. Even as the shame crept over me, I felt unburdened, like the nervous anxiety I'd been trying to manage for the last day or two had finally been discharged. My mother's already had two heart attacks. She's on a cocktail of pills.

As I lay in the dark, I could picture her clearly: lying flat on her back, head resting on her pillow; one hand laid by her side, the other over her chest, trying to keep very still, to calm her old, weak heart.

13

I DO LOVE MY MOTHER DEARLY, DESPITE EVERYTHING, BUT THIS particular issue is fraught for us. If she and I were to start talking, and I were to finally tell her the honest truth about everything I've felt over these past forty years? Well, I couldn't do something like that—not now, at her stage of life.

I don't want to sound as if I'm still consumed with anger at my mother—I'm not. At some stage of your life, you learn that you can't blame other people for everything; you have to take responsibility for your own actions. But it's also undeniable that, you know—there's been a lot for me to deal with. For example, the way they had me travel to Venezuela. The miracle is that I didn't die of a heart attack during the crossing—I truly thought I was going to be tied up and thrown into the sea to drown. I think that's why I have almost no recollection of where we went or how long it took, because I was in a sort of state of shock.

She and I have never spoken about it properly. After the breaking of the pact—the time she flapped her hands around her head as if flapping away a swarm of bees—she and I have spoken about it only a couple of times, and then only obliquely. She'd say things like, "Let me give you some advice. Don't say anything to Robert about your past." Or she'd say, "That's a good man you found for yourself there, you know. Men like that don't come along often."

At a certain point, I started writing letters. This was in the time before emails and the internet. I wrote letters to all sorts of government departments and hospitals and churches around Venezuela, trying to track down this child. When my mother got wind of what I was doing, she tried to keep her thoughts to herself at first, but they burst out before very long, in dark, ominous tones. "Dawn, girl! Mark my words, you're making a big mistake." Or, "You think men have changed? No man wants to have anything to do with another man's child."

When she said these things, I tried to press her for more information. I asked: Who made the arrangements in Venezuela? What were the nuns called? Hasn't any word made its way back to you about where the child was sent? But every time, what had seemed to be a window of opportunity slammed shut again. She said things like, "Dawn! Don't involve me in this! I want nothing to do with it." Or, "Trust me. You'll regret doing this one day."

I think of that time as my "Era of Letters." I still have the master copy of the letters I sent to government departments and hospitals and churches in Venezuela. I wrote them all out by hand. I'd bought an airmail letter writing pad from the post office, the paper very thin and lightweight, what they used to call onionskin. The writing pad had fifty or a hundred of these very thin pale blue pages, and there was a different sheet of much thicker paper at the back, white with thick black horizontal lines. You fitted that thick lined paper underneath the sheet of onionskin you wanted to write on, and the black lines showed through, to guide you along.

I remember all this very distinctly: I wrote so many of those letters. I was still practicing medicine, but I'd had Oscar by then too, and I'd taken several bumps down the ladder. The only work I could get at that time was a short-term contract in east London. There were no buses and I was having to spend an hour driving in traffic each morning to get there. I used to sit in my car during my lunch break, and after I'd eaten my sandwich, I'd copy out the letters in batches, and leave the addresses blank to add in later.

Rob and I were still living in the attic flat in Clapham at that stage: Rob was working long hours, and after I put Finlay and Oscar to bed, it was easy enough to get out my lists of addresses, and write them onto the envelopes. I kept them in a brown paper envelope in my drawer until I had a chance to take them to the post office. You had to physically go to the counter in those days, and put each letter on the scale, and check that it was under an ounce, and then the post office lady opened a big folder and flipped through pages of stamps, and carefully tore off the ones she needed to make up the right amount. For each of those featherweight letters to Venezuela, it would cost something like 60p in those days. It doesn't sound like much, but it added up. Money was tight for us then.

That makes it seem as if I kept it all a secret from Rob, and it wasn't quite like that. Rob was aware of these letters, although I discreetly kept them out of his way, and he discreetly pretended not to notice them. He seemed disinterested, if anything. If ever I left something lying on the countertop—a Spanish dictionary, or a page cut from a magazine, or my blue airmail letter writing pad—he might touch it with a forefinger, just enough to straighten it so he could see what it was. Once he understood that it was something to do with "all that," the faintest hint of a change might come over his expression—just a moment of some private thought, a stillness in the eyes or the way his lips were set together—but he'd say nothing. It was very strange. From him: nothing. Like he didn't believe the child was real; or he didn't believe I was really writing to hospitals and Catholic churches and government departments all around Venezuela, trying to track down her birth certificate or adoption papers; or that he didn't occasionally notice the postcards or letters that arrived addressed to me, from the few people who did write back.

So to answer the question about whether Rob knew: yes, he did know, but it wasn't something that could be talked about. There was still the shadow of "the Pact," and all the prior years of secrecy, and there was the fact that my mother had waved her hands about her head in distress and told me not to ask; and there was the contempt with which my brother had spoken that night on the patio. For all these reasons, I hid the blue airmail writing pad and the few letters that came back in response.

Of the handful who did write back, they all asked the same questions. In which district was the baby born? I didn't know. In which hospital? I didn't know. When was the birth registered? I didn't know. What is the child's name? I didn't know. I wrote back with the little fragments I had, in English, and in a terrible attempt at Spanish. I tried to say that I hadn't been in a hospital, that I had been in a house with nuns. I tried to describe the nuns, and to guess at the names so far as I could remember them. A Hermana Maria, and a Hermana Maria-something—maybe Maria-Theresa, or Maria-Pia. The one who might have been Maria-Theresa or Maria-Pia wore glasses. Another had a name that might begin with an *F.*

I sent these long letters off, and waited hopefully for replies. Someone must know these nuns, I thought. I wrote follow-up letters, adding the other things I remembered. The lady who took the babies away in her car—the car might have been green. I cut a picture from a magazine that looked a bit like the lady, or at least as I remembered her. She had been nice-looking, smiley. Light-colored skin, not white-white, but generally fair; a light-brown color, a toasted color. I wrote all this down, and sent letter after letter.

I can't help but laugh now at my own foolishness. It shows how little I knew about the world. I had nothing on my side. I had no idea where I had given birth, or what name the child was given, or whether her birth was registered, whether she was baptized; whether she was fed, whether she was clothed, whether she was given immunizations; whether anyone soothed her when she cried, or cared for her when she was ill. I knew nothing. And yet, I sat in my car, day after day, writing out those lines on my onionskin paper:

"Dear Sir/Madam, I hope you can help me. I am a mother who gave birth to a child in Venezuela, in November 1980."

I'm amazed at the determination I had then, the conviction. It was as if I believed there were a force behind those words: as if, by saying them, I were issuing a cosmic command. The problem, as any fool can see, was the passage of time. Because, as we all know, time is commanded by no one, not even mothers who gave birth to children in Venezuela in November 1980, and then foolishly, belatedly, realized they had made a terrible mistake.

I CAN REMEMBER ONLY ONE opportunity when I might have asked my father about Venezuela. It was the summer when Finlay and Oscar were seven and five, and we had gone down to Trinidad for a few weeks of vacation.

Outwardly, everything must have looked fine. Robert had got a more secure job at a different hospital, and we had just got the keys to the Wandsworth house, the one with the beautiful beech trees. All these years since I had qualified in medicine, I had been carrying on messily, patchily, but on this trip down to Trinidad in the summer of 1999, I was thinking of giving up work.

My mother disagreed with me. When I was down, on that holiday, she and I talked about it over and over. She said, All those years you studied? Just to give everything up? And after everything you've been through? I tried to make her understand. Being in England wasn't like being in Trinidad. I couldn't make it work, I said. I'd tried. She still didn't believe me. For every problem, she suggested a solution, and when I said that the solution was unworkable, she sighed and said I was too negative, and that other people made it work, and I must be able to find a way.

The years after the coup had been a difficult time for Trinidad. There had been a lot of emigration, and the people and businesses who stayed had just tried to secure what they had, and make it through one day at a time. By this particular summer, nearly ten years after the coup, the Bishops' companies were in fairly good shape again. There had been some changes. I won't go into details, but certain changes had been made for tax or legal reasons. Also, with my father and uncle getting on in years, there was the issue of passing the companies on to the next generation, and doing it in such a way that there wouldn't be fighting further down the line. I wasn't part of it all: Ryan was overseeing the legal aspects, and Warren was the one who had more or less taken over my father's role. The feeling wasn't one of everything growing and expanding: it was more shaky, more turbulent; there was a feeling that you had to live from day to day, month to month—year to year, if you survived that long.

We all went to Tobago for a week together, the whole family—my mother and father, and Warren and Suzanne and their children (they had four by then, two boys and two girls); Ryan and Samantha came over from Barbados, with their daughter. The house had been expanded and modernized by that stage. Now it had a pool, and a thing we called a gazebo in the garden, which could sleep four people. And there was an outdoor shower area outside the house, to wash off sand after the beach, and a shed outside as well for all the paddleboards and snorkeling flippers and oars and all that sort of thing.

The good old days. In the photos, we all look happy, and young, of course. I was thin, all the baby weight long gone, but I was too distracted to notice it, and I was in baggy shapeless clothes when, looking back at the body I had then, I should have been in tight dresses and high heels every day. My hair was shoulder-length, and it still had its natural color, a deep brown with copper tints that caught the sun, but I had no time for it, and in every photo that beautiful hair is tied back in a ponytail or a bun. Rob looked well, though. In the photos, he's in a deck chair by the pool with a beer and a book, suntanned, or holding up a fish he's caught. Finlay was seven that year, Oscar five. In the photos, all the cousins are a blur of colorful bodies and swimsuits in the blue water of the pool. Or half a dozen children tangled up on the sofa together, eyes tired from all day on the beach. In the evenings, the adults sat out talking until late at night, just like long ago, when we were children.

The talk at that time was about Venezuela, about how bad things were getting. You couldn't go Caracas anymore, Warren told us. (The rest of my family already knew all this, and he told the stories for my and Rob's benefit, late at night when the children were out of the way.) You arrive Caracas? They kidnap you! Just pull you in a car, and bam, vanish. Drive you somewhere out in the jungle, and demand money, and if they don't get it, they start chopping off body parts and sending them. It was all real, Warren said. Everyone knew it was real. The newspapers had been reporting about the kinds of things that had started washing up on our coastline: the bodies, and body parts.

THE TIME I'M THINKING OF with my father, we had somehow ended up on the beach together at the end of the day, after everyone else had gone in. The children had been there for a while, admiring the sunset and squeezing the last drops out of the day, and then I think my mother had taken them back up to the house with her, and I was left alone with my father. He was smoking a cigarette, and I sat quietly beside him. The sun had mostly gone down, and it was only because I was enjoying a rare moment of quiet that I was still there.

"Well, it sounds like things are going good for you in England," my father said, suddenly.

I laughed a little. I said, "It's not easy, you know!" I didn't literally mean it wasn't easy. I meant it in the Trinidadian way: as a sort of expression of respect for the difficulty of an undertaking, and maybe a bafflement about it, a recognition that the task is beyond our understanding. But that's a very complicated explanation for a phrase which, when spoken, manages to communicate its meaning very simply.

"I know it's not easy." My father broke it into its other, simpler meaning. "But you think life is easy for anyone?" He puffed on his cigarette and shook his head, looking out at the sea, as if talking to himself. "Life not easy for anyone."

"Well, it's certainly not easy with two little kids on my own," I said. "I haven't found it easy."

He waved a hand, annoyed, like he didn't want to hear all that again. He said, "Why you keep on talking about that? That's the only thing I'm hearing you talk about since you came down."

"Because—it's difficult!" I said. "I knew it would be hard. But I didn't expect it to be as bad as this."

"But all women have children," Daddy said. "Or nearly all women. And women just have to manage. Why you're making this big fuss?"

"Because I'm supposed to have a career?" I said. I was completely taken aback by this. I'd grown up expecting to work. And they'd expected me to work, surely. They'd paid for me to go to medical school, over ten years of bills. What was it for if not to work?

"Well, if you want to work, then work!" he said. "Who's stopping you?"

"Well, I have the kids!" I said. I almost laughed, I was so astonished.

"What about the kids?"

"Someone has to look after them!" I said. I began counting on my fingers all the difficulties; I was well rehearsed by now. They finish school at three. And half the year they're on school holidays. And then football after school, and scouts, and parents' evenings, and homework. And cooking dinner. And shopping. And ironing school uniforms.

He waved his hand again, irritably, as if to say, Stop, just stop.

He said, "Look here." He took a long pause, for emphasis. "All you have to do? Is work out what's best for your family. Do what's best for your family. Rob is on track to earn well, you could manage without your salary. If it's better for your family for you to stay home? Then stay home."

"But it's not just about Rob's salary," I said.

"What's it about?"

"I want to work! I want to practice medicine! What did I study all those years for?"

"Well, either stop or don't stop!" He was exasperated, as if he couldn't believe he was having to go over this with me. "Those are the options! Choose one! I don't understand why you're making this big song and dance about it."

"Song and dance?" I repeated. I couldn't believe what I was hearing. "Song and dance?" I made a big steups—it's what we call it in Trinidad when you suck your teeth to express annoyance. "Men!" I said. "Men don't understand."

He looked at me sideways. "You think men don't understand?" he said. "I do understand. It's you who doesn't understand."

"Up there," I said. "It's not like here."

Maybe he heard something in my tone, something I hadn't dared to say. He shook his head, and said, promptly, "Girl, you stay up there in England, eh? You see how Venezuela's going? This place will be getting like that just now. Wait and see."

We sat side by side on the sand. The sun had dipped beyond the horizon, leaving a slowly dissolving spectacle of color in its wake. The sea was restful, a molten silver.

It crossed my mind, after we had had this exchange and a silence had fallen, to ask him about Venezuela. I can see now that it would have been a good opportunity. He was already angry at me, so what, really, did I have to lose? But my attention was elsewhere. I was angry at the injustice of my situation with having to give up work, and I was wrestling with my father's distorted understanding of me. I sat there in silence, and fumed.

AT THAT TIME, I'D BEEN saving all the letters and cards from what I later came to call my "Era of Letters," and a few maps and pictures I'd torn out of a *National Geographic* magazine.

But not long after the trip I've just described, when I was unpacking in the new house, I went downstairs and got a big garbage bag, and came back up to the bedroom and stuffed everything inside of it. I was quite certain about it, just stuffed it in, thinking, rubbish, rubbish, all rubbish. It seemed so hopeless at the time: it felt like I'd reached a dead end. I tied up the bag and put it out in the bins, and came back inside. I felt lighter, and like I'd let something go.

Finlay would have been seven, and Oscar five when we moved to the big house in Wandsworth. My Auntie Pam had sent me some fabric from Trinidad—I still remember it: blue and white stripes, with a pattern of smiley-faced suns—and I'd sewn curtains for their new bedroom, and two cushions, one for each bed. The boys had helped me paint the new room, and put up the curtains and arrange the furniture, and I remember that when everything was done, we sat on the edge of one of the beds, with Finlay snuggled up to me on one side, and Oscar the other, and admired our work. It was just an ordinary room: a wardrobe, a chest of drawers; the two beds side by side, but it did look nice, with the matching curtains and cushions and quilts, and especially cozy, the three of us huddled together by the light of the bedside lamp.

I don't know how to explain the logic of what happened next, except to say that the spirit moved me. It's a Trinidadian expression, I think; nothing religious. It just means that I felt a certain way, and I don't know why I felt that way, but I just did, and when I spoke, I spoke with sudden courage and conviction. I said to the two of them (their little legs dangling down from the bed), "Did I ever tell you that you have a sister?" And their eyes widened, and they said, echoing each other, "A sister!" And Oscar straightaway pointed at the space between the two beds, and he said, "When she comes, she can sleep there." And he took one of the new cushions from his own bed, and he placed it on the ground where the sister's head would rest.

They asked if they would meet her, and I said, no, we won't. I said, she's grown-up. She's living her own life, she might have her own family now. Oscar, the more outspoken of the two, asked, but why isn't she here? And I said I would explain it better one day, when they could understand. They fell quiet then. The two of them watched me uneasily, aware of some new element of uncertainty having entered their world. I felt then that it should have remained a secret for longer, or possibly forever. I felt that all that I'd achieved was to make them feel slightly fearful and unsettled: something important about their world had changed, but they didn't know what. Maybe they thought: if this sister could be somewhere out there, seemingly unaccounted for, then couldn't that happen to them too? Was she all right, this sister? Was she a nice person? Or maybe she wasn't—maybe she had been sent away. I tried to speak cheerfully, to redirect them to putting away toys and books, and folding clothes. Oscar followed my lead. He still trusted me that way at that age: if Mum was cheerful, he seemed to think, then everything was okay. Finlay was more uncertain, more suspicious. And in the next few months, it was only ever Oscar who asked about the sister. Will she come at Christmas? Will she have a birthday party? And I had to tell him, we don't talk about her. And he said, why? And I said, your sister, really she's your half sister. I said, she has a different dad. And Oscar asked if, before Dad, I'd been married to someone else. (Children were quite alert to that aspect of life, somehow—they knew about these things from their school friends.) I said that it was something like that, and that seemed to make sense to him: that the sister somehow belonged to Mummy's previous life rather than to the one she had now, which was, after all, partly true.

14

DURING THOSE FIRST COUPLE OF YEARS AFTER WE MOVED TO THAT big house in Wandsworth, there were long stretches when I felt as if I'd made a sort of peace with the fact of not being with my daughter. She would have been turning nineteen when we moved house: more or less grown-up; arguably, she wouldn't really need me anymore. I said to myself, Dawn, not everything is your problem! I said, Dawn, don't you have enough on your plate without going looking for problems that aren't even yours?

I imagined her still in Caracas, still close to her adoptive family. She might have her own car; she might pick up her younger siblings from school. I imagined her standing in front of a mirror brushing her hair, arranging it in a side part, the younger siblings watching her admiringly from their positions on the bed. She might be doing a business degree at the university. Maybe learning English in the evenings. It was that happy vision that made it possible for me to live, most of the time, like an ordinary person. But then, of course, there were other times when the realization of her absence returned. It always arrived somewhere in my abdomen, the sudden shock, like remembering laundry left out in the rain, or children not picked up from school. Those were the nights I spent pacing the kitchen, hugging my arms, while Rob and the boys slept peacefully upstairs.

Over the following years, as Finlay and Oscar moved to secondary school, and my daughter would have been getting into her midtwenties, I began to feel as if she might be of the age where we could understand each other. I took to carrying on conversations with her, as a way to manage my worry. Sometimes when I was doing the ironing, or when I was folding a pile of clothes, I'd say, as if she were sitting on the edge of the bed nearby, "You're old enough now, you understand the bind I was in. I wanted to live my own life. And I was so young. I didn't know what I was doing." And in these fantasy conversations, she understood perfectly, and she said, "Yes, I do understand, I am just the same. I see now what you went through, and I'm glad that at least I'm here. At least you did that for me, so that's something." And I'd say, "Yes, and I wish I could have done more, but I wasn't able. I was so young. And my family. You understand?" And she'd say, or I'd make her say, "Of course, of course! I understand."

That was how the imagined conversation went sometimes. Other times, I'd stop, with the pile of folded clothes on the bed, or the iron still steaming on the board, and the lovely rosy dream would vanish, and I'd realize, Dawn, nobody's here. You're only talking to yourself.

BUT TIME PASSED, AS IT always does. The online world came into being. News sites. Message boards. Facebook. It was astonishing to us then: that people were able to reach across time and place to find each other again, where, previously, connection had seemed impossible. On Facebook, I found Angie de Vries, the girl who had lived in the house next to ours when I was a teenager, whose father had been a head honcho at Shell. She was living in South Africa. Her photos showed her happily married, with three happy children. She ran marathons, and sailed catamarans.

"I felt really bad about how things ended up," she wrote to me on Facebook. "We were so close and then it was like you dumped me. What did I do?"

"Gosh, I'm sorry," I wrote back. "I was so wrapped up with my own stuff. I never realized."

It seems strange now that I didn't tell her the truth—after all, by that stage, to be pregnant at sixteen was not as shameful as it had once been. But it's like one shame kept replacing the other: if one layer was peeled away, it only served to expose the next layer. I could admit to having been pregnant—that, now, was understandable and forgivable. But to have traveled to Venezuela in secret, in the middle of the night, and to have left the baby there with strangers; and for the Bishops to have been complicit, or to have orchestrated the whole thing—that was unsayable.

With the internet, things became searchable in a way they hadn't been before. You could find pictures of places. You could find maps. You could see satellite images; you could zoom in. Then, on nights when I couldn't sleep, I would tiptoe downstairs to the kitchen, and instead of walking around in the dark trying to control my breathing, I would sit at the table and switch on the computer. There, in the blue light from the screen, I'd type different combinations of words into the search engines, and study the images that came up. "Trinidad + Venezuela + boat + where." "Venezuela + nuns + hermana + pregnant + girl + where."

"Where" was always part of the question. Where had I been? Wherever I had been, my daughter had also been. If I could find that piece of the puzzle, I felt, I might be able to get somewhere.

FOR MANY YEARS, I HAD thought that I might have been in a region in northwestern Venezuela called Maracaibo, where the main oil fields are. It seemed like a place that had a natural connection with Trinidad: many Trinidadians go there on work contracts; and I had a recollection that my father and uncle had been there too, buying machinery and supplies. But I've looked at many photos of Maracaibo—first in copies of *National Geographic,* and then in tourist guidebooks, and finally online—and nothing about it looks remotely familiar. Also, it's way over on the western side of Venezuela, and I arrived on the eastern coast: adding up all the parts I can remember, of my journey there, and then my journey back to Trinidad again, I just don't think I can have been that far west.

And if I had been in Maracaibo, surely I would remember the smell. You notice the smell in any petrochemical area—the smell of crude oil, the mix of hydrocarbons coming out of the ground; the smell of steel, iron, grease, heat. And there's the way people move in those sorts of places—they have an alertness about them: working with volatile hydrocarbons demands alertness. In those oil industry places, people don't move in the slow, untroubled pace that you see elsewhere in the Caribbean;

they move on a different rhythm, more high voltage. Wherever I was with the nuns, I'm certain we must have been far from all of that. We were in the hills, with parrots in the trees. The humidity of the air carried the clean, good fragrance of forest, and rich soil.

Hills: to get to the house we had to climb a hill; and from the house, what we saw around us were hills. For many years, these hills remained safely in my memory. Even now, I can bring them to mind, or the feeling of being amid them. Sometimes when I'm alone, my right hand lifts, and the hand sweeps diagonally upward, as if to trace the curving flank of one of those hills: a slow, smooth movement, like those old people you see in the park sometimes, doing their tai chi; the slowness communicating, somehow, the enormous size of the mountains, or the way it felt to look at them or to be in their company; something about their grandeur and age, and the sense of awe that I felt then, and that I feel again whenever they come to mind.

I'll describe what I remember. Green. The dark, fuming, forest green of the tropics; the elemental green. Hills, or maybe mountains, shrouded most afternoons in cloud. Thick opaque sheets of rain came in, sheet after sheet, obscuring the hills. The slopes thick with trees; no roads; no houses that I could see, although, at night, there were yellow specks of light that must have been from other dwellings. In the mornings, the sunlight rested against those green flanks, like a butterfly rests for a moment upon a flower; and those mornings in Venezuela, I was not the only one who watched those hills, and that still, golden cloud of light; watched, and breathed lightly, and said nothing, as if for fear of disturbing the balance.

I've tried to draw what I remember, but it looks like a scribble, like someone lost control of a pencil.

But what becomes obvious as soon as you look at a map of Venezuela is that a huge area in the middle is all lowlands. There are mountains in the north, along the coast; mountains in the northwest, along the border with Colombia; mountains in the southern regions too, along the borders with Guyana and Brazil. But everywhere else is flat, Amazon-basin territory: low-lying, waterlogged land, prone to flooding.

Sometime after that, I got hold of a physical map of Venezuela, and with a pencil I crossed out all the areas I could say with certainty I had not been. That whole enormous area of lowland in central Venezuela represents about a third of the land area shown on the map.

Then, when I looked more closely at the topography of the mountains in the southeast, I noticed their unusual shape. In fact, they're tabletop mountains, plateaus: the tepuis. They're enormous, and distinctive: if I had been anywhere near them, I'm certain I'd remember. I took up my pencil again, and shaded this area out, on my paper map.

For so many years, I had assumed I would never be able to find my way back to the place I had stayed with the nuns: now, the area I had to search was reduced by half. This was a moment of real revelation to me: that a single tiny fragment of information I'd carried for so long with me, the memory of having been in the mountains, could wield a sort of power over a vast area of land.

DURING THAT PERIOD, WHILE SITES like Facebook and Google were coming into being, changes were happening in Trinidad too. People began noticing that there were more Venezuelans around than usual. In the past, there had always been a bit of movement between Trinidad and Venezuela but it always used to be a small-scale thing. Trinidadians—nearly always men—would cross over to the mainland for some subterfuge business, to pick up wild meats, birds, cigarettes, and bring them back to Trinidad to sell, that kind of thing. A lot of men had second families over in Venezuela, and they went back and forth quietly between these families: a discreet business on one hand, but widely acknowledged as a trend on the other, the subject of rum-shop banter and calypso lyrics. And if there was a reason to want to disappear—if a man had debts, or if he had jumped jail, say—then Venezuela was the obvious place. There had always been a trickle of people moving in that direction, from Trinidad to the mainland—but around the early 2000s, the tide began to turn. Once, I had made the journey myself, across those seven miles of choppy sea by night: now the flow of people moved in the opposite direction. Venezuelans—Spanish people, as they were called—began clustering in the coastal villages in southern Trinidad. They were ordinary people. They wore jeans and sneakers. The women had their hair brushed into neat plaits or ponytails. They had suitcases, mobile phones.

I WANT TO TALK ABOUT the summer of 2003. Finlay and Oscar would have been eleven and nine that year. Oscar had his birthday party in Trinidad, and we hired a boat to take us down the islands—a "yacht," as we called it, but a little one, maybe forty feet: there was enough space for a dozen kids to sit with their legs hanging over the edges, and for my father to have a barbecue going at the back. Oscar still remembers that birthday: how he and his cousins and friends spent all afternoon jumping from the boat into the warm sea; swimming in the warm clear water; and climbing back in only for the joy of doing it all over again. Finlay was eleven that summer: he was about to start at his new school after the school holidays.

My daughter would have been twenty-three. I imagined her still in the Caribbean—if not Venezuela, then perhaps Guyana, or Colombia. She had an office job, something secretarial, maybe in a government office; this was how I imagined her. She was reliable, conscientious; maybe she had her own car, bought with her own earnings. At lunchtimes, she hitched her handbag over her shoulder and went out to the hot bright street, busy with traffic and pedestrians and limers and vendors. She bought food from one of these vendors and ate it sitting on a bench under the shade of big trees.

That summer, if I remember correctly, I had given up my GP job, and I was looking at school-admin jobs I could do in the term time. I'm sorry to say that I didn't want to do these jobs: I was putting off having to do them. I was a qualified medic. I could treat people in cardiac arrest. I was authorized to prescribe life-altering medications. Allowing Rob's career to take priority was one thing; struggling for so many years to work and manage the kids, all that resentment and exhaustion and worry, was another. I had done all those, and I wasn't quite ready to climb down to the next rung of the ladder of humility, to start making coffee and battling with the photocopier and cutting worksheets into twenty slips of paper each saying A is for Apple. So that summer I didn't work: you can see it in my face, compared with photos from previous years, that I looked more relaxed. I was back on the pill, and it had made me gain weight. I'd stopped wearing my little short-shorts and tight T-shirts, and I'd started wearing loose cotton dresses instead. In the photos, it's those shapeless dresses that make me look old, even though I hadn't even turned forty by then.

Things were bad in Trinidad at that time, crime-wise. That was the year we started having to move around with bodyguards, and travel in a convoy of several cars whenever we went beyond Port of Spain. Later, I found out that Warren had a number of guns, one that he kept underneath the driver's seat of his car, another one in his desk drawer in his office down south, and another, I realized later, that he had always with him, on his person. (Where he got them, and the ammunition, I don't know, and I don't want to know.)

It was on that trip in 2003 that I saw for myself how much things had changed. For the first time, I was conscious of the color of my skin; I felt as if it marked me out as different in a way I'd never felt before. I still met people's gazes squarely—you have to stand your ground in a place like Trinidad, you can't just be meek—but there was a new discomfort to it, a feeling of hackles rising, and the possibility of something escalating. The first time I came back from a walk around the Savannah, I said to my mother, "Boy, things changed for true!" and she didn't even have to ask me what I meant, she just nodded, ruefully.

Warren and his wife, Suzanne, had built their house next to ours, at the top of the hill, so the two houses were literally right next door, and yet even going from one house to the other wasn't trivial. First we had to check the security cameras, and there were several; then we phoned to say we were coming; then there was the unlocking of doors, the relocking them behind us; then the quick dash out the gate, down twenty yards of road, and into the gate of the other house, down the driveway of that house; then the unlocking and relocking of doors again; and finally another phone call, to say that the person had arrived safely.

And even going to Maracas beach, an easy twenty-minute drive from our house, a place we'd been to countless times, a busy beach, with lifeguards and food stalls—even there, Warren and Suzanne didn't want us to go by ourselves, because they said it wasn't safe. They both took time off work to go with us, and then there was the business with who would go in which car, with which bodyguard. And when we were there, Warren didn't want Finlay to walk on his own from the sandy part of the beach to the shark-n-bake shop to buy a cold drink, a distance of a minute's walk. Rob went with him, and even then, Warren stood up and shaded his eyes to watch them walk to the food stall, and then watched them walk back.

Even the evenings on the patio were different. We still sat out talking, but everyone spoke in lower voices, and paused from time to time to glance around, checking for intruders.

Warren drank more; he was rougher, more plain-speaking, with less time for pleasantries. He would have been in his mid-forties then: in the photos you can see how he'd filled out, the way men do as they age. He was still broad-shouldered, strong, but with a gnarly, hardened quality, like an aging plank of wood. On the patio, all the talk was about the changed situation in Trinidad, the crime, the Venezuelans, the kidnappings.

"You see, people in Trinidad now," Warren said. "The bad-johns feel they gone big time. Before, Venezuela never used to bother with us, now Trinidad has strategic value."

By "strategic value," he meant drug trafficking. People had lost interest in oil, Warren said. He loosened up quickly with the rum, and I saw then the strain he must have been under, with running businesses and dealing with these new threats; and that a new division had grown between us, that he had hardened in a way I never would, because of these new circumstances. People weren't prepared to rely on oil anymore as a livelihood, he said. People were taking matters into their own hands. A whole new economy had sprung up, he explained, obviously illegal in theory but not in practice. Everyone knew what was going on, to enable the transport and logistics of the goods that had to be moved, the negotiations, the maintenance and protection of same.

"So people have discovered a new source of income, you see," Warren said. (I'm paraphrasing, but this is the gist of what he said while we were home on that trip. Every night it was the same conversation.) "And you don't need to have bothered to go to school. You don't need to have built up a business with blood, sweat, and tears over generations. All you have to do is take somebody gun? And stand here? And if anybody challenges you? Kill them! And just-so, you have money in your pocket! Life good, eh? Life real good." He was being sarcastic, obviously, but the hardening showed.

"But you know Trinidad," he said. "You know how Trinidadians are. You think that's enough for them? No! Trinidadians getting so boldface. They see, oho, if I have a gun, I could get rich? Wear all kind of gold chains around my neck? Well, why I have to stop there? That's what this whole kidnappings business is, you know. It's just greed. Boldface. The people already have plenty money from all the trafficking they're doing, but now they get a taste for it? They want more. That's why it's real trouble now. That's why we have to travel with bodyguards and have all this security and thing. Because anybody who has a bit of money? They're a target. All the people who run businesses in this country? Who been working hard, over decades? It's time to pack up and get out of this blasted place."

I had heard this sort of talk for decades, about how it was time to pack up and get out, but it was Rob, the relative newcomer, who thought Warren might be serious, and asked him the question.

"Are you going to move?" Rob asked.

"Me?" Warren steupsed. "Maybe I will one day." He paused, and I was aware of something not being said. My mother looked down at her hands.

"I'm not going anywhere," Warren said, and it was as if he were speaking to the others, continuing a conversation they'd had previously. "My life is here. My living is here. Here is where I'm earning a living. How I support myself and my family, my grandchildren—everybody is here. And to be frank, why should I go anywhere? I haven't done anything wrong! I haven't broken any laws! Why it must be me to lose my home and to lose the business I've been building up and my family has been building up for fifty years now, because somebody want to be a big man and run a drugs ring down south? Why I must do that?"

"Fair enough," Rob said. "Risky, though."

"Yeah, but life is risk," Warren said. "Crossing the road is a risk. You all in England, you wouldn't understand. People expect everything to feel safe in England. If it's not safe? If somebody cut your finger? Miss! Miss!" He put his hand up, mocking, as if playing a child in a classroom. "Miss! Johnny hit me! Not so? That's how it sounds, in England."

IT WAS WHILE WE WERE in Trinidad that summer that we took the trip to Caroni Swamp. "Swamp" makes you think of a dirty, manky kind of place, but once you get to see it up close, you realize it's quite beautiful. It's a mangrove swamp, twelve thousand acres—estuary, really. It opens out to the sea on the western side of Trinidad, the same Gulf of Paria that separates our island from mainland South America.

It's about an hour from Port of Spain: along the Beetham Highway as if you're going to the airport; then, by Grand Bazaar, you make a right turn onto the Uriah Butler Highway heading south. There were two lanes of traffic on either side of a low barrier, with a section of scrubby land as a shoulder, and occasional vendors at the roadside: ladies sitting beside plastic tables stacked with jars of homemade coconut cake, or fellas standing by a bucket with a rope end hanging outside the bucket, and if you looked closely you might see the slowly scrabbling movements of crab legs from inside the bucket.

The turnoff for the swamp was unmarked; I'd have missed it if I'd been the one driving. Into a narrow road cut through the bamboo, the car bumping along slowly through the potholes, the driver suddenly on alert, scanning the bush on both sides. The tarmac gave way to dirt, and finally we arrived in a clearing in the bamboo where there were a couple of cars already parked. There, we got out, and walked across the scrubby, pitted ground, toward a hut where a handful of people were standing waiting. Two pirogues tied alongside the wooden jetty were bobbing gently on the green rippling water.

As well as us, there was a family from the countryside, several adults and older children, and a handful of smaller ones. And two local women from town, well dressed, carrying binoculars and a flask of water, and a bird guidebook. When the boatman indicated we would take only one boat, the local children rushed on, with much laughter and squealing, and took the benches at the front. My mother hurried Finlay and Oscar on, and nabbed the next bench behind them, and Suzanne squeezed in with her. The two well-behaved ladies went behind them, and Robert and I ended up at the back, by the engine and the boatman.

The family from the country were very loud, cackling and shouting and joking about pushing each other out of the boat. But the woman and her friend with her binoculars glared at them and one said, "Hello, this is nature. We're in nature. You can't be loud like that." And the boatman, standing at the back by the engine, agreed, and he gestured at Robert, who was slathered in sunscreen and insect repellent, and said, "You all could see these things anytime. Look the people only here now from England. They want to see Trinidad, you all. Don't spoil it for them."

The boatman was a local fella, scruffy-looking and barefoot, but he really had knowledge. As we glided along water channels between the mangrove islands, he pointed out all sorts of wildlife to us—herons, woodpeckers, dragonflies, four-eyed fish, hermit crabs, and more. He knew them by their local and their Latin names, and he knew whether they were juvenile or adult, male or female; he knew their nesting habits and diets, the wingspans of the birds, how to identify their eggs. And he gave all his measurements in metric and imperial, standing calmly on the rim of the boat in his bare feet, but speaking as if he were a university professor. "Here in Caroni Swamp, the species of caiman we find is the spectacled caiman. A reptile, related to the alligator. The male can grow in length to a maximum of 2.7 meters or about nine feet, and a weight of forty kilograms or eighty-eight pounds." Everything he said was delivered this way, calmly, and with authority. The family in the front giggled and nudged each other. He was Indian like them, but he had knowledge, and it made them uncomfortable.

At one stage, the boatman brought us right into a particular mangrove thicket, so we could see a boa constrictor looped around one of the branches high above. The roots of the mangroves rose out of the mud, gray and ghostly. I found myself studying the root, and then reaching my hand over the side, and taking a firm hold of it. My palm closed around it. It looked like it should be sinewy and flexible, but my fingers curled around it and pulled, and it didn't move. I stared at the root, and then my hand drew back. I remembered walking once on roots just like those, in the dark, by torchlight. The memory came over me fully, just as if I were there again, in Venezuela. I remembered now that I had held the branches overhead, and with my feet I had put my weight on the sections of roots that came up out of the water, and made my way along, half crawling, half climbing. The men who had transported me to Venezuela when I was sixteen—they must have taken the boat inland, through the mangroves of the Orinoco Delta, to avoid the Guardia Nacional. This knowledge came over me suddenly and completely, from the feeling of the mangrove root against my palm. I looked over my shoulder, and instinctively met the boatman's eye. He studied me curiously.

As the sun began to set, the boatman put the engine on full throttle. He drove us out to more open water, with just the occasional mangrove island, and he switched off the engine, and it went quiet. We would wait here now, he said, for the scarlet ibis to fly back. He explained about the ibis, about how they built their nests, about how they flew across every morning to Venezuela, and back again to the swamp every evening to roost. For a few minutes, everyone on the boat was quiet too, enjoying the sunset, and the gently rocking motion of the boat on the water.

"But where're these birds?" someone muttered, after a minute, the older boy in the family at the front. "Like they're late! They don't know is time to come back?"

"We have a little while to wait," the boatman said, unperturbed. He was well able for these fellas. "They come at dusk. We make sure to get here in enough time so you all wouldn't miss them." He carried on, evenly, all in a day's work: "If you have any questions for me, you could ask. We've been working here in the bird sanctuary for decades now, we know the habitat well."

It was a little challenge, a test-me-nuh kind of challenge. From the group up front, one of the adults, maybe an uncle, turned and asked, politely, "How long does it take the birds to fly over to Venezuela?"

"It depends on a number of factors," the boatman said. He spoke without any hesitation. "The adult males are the strongest, and with the biggest wingspan, up to fifty-four centimeters or twenty-one inches, and so if there's not a strong wind in the opposite direction, they can reach across in about fifteen minutes. The smaller birds can take up to half an hour, again, depending on the winds. The youngest ones might need to rest, and they'll find something to rest on, a fishing boat, or anything floating out on the water. If they stop off there to rest, it might take them longer, up to an hour. But they always make it back here before it's dark. They come back to their nests for the night."

A silence fell again in the boat, people impressed by the quality of his answer, then a laugh broke out at the silence.

"Fifteen minutes? I didn't know they were so fast," someone commented.

"They don't all go that fast," another person said. "He said only the fastest ones take that time. The others are slower."

"But it takes over an hour in a boat," the first fella said. He said it in a low tone.

"An hour?" someone else scoffed. "What boat you traveling in that takes you an hour? Half hour max, man."

"Well, it depends," someone else said. "Depends what you're traveling for. And who chasing you."

"Ask him," someone else said. "Ask him. He says he knows everything. Ask him and see if he knows." They glanced back at him, but the boatman, behind me, aloof, said nothing.

The uncle turned himself around to face the back of the boat. "Do you know?" he asked, politely. "I know it's not technically about the swamp, but you seem very well informed. How long does it take for a boat to get across to Venezuela?"

"Depends on the distance," the boatman said, and for the first time, there was a note of knowingness in his voice, as if he were coming down from his teacher's desk and talking as one of us. "And it depends from where exactly in Trinidad, to where exactly in Venezuela."

Someone sniggered. I felt sick. A sweat had broken out all over my body.

At last, someone pointed up at the sky at a little moving red dot. People looked up, and started cheering, or exclaiming, "Look, look!" And a few moments later, there was another red dot, and then a little cluster of several red dots, and then we could make out the wings flapping. Up at the front of the boat, the children started loudly counting the birds as they came in. The women passed the binoculars to my mother, and my mother put the strap around Finlay's neck and helped him hold them up and focus the lens.

"Pirogue, nah," the boy said, while this was going on. He had turned back to face the boatman. "Like the bandits-an-dem, man. All the fellas running"—he cast a half glance over his shoulder—"running 'items' between Trinidad and the mainland. Specialist items."

"Depends on the exact distance," the boatman said, unfazed. "If you know the distance, and the speed the boat could travel, you could work it out."

"Well, the distance is seven miles," I said. I was surprised to hear my own voice. "Didn't we always learn that in school? Seven miles."

I was aware of the boatman studying me with interest, before he replied. "Seven miles is the closest distance in a straight line," he said, "from up near Chaguaramas in the northwest tip of Trinidad, to near to a village called Macuro, on the easternmost peninsula in Venezuela. But the boats don't travel that route, through the Bocas, because the water is too rough there, and they have strong currents that would drive them onto the rocks. They travel other routes."

"What routes do they travel?" I asked. "From where to where?"

The fellas at the front turned around to take a proper look at me.

"Mostly they go from south," the uncle at the front said, matter-of-fact. "Cedros, Icacos kind of direction."

"More Icacos," the other man said, correcting him.

"Both," the first man said.

"And where do they go?" I asked. "Where in Venezuela?"

The boatman looked at me. "A number of landing points," he said. "Depending on the circumstances." He uttered a name I hadn't heard before: it sounded like Girry-ah, or Giv-ya.

"Gih-ree-ah," I repeated.

The man said the name again, and I repeated it after him: Goo-ree-ah. Now I know that he was saying "Güiria," but I didn't know the spelling then.

"Not far from Macuro," he said. "Still on that same easternmost peninsula. And it has a road, to take you inland."

"Otherwise, you're going in through the delta," the uncle said, from up front. "That would take longer. And it's more dangerous. You're going upriver, against the current."

"And it has more predators," the older boy added, gleefully. "Jaguars and thing."

The conversation had been just part of the general chatter in the boat, while people marveled at the birds flying in, and counted them in their twos and threes and then their dozens. Suzanne and my mother turned and asked the boatman another question, I can't remember what it was, and the subject of the boat crossings between Trinidad and Venezuela was quietly dropped.

It was thick dusk when we got back to the little jetty, and we all clambered off the boat. The mosquitoes were out, big swamp mosquitoes, everyone slapping at their arms and legs and faces, and squealing and running to their cars. The boatman was impervious. A little cluster of people, his family, perhaps, had appeared, and two men were busy organizing the boats, tying them to the jetty, and unrolling tarpaulins to cover them with.

The boatman was standing in the open hut, with his money box full of cash open on a wooden table. His family were gathered around him—a woman who might have been his wife, and a few small children, all brown-skinned and with glossy black hair, their skin spotted by old scars of insect bites. A torch hung from a hook in the ceiling overhead, casting them in a shadowy light. The woman nudged him and pointed at me.

"Thank you," I said, to the boatman. "We enjoyed it. And all your knowledge."

He inclined his head, and gave a polite little smile. "No problem," he said. "If you have more questions another day, you know where I am."

As I walked back to the car, I was aware of a low murmur of the woman's voice, and then the boatman saying, "Shhh," and then perfect silence behind me as I made my way over the pitted dirt track, back to the car.

I'M NOT SURE HOW THIS made its way to my father, except to say that it's like the walls have ears in Trinidad. Two days after the visit to the swamp, my father spoke to me about it. I had gotten up early and come downstairs, and I was in the living room, in front of the panel for the security system, trying to decide whether to disarm it so I could unlock the sliding door and go out to the garden.

Maybe he had heard me come out of the bedroom, and followed me downstairs. He was in his shorts and a T-shirt, not yet dressed, not yet shaved, also barefoot, like me.

"Hey. Morning. What's up?" I said, because he seemed to have something in mind.

He shot me a glance, and I realized then that he was angry.

"It's just you?" he asked. "The kids are asleep?"

"Just me," I said. "I was going to go outside."

He beckoned, and I followed him where he led, through the kitchen and to the narrow area just beyond the kitchen, by the washing machine and some storage cupboards.

"I gather you've been going around asking all kinds of questions," he said.

I must have just stared at him blankly. I couldn't think what he meant.

"Out by the swamp," he said. "I gather you were asking the fellas some questions. About Venezuela."

"What?"

"What you were asking them about?" he said.

"I didn't ask anything . . ." I began.

"Oh, you didn't ask anything?"

"I just asked . . ."

"Oh, so you did ask something then? Which one? You asked, or you didn't ask?"

"Daddy. Stop. Wait. Give me a second, man," I said. "Ease up."

That put the brakes on, and when I was able to take a breath, I said, "Geez. I don't even know what you're talking about. By the swamp?"

"I gather you were asking about drug trafficking between here and Venezuela. Weren't you? You're asking about the boats? And where exactly they go, and how long it takes, and how difficult it is to get in through the delta, and all kind of thing. Not so? Was that you?"

He was shaking, he was so angry. I remember I stepped back from him, and I switched on the light, and then stood closer to the kitchen, so I wouldn't feel trapped.

"You can't just show up here and start digging things up," he said. "You have to think about the whole family, not just yourself. You don't realize that?"

"I am thinking about the family. I wasn't asking about drug trafficking," I said. My tone was matching his, the same vigor or aggression, to defend myself.

"Well, what were you asking about?"

"I was asking about me!"

"What about you?"

"Me. I went to Venezuela. Remember?" I knew I was turning red, but I couldn't stop it. "I was asking about me. Nothing to do with you."

He looked taken aback. "You mean from when you used to live here? All those years ago? Why you want to know that?"

"I've asked Mummy, but she won't tell me."

"But I don't understand—why're you bringing that up now?" he said. "What does that have to do with anything?"

I couldn't think of a way to answer him, and I wasn't thinking very clearly anyway. We stared at each other for a few moments.

"You must remember something," I said. "Where did you all send me? Was it Caracas? Maracaibo?"

He shook his head, made a small steups. "Girl, you making joke. That was so long ago. I can't remember that."

I stared at him. "You don't remember anything? Nothing?"

He watched me for a moment. "It wasn't Caracas," he said.

"Where, then?" I asked. "Maracaibo?"

"What's making you say that? What you know about Maracaibo?"

"Isn't that where you and Uncle Lloyd used to go?" I said. "I thought maybe you know people there?"

"You weren't there," he said. "You were closer. Eastern side."

He watched me with an expression I can't describe, and I waited, my heart hammering, for him to say more.

"Do you have the address? Or anyone's name?" I asked. "I think there was a Maria-Theresa—do you remember?"

"How could I remember?" he said. "You're the one who was there, not me. How you expect me to know? All I was concerned about is that you came back in one piece. Which you did. As far as I'm concerned, that was the end of it."

If I'd been able to, I would have stayed and asked more, but I was shaking, and I had to get away. I walked back through the kitchen and back to the control panel of the security system. I tapped in the code to disable the alarm, and then I got the key from the hook to unlock the door.

"Dawn," my father said, as I was pulling the sliding door back.

"What?"

"I know you said you're a big hardback woman and thing. But I could give you a little piece of advice?"

"What's that?"

"Don't bother with this." He waved a hand, as if to flick it away, but gently; he was trying to be kind. "You and Robert—it's a difficult stage for you all. He's working on his career. The children are young. Plenty young couples find it difficult at this stage, it's not just you all. It's not easy. You're looking for a distraction."

I didn't have a reply. I slipped outside to the patio, and from the patio, down the slope, away into the cool of the garden.

THAT CONVERSATION ENDED WITH SUCH gentleness that I was taken aback by what happened next. That evening, Warren, under the pretext of going out to pick up a KFC takeaway for dinner, took me, instead, around the Savannah, and then down Charlotte Street, to the entrance of the General Hospital.

"What's this? Where we're going?" I asked.

"Daddy wanted me to show you something," he said.

We went alone, just the two of us in Warren's car, without

a convoy or a bodyguard. At the entrance to the hospital, Warren stopped and rolled down his window. The guard came out of his wooden hut.

"Bishop," Warren said. "We going in the back. He knows we're coming."

The guard nodded, and raised the barrier for us, and waved us through.

We drove slowly along the smooth paved road through the hospital complex. Victorian brick buildings, with rows of arched windows and doors. The corridors were lit, and some of the windows showed that the rooms inside were lit. We passed a neatly mown lawn, with hospital signage lit by an electric light, arrows pointing in different directions, for radiology, cardiology, maternity, morgue. Warren drove past the main building and turned into a smaller side road.

"Where're we going? We're meeting somebody?" I asked.

"You'll see just now," he said. "It's not a nice thing. Brace yourself."

We stopped outside a low building, set apart from the others. It was one story, with breeze blocks along the front wall, and a roofed forecourt with steel gurneys lined up under the shelter. A man was sitting on a chair next to the gurneys. He stood up when Warren switched off the car, and under the electric light, I saw him swat away a fly. He had on long-pants and old leather slippers, and a T-shirt and an old baseball cap.

"It's open?" Warren said.

"Yes, yes," the man said. His hand moved again, to brush away another fly. "I didn't lock up yet."

A painted sign on the front door said MORTUARY.

"Um," I said, on the forecourt. "Um. Hello? What is this?"

"Come, come," Warren said. "It wouldn't take long."

I didn't want to move. I said, "What's inside here? We're meeting someone? What are we doing here?"

"Come," Warren said. He looked toward the fella and laughed. "She doesn't want to go in! She fraid!"

"Cover your nose," the man said, helpfully. "You have something to cover your nose with?"

"I could smell it already," I said.

Warren put his shirt up over his nose, and I did the same. The lights were on inside. In the first room, there were more gurneys and some black plastic office chairs. On one of the gurneys lay a corpse, partly covered by a pale blue sheet. The feet were exposed. I wasn't sure at first that they were feet—they looked like they might be vegetable matter—a tree root; something decomposing. But—I'm a doctor. We had to do autopsies. I recognized the smell.

Warren put on a glove, and lifted the sheet a little. I held my shirt to my nose. The person might have been black before they died; the skin was gray and green; flies on the feet.

I didn't want to open my mouth to speak. Warren opened the next door. I followed him in, reluctantly. The next room was cooled. The smell of bleach, formaldehyde. A mortuary body bank, the stainless steel drawers it open.

"I told you it wouldn't be pretty," Warren said. He put a finger into the hook of one of the drawers and pulled it open.

I said, speaking through the shirt pressed to my nose and mouth, "Who are these people?"

"Nobody we know in here," he said. "Here. Look." He unzipped the body bag.

I turned away. "I don't want to see this. Warren. Stop it."

He was already looking at the corpse. It was someone dark-skinned, but I hadn't glimpsed any more than that before I turned away.

"Come, come," he said. "Come and see. This is Trinidad now. This is what Daddy wants you to see."

I shook my head. I still had my shirt over my nose.

"Come," he said. "Come, come, come, come, come."

I'm not going to describe it. Except to make the general observation that in cases like these, you find yourself looking closely, in puzzlement, because you don't understand at first what you're seeing. It's not immediately recognizable as a body; more parts; damage, decomposition. You study what's in front of you, and only slowly can you make out the constituent parts, and then it's some time longer before you can work out how the body came to be in that state, and what acts must have been performed, and by what instruments. And your brain having worked out all this, not out of macabre curiosity, but just out of a natural puzzlement, you can't unsee what you've seen. You think of the person who's on the gurney, but also of the invisible person, or people, who carried out the violence, and you feel a sort of despair.

We left, at last. When we were back in the car, Warren opened the windows and drove fast, to let the breeze in.

"And now we have to go and get KFC for everybody!" he said.

"Why did Daddy want me to see that?" I asked.

"We want you to understand. You can't come down to Trinidad and start asking questions. All kinds of things go on that you don't know about. And it's better for you not to know. But—trust us. Don't make trouble. Just don't make trouble."

"I didn't think I was making trouble," I said.

"That's exactly it," he said. "You didn't understand what you were doing. That's what I'm trying to tell you. You don't understand. So you just have to keep your mouth shut. Understand?"

"Sure. I understand."

"Good. Whatever it is you want to do—don't do it here."

We were driving around the western side of the Savannah, handsome old buildings on our left, and the nighttime food carts lined up alongside the Savannah on our right. I angled my head to get the breeze from the window, to blow away the smell that still clung to me. On the Savannah path, people ambled by, or sat on benches drinking from cans, or eating from grease-spotted brown paper bags. Warren reached a hand out and turned the volume up on the radio. Music came on. He turned the dial again, a little louder, to drown out the silence between us.

15

MONICA SARTORI IS NUMBER FOUR FOR ME—MY FOURTH TIME going through this. The first one was in the pre-internet days, a girl in Ireland, eighteen years old. The second one was in the U.S., when she was twenty-five. We met, physically, in Boston, to go to a lab to get samples taken for the DNA test. You had to go in person, in those days, and sign everything in person. She was doing it without her adoptive parents knowing and we agreed that we'd each pay for our own travel to Boston, but I'd pay for our hotel room. But it was excruciatingly awkward. I met her at the Greyhound station, and it was just awful. We looked at each other, and neither of us knew what to do. I didn't know how to make it bearable, and I didn't know that it was up to me to make it bearable. We walked to the hotel together. I tried to make conversation, but she gave me one-word answers. We were both trying to steal glances at each other, to size each other up. When we got to the hotel room, she went into the bathroom and locked the door. It was just a disaster. We did at least manage to go to the biotech place to do our swabs, and when the result came back saying we weren't a match, I have to admit that a large part of what I felt was relief.

The third one was more recently, just a few years ago, in 2016: a woman who was actually still living in Venezuela. We connected on the forums: I contacted her first. At that time, 2016, Venezuela, economically, was a kind of disaster zone, and people were flooding out in all directions, over the hills, to Colombia, or across the sea, to Trinidad or other islands, even south, toward Guyana and Brazil. But this woman, her name was Carla, was still living in Caracas. She had a child, a young daughter. She sent photos, we did video calls on WhatsApp several times a day, when she had enough battery on her phone. There wasn't food in the groceries in Caracas at that time. They couldn't get medicines, the hospitals had to work on generators because there wasn't electricity. I sent her some money—several lots, by Western Union. Embarrassing, to have been taken in. We never got a test done. But in a roundabout way I managed to establish her age, and it wasn't her. So—a scam, I guess. You live and learn.

None of us know what we're letting ourselves in for, in this process. We just don't know what we're going to find out, or who we're going to bring into our lives. I read one long post one night by a man—I can't remember where he lived or what his exact circumstances were—who said he wanted to find his birth mother and run her over with his car. He said that he would pin her under the wheels, and that he would kick her head like it was a football. That image stayed with me. You think twice about putting yourself out there, as a birth mother, when you read things like this.

But Monica Sartori seems to be one of the lucky ones. Settled. Ordinary. She works as a research scientist at a pharmaceutical company. She's on good terms with her adoptive parents. She lives with her boyfriend. They go to music festivals in the summer. She writes nice, courteous messages, with lots of emojis. She writes a mix of English and Italian, and I just copy and paste the bits I need into Google Translate to work out the meaning. I write in English, and she says that she uses Google Translate to turn it into Italian for the bits that she can't understand. We've been communicating in this way quite merrily, all these past few weeks.

She's sent me several more photos now. Photos of herself when she was younger, and photos of herself as she is now, with views of her face from multiple angles, and even a picture of her wearing a bikini on the beach, to show her whole body. Also a photo of her and her boyfriend, and another one showing the view from the window of her apartment, all red rooftops and beautiful flowers in the window boxes, and green slatted shutters over the windows.

She and her boyfriend have been together for nearly ten years. They have no intention of getting married, or having children. She said that things in Italy are very hard, that it would be impossible to survive on just one salary. And both sets of parents (she said "parents," but she means her adoptive parents, in her case) live far from Verona, so if she and her boyfriend were to have a child, they would have no help, so it would be impossible. She wrote all this in English, quite willingly, prompted only by a tentative polite question from me—something along the lines of, "I'd love to hear more about you, whatever you feel comfortable sharing."

Because she's been so generous this way, so forthcoming, I've been doing the same—writing long emails, and attaching batches of photos. Maybe I shouldn't. The forums advise taking it slowly, and I know from experience that it would be sensible. But a part of me feels that you have to let the adoptee lead. Or, to put it another way, a part of me feels that, you know, here we both are, her seeking her real mother, and me seeking my real daughter, and whether or not we turn out to be a match, for the time that we're together, we can behave as if we really were those things to each other. Yes, we may both be disappointed when the result comes. But for now, if I write to her that she looks gorgeous in that photo that her boyfriend took in Rome; or that, yes, I think she should do the management training; or that I've thought of her every year on her birthday, November 19, and that I bought her cards, presents, wrote letters—if we're disappointed when the DNA result comes, those things still mean something.

Monica said that her adoptive parents thought they couldn't have children: that's why they adopted her when they lived in Venezuela for a period during the 1970s–80s. Later they returned to Italy, and there, when Monica was ten years old, her adoptive mother unexpectedly fell pregnant. Overnight, everything changed, Monica said. She felt like a guest in the house; she began to think that she might be sent away. When the baby, a boy, was born, it was worse. She sensed that her adoptive mother resented her presence.

"But I've never told them any of this," she wrote. "I couldn't. And they have been good to me. They always treated me well; I went to school. I lacked for nothing. It was just something I felt, in my own head. I was afraid that if I said anything, they would send me away, so I just stayed quiet instead."

"You're such a strong person," I wrote back. "Look at everything you've achieved! And you have such a kind heart. I'm proud of you."

I HADN'T SPOKEN TO OSCAR for a few weeks, but he rang that Sunday evening. He doesn't have a regular Sunday-evening slot, he just calls when he gets a chance, and we keep in touch on WhatsApp. It was afternoon for him in Pennsylvania: he said he and some friends had been out on a hike that morning, and now he was back at his house, packing up his things to go back to the lab. (This is how he seems to live over there: hiking, coffee, Frisbee, potluck dinners. And always at the lab, at all these odd hours.)

"But I thought I may as well call rather than text," Oscar said. "Since all these messages are flying around. Everyone's making plans!"

"What plans? What're you talking about?"

"Well I had Granny asking about Thanksgiving, and you asking about Christmas. Something going on?"

"No, no," I said. "I was only asking. Just information gathering. No plans yet. And I don't know why Mummy's talking about Thanksgiving."

"She said you and Finlay might be coming down to Tobago," he said. "She said I should come too. Get everybody together. But I can't do two trips—Thanksgiving and Christmas. Did you have plans for Christmas?"

"No, no," I said. "I was just checking what you were doing. No firm plans."

"Uh-huh."

We both stared at each other's images on-screen for a moment.

"And what's all this about a new girl?" Oscar asked. "Finlay told me. There's a new girl? In Italy?"

"Yes, in Italy," I said. "But don't get excited. We don't know anything yet. She agreed to the DNA test, I'm just waiting for the right time. I don't want to rush her."

"And is she, you know, plausible?" he asked. "Right age and stuff?"

"Seems so." I was trying to keep it light.

"Right," he said. He sounded disbelieving. "And how are you?"

"Me? Fine!" I may have said it a little too brightly.

He watched me on the screen. Then he shook his head. "Mum."

"What?"

"You know how you get."

"How do I get?"

"You should just let one of us do all this for you. Give them our email addresses. It's easier for us."

"But you all are busy," I said. "You have your lives. You are young. You have to focus on yourself."

"Tell her you need to do the DNA test. Or better yet, just order it online, and get it sent to her address. You have her address?"

"Not her home address," I said.

He narrowed his eyes again. "Is she definitely legit?" he asked.

"Yes, yes," I said.

"And you've seen a photo?"

"Yes, plenty photos."

"I'm being a bit hard-ass," he said. "But what we learned from last time is that you have to just do the test, get an answer one way or another. All the chitchat, and history, and maybe-this, maybe-that, it's all meaningless. Just get the DNA."

"I know," I said. "But there are people's feelings to consider too. You have to think about how it comes across, how it makes her feel."

"I'm happy to ask her," Oscar said. "Send me her email address. I'll contact her."

"No, no," I said. "No. I'll do it."

"You'll do it? You promise?"

"Yes, yes."

"It's in everyone's interests," Oscar said.

"I know, I know."

"So what shall I say to Granny?" Oscar said. "Are you and Finlay really going to go? If you're going to go, I'll try to come too."

"Well, last I heard, Finlay said no," I said. "He said he couldn't get time off."

"Well, apparently he can get time off now," Oscar said. "And Warren and Suzanne are going to come, and Granny, and who knows who else. They making a big lime."

"Well, that's news to me," I said.

"When is the last time you were down, again?" he asked. "Did you go for Grandad's funeral?"

"No, that was in 2020," I said. "Pandemic."

"Oh, yes."

We both paused there. I was beginning to think—but what

is all of this? All these people planning to come to Tobago, and I only intended it for Finlay to have a quiet few days?

"Well, let me know what you want to do," Oscar said.

"Sure. Let me have a think."

"Get the DNA test done," he said, firmly. "If you can get it done, I'll come to Tobago and meet you all there. Okay? Promise? And if it's her, we all celebrate. Okay? If it's not her? Well, it's not her. Go back to how it was before. No panic. Everything will be okay."

"Okay," I said.

"Okay?"

"Okay."

I put the phone down feeling unsettled. Of course, it would be great to see Oscar. And I could understand Warren and Suzanne coming—we hadn't seen each other in a few years, and they would feel that for a twenty-minute trip by plane, they should make the effort to come over to Tobago and see us. But my mother? As soon as Oscar said that my mother was planning on coming to Tobago too, I thought, hmm! Some kind of showdown happening here or something?

My mother is eighty-seven, as I've mentioned, and although she's mobile, she really doesn't travel anymore. She has her heart problems, and she has low blood pressure—she feels flying is risky for her. She needs a special mattress and pillow because of her back pain. She's busy with church and with her different groups—it's not easy for her to miss church on Sundays, because the church ladies rely on her to set up the church for Mass on Sunday, and for weddings and funerals on Saturdays. And she doesn't like leaving the house empty, even though one of Warren's children can go in every day to check on everything.

I did as Oscar had instructed. I messaged Monica, with the link to the biotech lab I'd used last time. I couldn't think of how to say it, and I knew Oscar was right, and that I shouldn't keep putting it off. I wrote, "I'm going to be away traveling for about a week. I wondered whether you feel ready for us to do the test. It's very simple, just a little swab that you do at home."

She wrote back, "I know how it works. I am a chemist."

In another message, she wrote, "I know it must be done. But it makes me feel sad. Like our relationship is conditional. I feel scared about what might happen."

"I understand," I said. "But we will have to do it sometime. Shall we go ahead? Whatever happens, please let's still stay in touch. We're fellow travelers on the same journey."

ASIDE FROM ONE QUICK TRIP for a nephew's wedding just before the pandemic, the last time I was in Trinidad properly was in 2016, when Robert and I were splitting up. Finlay and Oscar had more or less left home by then, Finlay was deep into med school, and Oscar was thinking about applying to PhDs in the U.S. I came on an open-ended ticket, and I brought three suitcases, instead of the usual one.

My mother wasn't one to hold back her opinion. In the car, on the way back from the airport, she gave it to me straight. "Well, you're surprised? The man had enough!" She meant Rob and our breakup. "No man wants to have anything to do with another man's child. I tried to tell you that."

My parents were living in our same house as always, the

same house on the hill. I had thought I would be made welcome, that I would somehow be able to slip back into the life I might have had—long late-night conversations on the patio, family get-togethers. But Warren was busy working. Suzanne was busy-busy. Even the children were busy-busy—they were now grown-ups, after all, and had their own jobs, cars, social lives.

It wasn't an easy return. My parents were both in their eighties by then: my father had for some years been in and out of hospital with prostate cancer treatment and hip replacements; my mother had no cancer, fortunately, but at that stage she had low blood pressure, and she had to monitor her blood sugar regularly. For my father's sake, they had moved to the old study downstairs, which was right beside the living room and kitchen. They had taken out the wood paneling and repainted the walls. My parents now had two single beds pushed together so they could be side by side, and on my father's side, there was a plastic under-sheet that crinkled and rustled, and a grab bar that swung out from the wall that was to help him get in and out of the bed.

As I settled back in to the house I'd grown up in, I was able to observe their daily rhythms. They shuffled around the house in shabby, mismatched clothes, their skin as thin as paper, bruised by collisions with door handles and table edges; cut by the most minor of sharp edges—on paper clips, bottle caps, or twist ties for the garbage bags. Paid helpers arrived at various times of the day: a patient, gentle young man called Eduardo came at ten o'clock to help my father get up for the day, and he came back again at six o'clock to help him get ready for bed. A lady called Mercedes, middle-aged, with dyed dark hair and swollen legs, came at eleven and stayed until four. She swept and mopped, and carried bundles of sheets out to the washing machine, and she sprayed and wiped the kitchen counters, and scrubbed the inside of the oven. The other maids had always spent a lot of time sitting on a chair under the shade of the guava tree just to the side of the house, but Mercedes never sat down, despite the swollen legs. They were both Venezuelan, Eduardo and Mercedes, and so was the new gardener, an older man who went by the name of Johnnie, although my brother said his name was something else, but that a lot of the Venezuelans were taking English-style names so as to try to fit in. Johnnie didn't speak any English at all, but he managed well enough. When he arrived, he buzzed at the gate, and he went around the side and collected the tools and began work. He swept the patio and hosed it down, knelt down in the hotsun and took out the weeds and moss growing in the cracks. Then he cut back the bushes, not with a cutlass as the Trinidadian gardeners used to do, but with long-handled shears, carefully, and dropping the piles of cuttings onto a sack laid beside him on the ground.

"The Venezuelans are good workers, eh?" my mother said. She said this several times during my first few days, usually when she was in the kitchen, looking through the window above the sink, and gesturing to where one of them, Mercedes, Johnnie, or Eduardo, was visible doing something outside. "They work hard!"

It felt surreal to hear her talking so freely about Venezuela, when, for me, the word had been practically unutterable. It was surreal to see Venezuelans, actual people from Venezuela, here in what had been my own house.

MY FATHER WAS UPSET AND angry to have me back. He said, belligerent, on the sofa, with the cricket on the television, after the maid had gone out of the room: "But why you had to go and leave him for? And you had everything set up for you?"

"What you mean 'set up'?" I asked.

"Set up! You had everything! You had a nice house, you all had enough money. You had your whole life up there. Children, everything."

"But the children are grown-up," I said. "They're at university. They've moved out. They have their own lives."

"But that's what I mean!" He was getting irritated and upset by my stupidity, by my refusal to understand him. "Raising children is the hard part. You all got through that, now is time to enjoy your life a bit. Now you get a reward for all your hard work. If you still have your health, God willing, which you all do, then now is time for your reward. And you thrown it in the bin!"

Both of us faced the television. West Indies was playing England at Lord's.

"That's where you should be," my father said, pointing at the TV. "You should be there, in England. Not here."

I sat without speaking. My father glanced at me once or twice before he spoke. "This thing with the child," he said. "The illegitimate child you had. In Venezuela."

I couldn't make myself speak. I raised my eyebrows instead.

"Why won't you let it go?" he said. "Everybody keeps telling you the same thing. Just put it behind you. What you think you can do about it now?"

I remember shrugging. I felt embarrassed then—at shrugging, and at being spoken to this way by my father. I should have stood up to him, but I didn't have the words.

"You wouldn't let it go, and now your marriage is falling apart," he said. "And you had everything set up for you."

It sounded like there was more he wanted to say, like there was something he wanted to get off his chest.

"And now you're back here. Why you're back here for? I feel you came here to blame me for something," he said. "Eh? That's how it is? You're blaming me for what you did?"

"No," I said. "No. Not at all."

"Because let me tell you something. You wanted to go to Venezuela and give the baby away. That was what you wanted. I didn't tell you what to do. It was you."

"I'm not blaming anyone," I said. "My actions are my responsibility."

"So why you changed your mind? After you already decided. Why?"

He said it with the frustration of having lived with that question for a long time. And so when I answered, it was honest and instinctive, just trying to find words I'd never had to find before.

"Because it was the wrong thing," I said, finally. "I made the wrong decision."

"But how do you know that?" he said. "Look at your life—I mean, up until recently, with all this nonsense that you've been carrying on. It wasn't the wrong decision. It wasn't."

He stared at me, waiting for me to speak. "How can you tell me it was the wrong decision?"

"I don't expect you to understand."

"Understand what? What I wouldn't understand?"

I laughed. Out of discomfort, mainly. I'd become unaccustomed to this sort of directness. And because even as the words were forming in my mind—about how it feels to be a mother, or about what I now understood was a mother's duty to her children—I was hearing how they could be used against me.

I said, "You know something I've figured out? I'm not accountable to you. I don't have to answer any questions."

He took a moment to absorb that, and when he spoke again, it was like he was voicing a conclusion he'd reached privately some time ago, and the fact that he was sharing it now meant that something had come to an end.

"You see you," he said. "How it seems to me? You lost your way. If you had stayed here, your life would have been one way. But you made your mistake, and your life took you down a different path. We couldn't guide you in England. We weren't there. And you lost your way, and now you're back here looking for something, and I don't know what you think you're going to find here."

I didn't say anything. I looked at the TV screen, instead of looking at him.

"Am I wrong?" he asked.

It was infuriating. It made me feel like a child, and I was a grown-up woman. I said, with a shrug, to convince myself that it didn't matter that I was agreeing with him, I said, "That I lost my way? You could say that. Sure. I mean, yeah." I gestured around me as if to say, Look at where I am.

"You should have put all that behind you," he said. He waved a hand, to communicate the unspeakable. "But, anyway. Your life. You reap what you sow."

We turned back to the TV screen, both fuming.

"It might not have been wrong for me," I said, after a gap. "I mean, who can say? But it was wrong for her."

"They will have looked after her," he said. "Children don't need that much, you know. They don't need a lot of fancy things. You all didn't have fancy things, and you all did fine. Not so?"

"That's not what I mean," I said.

"What do you mean, then?" he said. His manner was skeptical, challenging, and it made me even angrier.

"I don't know what you think the point of making all this fuss is," he said. "All this was so long ago."

"This is what I mean," I said. "You can't understand." I jabbed my thumb at my chest. "I know what I'm talking about. I am a mother. Let me tell you. Mothers go into burning buildings."

I was aware of my voice getting louder, more aggressive. "Mothers will fight off lions," I said. "I know you're going to say there are no lions, but what I'm saying is, we'll fight them. Any mother will tell you the same thing."

"That's what women like to say," my father said. "How they would fight lions. How you expect anyone to take you seriously when you talk nonsense like that?"

"Babies?" I said. I spoke slowly, firmly, through gritted teeth, and used simple words, as a last-ditch effort to get through to him. "Babies belong with their mothers. That's where they belong. I should have kept her with *me*." I pressed my thumb to my chest. "Me."

It landed, at last. His expression changed.

I glared at him for a few moments more, and then I turned back to face the television.

"Actually, it was you I should have been fighting," I said, with a little laugh, after a few minutes, when I had cooled down. "You were the lion. I didn't realize it back then."

THE DNA SAMPLING KIT IS pretty straightforward. It feels very much like the Covid tests we all had to do, back in the days of the pandemic, except that you swab the inside of your cheek, rather than your nose, and there's a small test tube or vial, to send the swab in.

I unwrapped the package on my bed, and out of habit I went to the mirror in the bathroom. The swab was a thin plastic stick about the length of a pencil, with a cotton wool pad on the end, like a long Q-tip. With my right hand, I held the plastic end, and with my left, I hooked a finger into the side of my open mouth and pulled it wide. I pressed the cotton bud against the inside of my left cheek. A ninety-degree turn. Then another. All the way round. That was it. I pulled the stick back out, and slid it into the test tube container.

Back in the kitchen, I did the remainder of what had to be done: slid the vial into a plastic ziplock bag; unpeeled a label from the sheet and stuck it onto the plastic bag; signed my name at the bottom of a page; ticked a box to give consent to this, and to this, and to that; and then slid everything into the envelope, and sealed the envelope up, ready for the post office in the morning. I took a picture of the sealed envelope on my kitchen table. I opened WhatsApp and attached the photo, and tapped out a message: "Done!" and I added a fingers-crossed emoji. But halfway through, I thought the better of it. I highlighted what I'd written, and tapped delete. I put the phone down. I sat there at the table for a while, looking at the envelope, and then I lifted my eyes to the room more generally. The sun shone through the glass of the French doors, lighting up a section of the living room, and revealing dust on the surfaces of things—the lower shelves of the coffee table, the blank television screen. I studied the backs of my hands. The nails a little long and untidy. The skin a little dry. The faint dent around my ring finger, where my wedding band used to be. Then my right hand reached out to take hold of the envelope: I let my hand sit there for a few moments. And then I got up and put on my coat, and I headed down the road to the post office.

16

LONG TIME AGO, CROWN POINT AIRPORT IN TOBAGO USED TO BE basically just a landing strip in a field. In fact, most people preferred to take the ferry, rather than suffer the turbulence of the little propellor planes. But now it's all modernized, upgraded to the fancier-sounding "Crown Point International Airport," with a full-length runway that can take the big jumbo jets.

The airport is right at the southwest tip of the island—right on the edge, so that as you come in to land, you look out the window and you're seeing bright sparkling blue ocean, and everyone in the plane is getting excited, looking out the window, because it's like, yeah! The Caribbean, man! We leave winter behind, and—look sunlight! Look ocean! Look all the coconut trees, man! And as the plane comes down, you see all the little pirogues bobbing on the water, and people looking up from the beaches and waving at the plane. And it feels like you're about to land in the water, and then out of nowhere, suddenly you see white waves against the rocky edge of the island, and then the gray of the tarmac of the runway, blurry, and a bit of ordinary green grass just beyond the tarmac, and then bump, you're on the ground.

Finlay had been asleep for most of the flight. We were in economy class, terrible legroom, but as soon as the meal tray was taken away, he'd folded his arms and leaned his head back, and that was it: eyes closed, fast asleep. I think it must be a skill he's learned. Maybe he sleeps like that in his car when he's between shifts. Still, he looked tired when he woke up after we'd landed. All around the plane, people were rubbing their eyes and taking in their new circumstances, exclaiming that the sky was so blue, and pointing at the sea, saying that the sea was so close, it was right there. A child in the row behind us was laughing at the goats tethered to trees just beyond the wire mesh fence. I pressed myself back in the seat to give Finlay space to see past me out the window.

I nudged him with my elbow. "We reach, man! Tobago! We're here!"

He ducked his head to look out past me, squinting because of the brightness. I saw his shoulders relax, the tightness already leaving his body. I rubbed my hand over his back.

"And it'll be nice to see Oscar," I said. "The two brothers. Together again."

He nodded, amicable. Then he raised his eyebrows: "The Bishops!" he said.

IT DIDN'T TAKE LONG TO unload us from the plane. When you reach Tobago, all the fussiness and rules that you have in other places just evaporate. Somebody opens the airplane door, and that's it. Everybody gets out. Down the rickety steps, across the hot tarmac in the bright afternoon sun. You're already there. The sea is right there. The heat is there, and the sun, and the breeze. A few airport staff were there in their uniforms, lounging in the shade and talking to each other. Occasionally they glanced up at all the people streaming off the plane, and waved.

At passport control, the lady looked up at me through the glass. I didn't recognize her, but she must have recognized my name from the passport.

"They all here already," she said. "Two women came yesterday, who's that? Your mother and Mr. Warren's wife, the Indian woman from south. And Mr. Bishop just came in not long ago. I saw the small plane landing. He's probably still out in the car park."

"Good, good," I said. "And this is my son," I said, indicating Finlay next to me, because I could tell she was wondering.

"Oh hoh!" the lady said, smiling at Finlay. "But he's been before, eh? I know his face."

"Yes, yes," I said. "Plenty times."

"Plenty rain now," the lady said, sadly. She was stamping all the forms and scribbling her initials on bits of paper as she spoke. "If you want to sunbathe, go in the morning. Rain coming in the afternoon. But you know that."

"I know," I said.

She slid back the passports and smiled again. "You look like you need some sun!" she said to Finlay. "You all living in England?"

"England," I answered. "London. And the other one's coming from the U.S. this evening."

"I wouldn't be here," the woman said. "The U.S. flight coming in half past seven. I finishing at five."

I felt nervous, pulling my suitcase out to the exit. It had been a few years now since I'd been home. Finlay and I came out to the arrivals area: it's sheltered with a high roof, but basically outdoors, near the car park and a little strip of local shops. They were standing just beyond the barriers, easy to spot amid the handful of taxi drivers. My mother and Suzanne, and one of the grandchildren with them. My mother looked lonely, somehow, without my father.

"But you all didn't need to come all this way," I said, to my mother and Suzanne. I'd let go of my suitcase, and was moving toward my mother, gently, with my arms open. "You all are busy. I didn't expect you to drop everything and come to see us. We're only here five days."

"How you mean?" My mother, offended, stern, surprised, reprimanding, like she had to remind me about a basic fact that so many years in England had made rot away from me. "How you mean! But you are my child! I am your mother! Of course I will come and see you!"

I'd seen her on video calls, but it was different seeing her now in the flesh, and feeling the knobby ridge of her spine under my fingers. We've always had the habit in our family of keeping airport hellos and goodbyes lighthearted. Every hello is just, "Hey, how you going," as if we had seen each other just the other day. And every goodbye is like "All right, I'll check you later," as if we would see each other again later that same afternoon. But now, at the airport in Tobago, with people still streaming past us through the doors, and men touting their services for taxis, my mother and I held on to each other for what seemed like a long time.

"But, Dawn, you're so thin," my mother said, when we released each other.

"She's looking good!" Suzanne said.

Suzanne and I hugged hello, and then I hugged the little girl.

"Look how big you are now!" I said to her—this was Lisette, Suzanne and Warren's third granddaughter, now five years old. "And oh gosh, so cute! I could just eat you up! You'll sit by me in the car?"

"I could stand to take some tips from you," Suzanne said, laughing. "Look at me. I need to lose a few pounds, eh?" She patted her stomach; she was thick around the middle.

"But Dawn is so thin!" my mother lamented again. "It's like she's hardly even there."

"Look Finlay!" Suzanne said, hugging Finlay. "How are you! We're hearing how they've been working you hard up in England, man. Hard! What's happening? Everything's okay?"

"He's skinny too!" my mother said. "You all don't have food in England, or something? What's going on?"

"Well, we'll eat now we're here!" I said. "We came hungry! Anything you have for us to eat, we'll eat."

"Good!" Suzanne said. "We're ready for you all. Food already cooked, beds made, everything done. We red and we ready."

Warren was walking over from around the side. He must have been talking to someone else while he'd been waiting for us. Warren looks just like my father did at this age. He's in his early sixties now, not quite retired, or not officially retired, although he's handed a lot over to the sons. (There are so many businesses now, it's almost like each of them can take one for themselves.) He was only in shorts and slippers, but he looked smart, and well. The shorts were smart, chino-style shorts, in a pastel color; the shirt was a collared polo shirt, in pale banana yellow, with the Ralph Lauren logo. He had come up closer to Finlay, and he greeted him first: a firm handshake, one of those handshakes that older men sometimes give to younger ones as a test, while looking into their eyes to see what they're made of.

"Finlay!" he exclaimed. He voiced it as if he were at the beginning of some longer statement, so that Finlay didn't reply, but just shook his hand vigorously, waiting for him to continue. "Finlay!" Warren said again.

And then he turned to me. I opened my arms and approached him, intending a gentle hug, but once we were pressed together, he wrapped his arms more closely around me, and squeezed me tightly. "What is this?" he demanded. "What, you didn't come to Trinidad to see us, and now you don't even want to hug me? And I am your brother? Wha' happen to you, girl?" For several seconds, he squeezed me close to him, tightly.

On the drive to the house, my mother and Suzanne sat in front, and I sat in the back, beside the little girl, Lisette, in her booster seat. Finlay was with Warren in the car just up ahead. It's not a long drive: about twenty minutes along the coastal road on the northern side of the island. Everything was the same as before—although, I have to say: it always feels like every time I come back, everything looks even smaller than how I remember. Little low houses and shops lined the road. Little mini markets, with clusters of bananas hanging on strings from the wooden struts that made the roof. Stray dogs gathered in companionable packs, as if taking comfort from each other. And young fellas gathered too, at street corners and outside certain houses. Children sat by windows, looking out. They looked as if they were used to those positions, as if they expected to spend many hours there, or to return there day after day.

In our car, Suzanne and my mother gave me a rundown of how things were at the house: which rooms they'd organized, what they'd made for dinner; that a bird had gotten trapped in the maid's room and there had been feathers flying all over the place as they tried to shoo it out. My mother's helper, Mercedes, the Venezuelan lady, had come over from Trinidad with her. She had stayed back at the house with another grandchild, since not everyone could fit in the two cars.

Warren slowed often to toot his horn at fellas on the roadside and call out hello. Everywhere he passed, people turned and raised a hand back in greeting.

"Right, Mr. B."

"Good day, good day."

"Take it easy, Mr. B."

When we reached the house, Warren's car stopped in front of the gate, and Finlay hopped out to open it. While we were stopped in the lane, waiting behind Warren, a silence fell in our car.

I leaned forward. "Look, just to say one thing, quickly," I said. "About the girl. Right? I don't want to talk about it here. I'm trying to put it out of my mind. I did my DNA test, I'm just waiting now. That's all. Okay?"

"When you get the result?" my mother asked. She sounded more eager than I expected. I'd been preparing for her to pounce on me, to ask me why I was wasting my time on this again.

"About a week," I said.

"So, when? A week from when? From now?"

"About a week from now. Yes."

"When you sent it in? Which day?"

I gritted my teeth. Interrogation! Already! "I sent it in last week. Last Wednesday."

"So they'll get it, when, by Friday, eh? So if it's a week, you might get the results on this Friday. Not so?"

"How you sent it? Same day?" Suzanne asked. "If you sent it same day, you send it Wednesday and it arrives same day. Then the results come earlier. They might come while you're here."

"How you sent it?" my mother asked.

Ahead of us, Warren's car began to move forward into the driveway.

"I sent it next day," I said. "But listen. This is what I mean. I don't want to talk about it. We're only here for five days. Finlay's here to relax. And Oscar's coming all the way from the U.S. I don't want this to spoil everything. I can't do anything until the results come, so I just want to put it out of my mind."

"Right," my mother said, agreeing.

We were driving through the gate just then, coming into the beautiful garden. Mercedes was by the lime tree on that front patch of grass. She was holding the edge of her T-shirt up, using it as a basket for the limes, and waving at us arriving with her other hand.

"It mightn't spoil things," Suzanne said. "It might be her. You might be celebrating."

"No, don't do that," my mother said. She was speaking to Suzanne. "Dawn is right. Let her put it out of her mind."

Suzanne parked next to Warren's car under the shade of the carport. As we were unclipping our seatbelts, and people were beginning to get out and stretch their legs, my mother turned in her seat and said to me, "Girl, you making me laugh, you know. You think you brought Finlay here to relax? Finlay brought *you* here to relax!"

EVEN NOW, A BIG HARDBACK old woman of fifty-eight, whenever I get to the beach house, the first thing I do is leave my suitcase in the hallway and go look around, checking everything is the way I remember. The living room was just the same: the same smooth wooden floors, the same feeling of space, with the ceiling fans whirring overhead, and breeze coming in through the open windows, and through the open doors out to the patio.

I love the patio in Tobago. We built this patio the summer I was eleven, before I started secondary school. It's open at the sides, but sheltered by the cup-of-gold vine that grows on a roof trellis overhead. From here, you see the garden, everything bright and full in the sunshine, grass, flowers, small fruit trees, and then the gently swaying coconut trees, the delicate blue sparkle of the sea. As I stepped out onto the patio, three or four birds darted away—I recognized them by their colors, the little yellow and black-and-white bananaquits, the gray-green tanager—and I paused, midstep, at the sound of a low hum. A hummingbird, not much bigger than a bumblebee, withdrawing itself carefully from one of the trumpet-shaped flowers. I watched the little glittering body, the blur of wings. It held itself steady for a moment, as if considering the options, and then it moved toward the next flower, the petals splayed open in welcome. It disappeared inside, became a shadow behind the bright yellow petals.

The pool was on, the surface rippling and lively. Farther

along, the gazebo with the door open and louvers swung open, someone's swimsuit already hanging on the line. The grass had been recently cut; the smell was still fresh. The guava tree was in season, yellow fruit among the dark green leaves; kiskadees and mockingbirds and ground doves gathered nearby like teenagers, jostling and squabbling over the ripe fruit.

The house has changed a lot since the olden days. It's still just one story, but it's much bigger than it used to be, and we've had over thirty people staying here at once, sleeping on bunk beds and mattresses on the floor, hammocks—wherever. The layout is simple. The kitchen and the main living area are in the middle, with corridors off to the left and to the right, what we call the left wing and the right wing.

Warren and Suzanne were in the biggest bedroom at the end of the left wing: it's air-conditioned, with its own bathroom, and it's where they usually stay now, when they're here. My mother and I were in the big room on the right wing, the room that she and my father always used to have when he was alive. There used to be a double and a twin in here, but when I came in, I saw that the double was gone, and now there were three twin beds, all lined up the same way like a dorm room, one, two, three, separated by bedside tables. My mother was setting herself up at the bed closest to the door. The window next to her bed looked out to the carport and driveway. As well as the wooden bedside table, there was a white plastic trolley with her boxes of medications. She was unwinding the electric cord of her blood pressure monitor to plug it in.

"But where is Mercedes going to sleep?" I asked. I was standing in the doorway with my suitcase. "Do you want her in here with you?"

"No, no," my mother said. She pointed to the other twin beds. "Well, we could all fit. But she'll sleep in the maid's room."

We call it the "maid's room" even though there's no maid. It's a single bedroom with its own door from the carport.

"She wants to sleep there," my mother said. "She needs her space too, you know. She doesn't want to be jam-up in here with us every moment."

"Right," I said.

"Take whichever bed you want," my mother said. "Take the end one. Then we have the middle bed to put things on."

She sat on the side of her bed. She held the handle of the trolley to steady herself, and with the other hand, she reached forward to push the plug into the socket in the wall. I watched her from the doorway. Her thin hair; the loose, wrinkled skin of her arms. When she sat back, she stayed still for a few moments, her fingers still wrapped around the handle, catching her breath. She glanced at me over her shoulder. I smiled and wheeled my suitcase in, and set it at the foot of my bed. I was beginning to realize that maybe she was as anxious about the test result as I was; that she wanted the absence to be filled as much as I did.

MANY YEARS AGO, WHEN I was pregnant with Finlay, a woman said something to me. The woman must have been a friend of my mother's. We were at a buffet breakfast in a big hotel for some occasion; everyone was milling around with plates of scrambled eggs and pancakes; it was happy, cheerful, busy. Everyone was congratulating me and asking how I was feeling. And this woman, I remember, she had come to give me her congratulations too, but before she spoke, her eyes had flickered over my body. I realize now that she must have seen it wasn't really my first baby. It shows in the body; a loosening, or a broadening: women see it. But she asked, politely, "Your first baby?"

I said yes, and that I was having a boy. She gave her congratulations, and then, for some reason, she took my arm. And she said, "Let me tell you something. You will love your son."

"Yes," I said. "I know." I wasn't being sarcastic: you learn to accept these offerings from older women when you're pregnant. The irritation at feeling patronized gradually wears away, as you begin to perceive a connection between you that was invisible before.

And, still holding my arm, she said, "No. You don't understand yet. You'll understand later. Wait and you will see. You will love your son." She put the emphasis on "love," as if this ordinary word would take on a new meaning as yet unimagined. "When it comes, remember it was me who told you."

I've thought often of that woman, and those words. The way she spoke, with emphasis on the "love," "You will *love* your son," as if it wasn't the ordinary word I was used to, but something different, something as yet unknown. And that first evening in Tobago, her words returned to me again, as they often have over these many years.

Oscar arrived, more handsome than ever, full of energy and good cheer, and Finlay seemed to reawaken, to become his previous self, as if life held some possibility again. Oscar came with no suitcase, just a pair of swimming trunks in a school knapsack, and after hugging everyone hello, he got changed, and he and Finlay went straight out into the garden, and climbed down the rocks to the beach, and the two of them barreled straight into the sea, each one trying to make a bigger roar and splash than the other.

It was just like old times. Warren did the meat on the grill. Suzanne and Mercedes got everything else ready in the kitchen. My mother and I stayed with the grandchildren by the pool: I was in the water with the two children with their arm floats and lilos, and my mother was in the shade of the patio, with her chair pulled to the edge so she was close enough to join in with the chat. Finlay and Oscar stayed down on the beach until sunset, and when they came up, still dripping, Finlay already looked like a different man. My mother saw it too. I saw her study the two of them as they walked side by side along the grass toward the patio: she had to crane her neck a little to see past the smoke from the grill. She took a good look at them, and then she sat back, satisfied.

I've always been good about taking pictures. It's impossible to be completely unobtrusive—it's not like I can camouflage myself and go and hide in the bushes—but I'm an easygoing presence with the camera, and swift. I kind of just glide around, saying, "Hey, smile!" and people turn and smile for the photo, and then inevitably the smile turns to a laugh, and then they go back to whatever they were doing. I love it. The photos are for posterity, to take out and look at in future moments, but I like how they subtly change the "now" as well. Each click of the shutter is like a little reminder: we're all here together *now,* we're happy *now; now* is a moment that will never come again.

I sent one of the photos to Monica. The grandchildren had gone inside to bathe, and I was sitting by the edge of the pool with my feet dangling down into the water. I had a bottle of

Carib next to me, and I was feeling happy and relaxed; a little tipsy, I guess, with the Carib. And I opened up the thread of our WhatsApp conversation, and I clicked on a photo to send to her. I wrote, "This is our house in Tobago. Maybe one day you'll join us here."

I waited for the little tick in the corner of the message to appear to say it had been sent. One gray tick appeared, and then a second. I was a bit slow-witted because of the beer, and I just held the phone in my hand, still looking at the same screen, half smiling to myself. Then the ticks turned blue, and then I saw the three dots to show that she was writing back.

"I hope so," she wrote.

I put the beer bottle down so I could hold the phone and type. "You would be so welcome," I wrote.

"We're all on tenterhooks for the result," I wrote.

"Everyone is here," I wrote.

I was feeling so happy and full of love for everyone. I selected a handful more photos, and sent those to her too.

WE ATE OUT ON THE patio. We do have a table out there, but the way we do it is just to put the food on the table like a buffet, and everyone comes and takes and eats from plates on their knees. It's more free-flowing that way. People can go where they want, the children can move around, Warren could get up and check the grill. The conversation at these things tends to be a bit of a hubbub—everyone talking at once, and then hearing snatches of another conversation and jumping in, so there's a lot of having to say things twice, or three times, for the first listener, and then for the second listener, and so on. And Trinidadian families don't do the polite-polite kind of thing: it's more a no-holding-back kind of talk, which is a shock when you're not used to it, but it has its good side.

At a certain point, for example, Warren said to Finlay, "Finlay! Why you don't come and work in the Caribbean for a while?" The two of them were by the table, Finlay holding his plate, helping himself to more food, and Warren just with a beer bottle. "Why you don't go Barbados? All the foreigners there. All the English tourists. When they get sick, they'll like to see an English doctor. Makes them feel safe. Talk about the NHS. You'll take a little sunshine. Find a nice Caribbean woman. Caribbean women nice, you know! They's know how to treat their men!"

I don't know what Finlay said in answer to that; I just suppressed a smile and tried to remove myself, so I wouldn't inhibit the conversation. But not long later, when I tuned in to what they were saying, I heard Warren dishing out all his advice, to both Finlay and Oscar at once—but aimed more at Finlay, I thought.

"Let me tell you something," Warren was saying. "The secret is confidence. Never apologize, never explain! Like the Queen! And if ever you've made a mistake? Don't say it! And the other secret? Is doh fraid anybody. It's like dogs."

Warren has a long spiel that he comes out with sometimes, about how it was so good to grow up with dogs, and how dogs can sense fear, and how if you learn to master your fear, you can handle any situation.

From time to time, the general conversation would turn to something else: corruption, crime, all the usual topics. Blasted Jamaicans, blasted Americans, blasted Syrians. But usually, whenever there was a lull, someone would comment again on Finlay and Oscar.

"They're too handsome," Suzanne said. "Look at the two of them. Handsome! Finlay, you need to take some sun. And get some exercise. You're looking scrawny. It's not good for you."

"But the child is working all the hours God sends!" my mother said. "That's why!"

I saw Finlay sigh at being called "the child," but he's heard this sort of talk often enough to know it's harmless, well meant. And while it might seem patronizing on one hand, it's nice too, to be sitting at the feet of one's elders, to feel protected, accepted, even with flaws.

"But look at Oscar. How Oscar getting up at five in the morning to run all-kinda-five-miles and thing. You should be doing that too. You're still young. The time is now, you know! When you're young, you always think, oh, tomorrow, next week, but time goes by, you know. Next thing you know, you wake up and you're fifty years old."

"Oscar's always been the sporty one," Finlay said.

"Yeah, but just because he's the sporty one don't mean you can't exercise," Suzanne said. "He doesn't have a monopoly on sporty. You could exercise too. Get a personal trainer. You have personal trainers in England? It's getting popular here now. In the gym, even on the Savannah early morning, when it's cool. They just make you do it. You set a time? Whatever time you have? Tell them to come then."

Finlay got up to get a drink. This kind of talk makes you want to stand up for yourself, it ruffles you. But it's good. It's too easy to hide in England, where everyone can see what's wrong but nobody dares to tell you. Sometimes you need someone to poke you a bit, stir you up. It makes you take action.

"Nice idea," Finlay said. "But I don't have any regular time. That's the problem. Everything changes week to week."

"But, Finlay!" Warren said. "How you could live like that, man? That is no way to live. Listen to me. Don't spend your life like that. However much money you might make? I'm telling you now, it's not worth it. I'm hearing you talk, and you're only working-working, and you have pressure on your tail, and meanwhile, every year, you're getting older, and older and older. Don't do it."

"How you could say that?" Mummy said. "You don't know how much money he might make. That is how life is. You have to work hard early on, and then rewards come later. Not so? That's what he's doing. Medicine is like that. You didn't take that path, you took a different path, but you have to leave young people to make their own choices."

"I'm not forcing him into anything," Warren said. "But he is my nephew. My flesh and blood, man. I giving him the same advice as if he was my own child. But it's only advice. I'm not forcing anybody to do anything."

"Yeah, thanks," Finlay said. "Appreciate all the advice." He looked a little flushed, but he was smiling. "Doh pressure meh!" He said it in the Trinidadian way, in the same rhythm as the old-time calypso.

Everyone laughed, and people chanted the next few lines of the song. It's from long-time ago, but it's like the lyrics have made their way into everyday language, as a way to say: Back off, leave me alone.

"That's right," Warren said. "You see? Just stand up for yourself. That's all you have to do. You see, if you lived in Trinidad, you would learn."

LATER, AFTER DINNER WAS FINISHED and everything washed up, I went down the corridor toward the bedroom, and I heard my mother's and Mercedes's voices inside. They were saying the rosary together. I recognized the sound it made: the low murmur, the two voices speaking at once, the rhythm of the words. My mother was sitting on the edge of her bed, in stiff pajamas, looking freshly bathed, her hair still damp. Mercedes was on the empty bed in the middle. They each held rosary beads, and they glanced up at me as I passed. Halfway across the room, I realized they were praying in Spanish: I couldn't help turning my head, drawn by the sound of the words. In Venezuela, I'd only caught fragments: Ave María. Elsen-yore-escontigo. Mujeres. Jesús. Now, I understood them fully. It was as if they were mine, returned to me; or as if I myself were returned to that earlier time, to the sheltered area outside the nuns' office where we gathered in the evenings to pray together.

"Come, Dawn," my mother said, gesturing. "Come and sit."

I put up a hand politely, saying no, and I went toward my bed. Without taking off my clothes, I got under the sheet and lay down and closed my eyes. The sound of their prayers carried on in the same low murmur for ten or fifteen minutes until Mercedes left, and my mother switched off the light.

Later, at some point during the night, I woke to the dark, quiet room, the unfamiliar bed, and I didn't immediately know where I was. For a time I thought I might be in Venezuela. I thought I was in the room I'd slept in with the other girls, with the mosquito net over the bed. I reached a hand out in the dark to feel for it, but my hand met empty air. I remembered the room. Sometimes this happens, moments seem to return in their entirety. I don't know how or why. Maybe it's whatever it is that stops women my age from sleeping well, or gives us our hot flushes or night sweats. The iron bedsteads. The pattern of the burglar-proofing bars over the window, a boxy pattern, with right angles. I could walk through it in my mind. There were four beds, two against that wall, and two against the other wall. Hot in the mornings, with the sun coming in that window.

Gradually, I came back to where I really was. Tobago, the beach house, the room that used to belong to my mother and father. Finlay and Oscar were here, under the same roof. Warren was here. Suzanne. My father was missing; he had crossed over. My mother was still here, right nearby, in the same room. No longer young. That was the sound of her breathing. And the girl in Italy: a half-formed presence, a maybe-maybe. In a few days, we would know. In this way, in the dark, with only a faint glimmer of moonlight through the curtain, these pieces of my life gradually came together.

17

I WAS ALONE WHEN I READ THE EMAIL WITH THE RESULTS FROM the DNA test. It comes with a long preamble, and attachments to useful resources. You have to click the link, and enter a password and then give consent to something else. Of course you just click, click, click through all the screens, because you're desperate to get to the answer. It was 4:30 A.M. in Tobago: 8:30 A.M. in London, 9:30 A.M. in Italy for Monica. I was on my phone, sitting on the bathroom floor so that I wouldn't wake my mother.

Less than 1 percent probability. Not related.

I studied the words closely, just to make sure I was reading it clearly. Then I turned the screen off and rested the phone facedown on the bath mat. I felt overcome by a sudden weariness. I drew my knees up to my chest and rested my forehead on my knees. Out in the garden, birds were singing, announcing the dawn.

A part of me felt as if I'd known all along that Monica wasn't the person I was looking for. I'd never seen any real resemblance in the photos, although maybe I'd tried to persuade myself I had.

I'm being completely honest: I'll admit that a part of me just felt really fed up with this whole saga. This is one of the things that I'm ashamed of: that there have been times, as now, when I felt bitter about how the mistake I made at sixteen has affected my whole life. How it feels like it's taken chunks out of my life, and it still hasn't stopped. Here I was, at fifty-eight, on a bathroom floor again, weeping again like a sixteen-year-old girl. My imaginary women in the kitchen, telling my story, would be shaking their heads at me. Dawn Bishop, who made a mistake, and then wasted her life searching for a child she would never find.

I sat with my face in my hands and spoke aloud, through my fingers. "Dawn. Just stop! Get off the stupid forums. Delete the Hotmail. Delete everything. Just. Stop it!"

Eventually, I got up, and I splashed some water on my face at the sink, and glared at myself in the mirror. Then I did my exercises. Ten touching toes. Ten side-to-side squats. Ten circling my arms like a windmill. And then I went out, quietly, so as not to wake anyone up, and went through the house and out to the patio.

A perfect Tobago morning. The sun only just now rising, shafts of gold over the tops of the trees. On the patio, with the hanging vines from the trellis overhead brushing my shoulders, I started an email to Monica, but I kept making typos, and after a few minutes I abandoned it. I walked across the grass and went to the gap where we climb down to the cove below. It was still early, the air calm, with no wind. I tapped the button to record a voice note instead, and held it down while I talked.

I said, "Hi, Monica. I'm sorry this is in English. I hope you can find a way to translate it if you need to. I just wanted to say

I'm sorry about the result. It's disappointing. I've been through it before, so I'm kind of used to it, but I know it's new for you." (I paused there, and I nearly let go of the button to abandon the message, but I held on.) "I hope you don't mind if I give you some unsolicited advice. I know you want to find your mother. I understand." (I paused.) "But, do you know what? If I could speak to my own daughter? If I could get a message to her? I'd tell her: don't spend your life like this. I've been doing this for years now. It's like a wild goose chase. Just—live your life. Go do all your amazing things. That's what your mother wants you to do, trust me."

I paused. My finger let go of the button. The phone made a little noise like it was swallowing the message, and then it sent. I looked up. I was by the fence still, just above the rocks and the beach. I looked back at the patio and saw my swimsuit from yesterday hanging on the washing line, where I'd left it. I could get changed out here, and then go in for a dip.

On my way back across the grass to the patio, I recorded a new message. "I forgot to say. You're welcome in Tobago anytime. It's nice here. Anytime you want, just come."

I climbed down the rocks, and I got changed on the beach. There was no one else around, just the little private cove, and our wooden jetty, and our one boat moored a little ways out, on a rope attached to a buoy.

The water seemed cold at first. I waded in up to my knees, and then my hips, and then my shoulders. Then I swam across to the rocks, keeping my feet up in case of manta rays, and then back across, parallel with the shore. I wasn't thinking anything. I was just moving my arms and legs through the water. I had warmed up by then, and it was like swimming in silk. Oscar came to the top of the garden: I saw him on the ridge. He was looking in my direction, but over my head. He was in his running clothes. He held a hand up to shield his eyes from the sun, and for a few moments, as I treaded water, he looked at the bright expanse of light. Then he lifted a hand and waved at me. I waved back. Then he disappeared from view. I turned onto my back and drifted for a while, before I swam back.

I came out of the water and sat on the sand. I sat for a while with my hands wrapped around my knees, and when they were dry, I rested them at my sides, brushing my palms against the top of the sand, away from me and then toward me, and then away from me again.

IT WAS STILL EARLY WHEN I walked back through the house, and into the bedroom. I meant to go in quietly without waking my mother, but when I pushed open the door, I saw her lying on her back with her eyes open.

She shifted her head a bit, and then she sat up, resting her head back on the pillow. She was watching me root around in the suitcase for something to change into. I was still in my swimsuit, with a towel wrapped around me.

"What happened?" she asked. "You look like you had news. You got the email?"

"Yeah."

"Oh. Not her, uh?"

"No. Too bad, huh?"

"That is too bad," she said.

After a moment, she went on. "Try not to let it get to you," she said. "All this searching and DNA-matching business. Twenty-three-and-me, all those things. It's getting easier all the time. People are finding each other. It's happening more."

I'd found some clothes, and I held them in a bundle to take them into the bathroom to change. But it felt like I suddenly ran out of steam. I just sat on the edge of the bed, and looked at her.

"Don't give up hope yet," she said.

I had to laugh. "But, Mummy!" I said. "You don't remember? You-self were the one telling me not to waste my time on this!" I shook my head. "Good grief, man. First people want you to do one thing, and then they want you to do the opposite thing."

"Well, people change their minds," my mother said. "Look at you. You've changed your mind about many things."

I shook my head again, and I said, "You know something? I'm thinking that I'm not able with this anymore. I overs." I dusted my hands together, as if to say that I was washing my hands of all this.

"That's how you feel now," she said.

There was a pause.

"You'll feel different in a little while," she said. "After you recover."

I sighed deeply, and she waited.

"Girl?" I said. "It's not easy!" I meant it in the way only Trinidadians would understand, the marveling at how strange the world was, how incomprehensible.

"It's not easy," she said, sorrowfully.

There were footsteps in the corridor, and we both looked

toward the door. Mercedes poked her head in. "You're awake?" she said. "I'll bring the toast. Toast, yes?"

"Yes, toast, thanks," my mother said.

Mercedes glanced at me sitting on the bed still wrapped in my towel, but she didn't say anything. After she left, there was another long pause. It was my mother who spoke next.

"You know. Long time I've been wanting to say something to you," Mummy said.

Something about the way she said it made me nervous. "Okay," I said. "What's that?"

She studied me for a moment, and then she said, "Come closer. You feel too far away."

I came around to the middle bed, and sat on the edge facing her.

"After you were down last time," she said. "When you and Robert separated. When Daddy was still living at home."

I suddenly felt sick. I felt I couldn't bear to hear whatever it was she was going to say.

"Well. You know what he did after you left? Nobody told you? Warren didn't say?"

"No. What did he do?"

"He looked into it. And he found out the address of where you stayed in Venezuela."

This was the beginning of what turned out to be an hour-long conversation. During the time that we sat talking, Mercedes knocked again, and came in with tea and toast for my mother. She set out my mother's medicines on the trolley for her to take with the food and then went away again. I heard Oscar come back from his run and Finlay get up and go to the kitchen to get breakfast, and then Warren and Suzanne and the girls, and everyone chatting and moving around, and then the sound of splashing from the pool.

My mother related the story of how they had got hold of the address: a long complicated story involving old phone bills from 1980, which were still in storage in one of the offices in San Fernando, and Mercedes—the same lady who had just brought my mother tea and toast—calling the phone number and speaking to them in Spanish, and asking about a house with nuns and girls having their illegitimate babies. When I said that it must be the wrong place, because the house I'd stayed in hadn't had a phone, my mother nodded, pleased that I remembered, and said, no, there hadn't been any phone at the house.

"But wasn't there a church nearby?" she asked. "That's what I understood. That's how I imagined it."

She was right: there had been a church. I had mopped the floor: I had folded up the padded kneelers and pushed the mop along the lengths of the pews.

"Well, anyway, Mercedes spoke to them, and she asked them who they were, and it turned out they were the church. It was a man she spoke to, I don't know if he was a priest or someone else, but she got the name of the church, and the address."

"The name of *the* church?" I said. "You mean the one close to the house?"

"The church close to the house," she said, confirming. "She asked him about the house, but he didn't know. But it must be somewhere nearby there."

My mother paused there and studied me, and she seemed satisfied by what she saw. I don't know what showed on my face: I was too stunned by all this to be able to speak. She turned to the trolley where Mercedes had left her pills and the tea and toast.

"I'm not finished yet, eh?" she said. "I have a little more. Let me just swallow this down, otherwise Mercedes will come and hassle me to eat. You know how she is." She took a sip of the tea and then she held up a finger. When she'd swallowed, she said, "What I mean about finding the address—you could go over there. Sorry, I told you that whole long story about the boxes in storage and the phone bills, but the point was to say that if you want, Warren could take you over in the six-seater."

"Take me when?"

"Well, whenever you want," my mother said. "But why not today?"

"Today!"

"Why not? Warren is here, the plane is already here in Tobago. It's not far. The two of you could go. Go and come back before it gets dark. The plane can't fly at night anyway."

"Fly . . . to Venezuela? Are you serious?"

She held up her finger again and I watched as she popped the other pill onto her tongue and swallowed it down with tea. She picked up the plate of toast and took a bite and then she put the plate down again.

"Sorry," she said. "I'm talking with my mouth full. Look, I know it's overwhelming. I should have said it earlier, given you more time to absorb it. But I thought maybe the girl in Italy might be her, and then it would have been a different story." She shrugged, sadly. "If you want my advice. I think you should go over. But it's up to you."

"Right," I said. "Sorry, I can't really process. I have a lot of questions." I put my hands to my forehead as I was speaking: it seemed to require all my concentration just to get these few sentences out. "You keep talking," I said. "You look like you have more to say."

"A little more," she said. She put the toast down and wiped her fingers on the napkin. "This isn't really relevant to you," she said, "I mean, not directly. But I just wanted to tell you anyway. Just so you don't feel we're hiding something from you."

I noticed a change in my mother as she began to speak again. A blotchy flush came over her face, and her hands turned bluish and mottled.

My mother told me that there was a woman in Maracaibo who used to write to my father. I didn't understand at first what I was hearing. The story was disjointed, something about a woman. Every time my mother said "this woman," there was a slight edge of contempt in her tone. I sat there listening to this stream of words, not understanding why it was so upsetting for her.

"Wait," I asked, eventually. "So who is this woman, exactly? Is this someone he knew?"

"It was a long time ago," my mother said. "He only met her once or twice. This was before he and I were even married. When he and Lloyd and Frankie used to go over together to Maracaibo. She kept writing to ask for money, you see." Here my mother paused. "For the child, supposedly."

"Right," I said, slowly, again. "For her child? This lady had a child?"

"Well, she claimed it was for her child," my mother said. "Daddy's child. That's what I'm saying. All these years she was writing, writing, and saying he had a son in Venezuela, and how he should recognize the son."

I stared at her and she nodded slowly, observing me. My own hands turned cold and then the cold spread to the rest of my body.

"But, let me get this straight," I said. "*Was* there a child?"

"Yes, it seems so. We think so."

"And I'm not getting confused—you're not talking about my child, my daughter. You're talking about a different child altogether?"

"Yes, you have it right. I'm not talking about your daughter. This was long before you went over. And this was a boy."

"So she did really have a child?" I said.

"Yes, she did have a child. A boy. He's dead now. He died in a car accident."

This came out matter-of-factly. She clasped her hands and then unclasped them. "I don't think it was really his child," she said. "He always insisted it wasn't."

"So Daddy," I said, slowly, "Daddy had—what? An affair? An outside woman?"

"He always said he didn't," my mother said. "He said the woman was getting him confused with someone. You know how some women are—they sleep with so many men, they can't even be sure which one is the father!" She made a little laugh, and then stopped herself. "Or, you know. More likely, she was just after his money."

I shook my head slowly.

"What?" Mummy said. "You're shocked?"

I was confused, mostly. And sad, about the boy. And, unexpectedly, ashamed—not just for myself, but for my mother. I said, "I feel like I'm hearing the music to Young and Restless playing. Like Cricket and Bradley should be walking in here just now."

She smiled at that, and I smiled too. It helped a bit.

"Look," my mother said. "This was a good while ago now. That's what I mean when I said it's not even really relevant. But I just wanted to tell you anyway, so you would know. That's why, with Venezuela, Daddy felt he had to be careful. He didn't want to put out feelers for you in Venezuela, or try to trace down the people who had helped him and Uncle Lloyd make the arrangements for you, because of this woman who used to be hounding him."

Mercedes came to the door again, and poked her head in, apologizing for interrupting. She said that she was going to go into town with Suzanne to get a few things from the grocery. She and my mother began talking about what was needed. I gathered up my clothes and fixed the towel, still wrapped around my body, and said I'd better get into the shower.

I felt shaken, as if I didn't fully recognize myself. Nothing was certain anymore. Maybe my father had had a secret affair with a woman in Maracaibo, or maybe he hadn't. Maybe the boy had been his son, or maybe not. Maybe we had a half brother, or maybe we didn't.

It was this latter fact, the existence of the boy that was the biggest shock, the possible half brother. I should have recognized the way I felt in that moment: after all, I'd read about it often enough on the forums. Being called into a room for a quiet conversation. The feeling of seasickness as your sense of yourself unraveled, so that when you got up to finally leave the room, it felt strange to be putting one foot in front of the other, as if your foot weren't even your own, but belonged to someone else.

I made my way back to the bathroom with my towel and dry clothes. I was still in my swimsuit, now mostly dried off, but still sticky and sandy from earlier. Out of habit, I checked my phone. An email had arrived from Monica, in English.

The tone was polite and faintly distant; all the warmth of our previous chats replaced, now, with something probably copied and pasted from the website. "I need to take some time to absorb the disappointing news. I may be in touch again at a later date, but in the meanwhile, I'm writing to wish you all the best, however you decide to go forward."

18

I'M NOT A RELIGIOUS PERSON AT ALL, BUT SOMETIMES CERTAIN words or phrases just offer themselves to you like they want to be spoken: that with one hand God giveth, and with the other He taketh away. I'm sure there are other ways to say the same thing, but it's the only one that occurs to me right now.

Warren and I were at Crown Point International Airport, waiting to get on the tiny six-seater plane. The pilot hadn't arrived yet, and the two of us were standing on the tarmac, close to the plane to get in under the shade. I don't know if you've ever seen one of these planes up close, but they do not fill you with confidence. There were dents and scratches all over the bodywork. Paint peeled off. Rust. Silver duct tape. It looked a bit like a car, but more battered. The idea of flying it over seven miles of sea, and then mountains, was making me think I should have brought the Xanax, and that I should take two whole tablets to get me through this. But I didn't have anything with me. Warren had said to travel with nothing—no ID, no money. He had his phone, and everything else was arranged.

To keep my mind off our impending doom, I was trying to

chat to Warren about something other than the airplane. I asked if he knew that Daddy had gone looking for the address in Venezuela, and if he had been there when they hunted through the old phone bills in the office.

"I wasn't there for that part," Warren said. "But I knew he had started asking around. He felt bad about it. Last time you were down, after you and Robert split up. That's when he started."

"And what about this woman in Maracaibo?" I asked. I felt queasy just talking about it out loud. "What do you think? Was it his son or not?"

"Who knows?" Warren said. "The woman wrote him every year, Mummy told you that? And she turned up once in south."

"Wow. No, Mummy didn't mention that part," I said.

"Oho."

The pilot was coming out to the tarmac now, walking briskly. He looked up at the sky, and then waved at us cheerfully.

"There's more to it?" I asked.

"I don't know. What did she tell you?"

"She said the boy died."

"Yeah. I think that's true. The letters stopped after that."

I wanted to ask Warren more, but the pilot was already there, reaching out to shake Warren's hand. He shook my hand next, and then he opened the plane door and climbed in, almost like you might climb into a car.

"Good Lord," I said, looking inside the plane. "This is it? No—helmets or anything?"

"Come, come," Warren said. "It'll be fine. Doh fraid! This plane is nearly as old as you and me. It's taken plenty bumps, and it's still going."

The pilot must have been trying to make up for his lateness, because he switched on the engine as soon as he got settled in the cockpit. I buckled myself in and held the armrests of the seat. It was a relief, in a way, that it was too noisy to speak. The engine hummed and droned, everything rattling furiously with the energy of it.

The plane taxied down the runway, rocking from side to side in the slight wind. We reached the end, the turnaround spot, and the pilot lined the plane up, and then he turned and gave us a thumbs-up. Warren, sitting back comfortably, gave a thumbs-up back. Then the pilot turned a knob, and—man! The engine started to roar. I would have put my fingers to my ears if I'd been able to let go of the armrests. It felt like the plane was going to explode. I closed my eyes and then opened them again: I couldn't tell which way was worse. I wanted to ask Warren how long we'd be in the air for, but I couldn't make myself speak in time.

The pilot pulled a lever and the plane moved forward. I sensed we were trying to speed up, but we weren't going very fast, only maybe as fast as a car. It still felt like it would explode. I shut my eyes. I did my deep breathing. I thought, the first time I went to Venezuela I thought I was going to die, and now it was happening again. This time, I felt, death was certain. We were speeding up. Any moment now the plane would explode. Or we would reach the end of the runway and just fall into the sea. I looked at the door to see how to open it if it came to that. And then, at last, the plane was tilting, the nose straining to lift up; and then we were up, the ground falling away. I think this must be why I have God on my mind today. We were airborne for now, yes, but being high up only meant that we would all die when we crashed back down. I was saying my prayers.

I don't know how long the journey took. All I remember is adrenaline. Everything loose flapped and blew in the wind; my hair whipped at my face. We must have been low to the water, because when I dared to look out the window, I saw the plane's shadow on the sea surface, and white frills on the wave tops. Seagulls rested on the surface of the water, rising and falling with the swells. Warren shouted in my ear once or twice, but otherwise, we didn't speak. Mostly he sat back as if he were on a day out, as if he were escorting a tourist on a tour. After a while—thirty minutes? More?—the solid form of the land materialized out of the haze. It was just like Trinidad—the same dark green, the familiar outlines of the trees. But as we got closer, I got a sense of the different size of it, that we were on the edge of a continent, rather than an island—how the land had no end; how it went on and on and on, as far as the eye could see.

I'd begun to acclimatize to the noise and turbulence, and at some stage I'd let go of the armrests. The plane began to descend. You could see more closely the different kinds of trees, and the coconut trees trying to rise up past the others, the thin long necks, like tall gray bones rising up from the forest floor. Then we were close enough that I could see the ground beneath the trees, and that it wasn't carpeted as it had seemed from farther away, but that there were gaps between the trees. Then there were channels between the trees, where people must have made paths. Then it felt like we were going too fast; the tops of the trees beneath us were sickeningly close and I understood where the scratches and dents must have come from.

The plane was tilting side to side. It looked like we were going to crash into the trees. I squeezed my eyes shut. I tried to curl into a ball, like the brace-brace thing they tell you in big airplanes. Then we hit the ground. Bounced. I thought we were being smashed up. Things were sliding and banging around inside the plane. Then we were skidding and swerving, and I realized we were on the ground, and at some stage I opened my eyes, and saw that we were in a sort of clearing. Warren was calling out to the pilot in Spanish, castigating him for the poor landing, and saying he nearly killed us, and he had his sister here from England. By the time I could really take in what was going on, we were stationary, and the pilot was standing in the open doorway of the plane, and taking a swig from a rum flask while he looked around.

We had landed in a clearing in the middle of the bush. Warren said something like, "Stay in the plane for now." I didn't catch everything he said. I think he meant that there might be trouble, and better to stay in the plane. The engines were off but I still felt the thrumming all through my body, and I could still see clearly the green blur of the treetops when I thought we were going to crash.

Eventually, though, we did get out. I remember my legs shaking. The pilot hadn't folded out the steps, so we had to jump out. The ground where we were was just packed dirt, but in other places there was old tarmac, mostly cracked up.

To the side of the landing strip, there was a little wooden shelter, almost like a bus shelter. The walls were made of planks of wood, painted blue. A galvanize roof, unpainted. Maybe a dozen people standing around. Ordinary-looking people, country people, I guess. A woman in jeans and a tube top. A few men in trousers and clean T-shirts; a few others in slouchy short-pants and slippers. Most people holding their phones, and they looked up from their phones to study us, and then back at their phones.

The pilot was already by the blue wooden hut. He was speaking to a man sitting on a chair in the shade of the galvanize roof of the shelter. The man got up and patted his trouser pockets. He nodded to us, and the pilot turned and waved, to tell us to come over.

"It's just like Trinidad, eh?" Warren said.

I don't know if I made any response. I was still feeling dizzy from the plane, and I was feeling ill, being here, and not knowing what was ahead.

"You're okay? You're going to vomit?" Warren said. "Go so." He pointed to the side of the landing strip, toward the bush.

I walked a little way toward it, but my legs were still shaky. "How far to get to the car?" I asked.

"It's right there," he said. "He's waiting there. Five minutes' walk, not even. And then we'll be in the car."

When we got to the bus shelter, I saw that there was a dirt path through the bush. I looked down at my sneakers and long-pants, and realized—Yes, that's right, I did walk. Before, I'd only remembered the cars, and the vomiting by the side of the highway, but I'd walked too—now that my body was doing it, I remembered. I had walked in the dark. I must have been either half-asleep, or drugged. I felt sick again. I paused and looked at the ground, with a hand to my stomach. Then I walked on again, following the men.

We came to another clearing, and a jeep parked in the clearing. The pilot spoke to the driver-man, and Warren spoke too, and they looked at their watches and spoke in Spanish. I understood what they were saying, and that in itself was profoundly jarring, as if I were being returned to an earlier moment of my life, but with the fog having cleared. We had to be back here before two o'clock, they were saying. There was rain coming in the afternoon. The pilot could fly in the rain, but it would be turbulent. More turbulent than the first journey. Better to leave earlier, before the rain came. He couldn't fly at night. The plane had no lights.

The driver was a Venezuelan man: he looked indigenous, maybe in his thirties, clean-shaven, and with tidily cut hair. The jeep looked well used; there was a strong smell of gasoline. Warren sat up front next to him. I got into the back. My seatbelt half worked: it clicked together, but had no elasticity in the belt. In the carry space behind me, there were two spare tires, and some tools, and a cardboard box with two green jerry cans held upright. The pilot waved to us from the clearing as we set off.

I don't remember all of the journey to the church. It was a long drive, a few hours. Rutted dirt roads, where bush scraped at the sides of the jeep as we drove along. Trees dripping with ripe mangoes, just like Trinidad, wide saman trees in full flower; squat, broad-leafed banana trees; tall, graciously swaying coconuts. Then tarmacked roads, with fruit-vendor shacks by the roadside, people ambling along in twos and threes.

THE DELUGE OF INFORMATION FROM my mother. My father, perhaps, wasn't the person I thought he was. The woman who had written him letters. A child who might have been a brother. On one hand, nothing had changed; on the other, I felt as if I didn't recognize myself, as if I didn't know who I was. I kept trying to pull the pieces back together, to remake myself. I was Dawn Bishop, daughter of Kenneth, granddaughter of Frankie, he who had built up a business from a few acres of citrus trees. I was Dawn, who had made a foolish mistake, and had left a Carnival fete and gone down to the beach with a tourist, and got ketch. I was Dawn, who had lost her way. But everything else—all the rest were fragments floating in space. The fact that I had blindly trusted my father; that I had tried to please my parents. That I had gone to England—why had I gone to England? That we had even been a family of five—had we even been a family of five? I didn't know anymore what was true. All that could be said was that I was a person in the back of a car, bumping along an unpaved road; that the air was warm and humid, and the trees were familiar trees, just like in Trinidad; that everything again was just like Trinidad, so that I wanted to touch someone's arm again, and ask, But where are we, really? Are we in Trinidad or Venezuela? Venezuela or Trinidad?

Warren and the driver talked a bit, up front. I sat quietly in the back. My eyes hooked on certain things at times: street signs, or little galvanize shacks, or people's faces. It seemed incredible that I hadn't come here before now, when it had been so close all this time. A mixture of shame and anger and confusion hovered nearby, but I pushed it out of my mind. I let my eyes rest on the trees, the broad leaves of the banana trees, the graciously swaying coconut palms. The road widened out. Ahead of us, the land rose toward the mountains, green, green, with wisps of cloud laced across their flanks. The air was thick and humid, threatening rain, and now it began to drizzle. The smell of the wet land mixed with the smell of gasoline from the canisters, and it was all just like the first time, except that now it was daylight and I could see where I was.

AS WE BEGAN GOING UP the hill, I felt it in my stomach, something familiar about the curve and incline of the road. On the low flank of the hill a first little house, white, with a red clay roof, a Venezuelan house, and in the land all around it, the garden, corn planted in rows, and smaller plants in rows, tended with thin bamboo sticks. An old man standing in the slanted field. He straightened up, and watched us as we drove by. I slid forward in my seat, I don't know why, maybe to call out to the man, or maybe just because I was amazed at what I was seeing. I grasped the back of Warren's seat.

"What? You want to stop?"

The man was behind us, leaning on his rake, still looking in our direction.

"No," I said. We didn't have a lot of time. "Let's keep going. It's up ahead, right? If we can't find it, maybe we can come back and ask him."

"I have it here," Warren said. He had his phone out, tracking our coordinates. "Point seven miles. We're nearly there."

THE CHURCH WAS JUST BEYOND a steep hairpin bend, on a gently sloping stretch of road. As soon as I saw it, I remembered it. That the entrance was not from the road, but from the right-hand side. I remembered that once you went into the church, you'd almost immediately have to go down a few steps. It was the way they'd built it because of the slope.

"I've been in there," I said. It was startling, the way the memory or knowledge seemed to return to my body, like a kind of electricity.

Warren made the driver pull over and I walked to the edge of the road and looked at where we were. This definitely was the place. I remembered sitting on the church steps waiting for someone, the smoothness of the stone under the soles of my shoes.

Warren tried to call the pilot to update him on where we were. The driver got out, and disappeared around to the back of the church.

"I don't know if anybody uses this church," Warren was saying. "Does anybody live here? Mummy said nobody answered the phone number they had, the number doesn't work."

I don't know if you've ever been in this sort of situation. A type of spatial memory, I guess. Somehow, you look around and you know which way to go. I left Warren and I began to follow the road farther up the hill. After a few minutes, the paved road carried on, and off to the left there was what looked like it might be a road to a farm, or a disused track. All the way up the road we'd taken, there had been wooden electricity posts at intervals, and thick black wires sagging between each pair of posts. The electricity cable carried on along the paved road. I felt drawn to the path, but there was no house there. Warren and the driver were still back at the church, out of sight.

I turned down the track. It was cracked-up tarmac, overgrown by weeds. I walked along slowly, wonderingly, because something about it was again so familiar, even though it surely was the wrong place. But I had a feeling of knowing this place before, a lifetime ago. The smell of the earth, maybe, or just off to the left, the shapes of the hills. Then I realized what it was: the trees were different. The ones that must have been big forty years ago were gone; the ones that had been only young back then had grown tall.

The track grew more heavily overgrown, so I had to lift my knees higher as I walked, to step through the tall weeds. I noticed a ditch on the right, running alongside the road. I stopped to look more closely. Here and there I could see past the weeds: the base of it was curved concrete, like longitudinal sections cut from a concrete cylinder, and laid end to end. I didn't remember that: maybe I'd never seen it while I was here, or maybe it was put in later. The path carried on for another ten or twenty yards, gently uphill. The top of the path was as dark as the mouth of a cave, obscured by tall trees and thickly growing bush.

I carried on along the path to the top, where there was a narrow gap in the bush, almost like a tunnel. And there, just beyond the mouth of the tunnel, was the gate. Smaller than I'd remembered, and rusted and battered and misshapen, but still flecked with white paint. Overgrown by the same corallita that grows in Trinidad, the same love vine, all green tendrils and brilliant pink flowers. The gate was sealed shut by the profusion of flowers, but the fence on both sides was gone, and I stepped over the curls of wire fence that had been peeled back, and into the garden.

The driveway was overgrown with weeds. There had been flowerpots all along here, and handsome plants. I walked alone, seeing not the flattened land, blurry with rain, but seeing it as it had once been, with the white border to the driveway, the clean drive, the clear sunshine of that first morning, the newness of arrival, of the Hermana walking with her arm around me, the little dog trotting beside us. "Venezuela, Venezuela," she had said. I seemed to remember now that as we walked, she had put her hand against my stomach, and we had stopped walking, and we had stood like that for a moment, her with her hand on my stomach, feeling, listening, and that her face was lined, and she was smiling. I paused on the drive, and my hands moved as if to touch her shoulder again, as I'd done so many years before.

Most of the house was gone—just a few partial walls remained, here and there, open to the sky. The ground was rough concrete in places, and earth and grass in others. As I got closer, I saw ruts or marks of tire tracks on the ground, as if maybe someone had kept their vehicle here, used it as a sort of shelter, possibly with those sheets of rusted galvanize for a roof. But there was no doubt that this was the house. I remembered the stairs, just outside the door to the kitchen. There was even a little bit of tiling still on the floor of the kitchen, the same black-and-white checkerboard pattern that I'd remembered all these years.

I walked along the edge of the room, and I passed my hand along the wall as it used to be, and it was as if I felt the brick wall under my hand instead of empty air. A few feet along, and then a corner, and here was the paved rectangle of a front porch—now grass, but I could imagine the porch, terra-cotta tiles, the outdoor table, a hammock. It was here that we sat and sang together, with one of the nuns playing guitar. A memory of her returned clearly: playing the guitar in trousers and a T-shirt, and a crucifix on a chain around her neck, and a handkerchief tied over her hair. It was all so vivid, almost as if I was sitting cross-legged on the ground and smiling with the other girls, instead of standing on my own in that derelict garden, in the rain.

And then I was darting around, almost dancing, touching my hands to the moss-covered bricks, and running my palms along the surfaces of the walls. The kitchen was here, the table where I sat on that first morning, the long table beside the other girls, was right here, beneath my feet. The small dark bathroom where I had changed out of my wet clothes on that first morning, it was here, and to prove it, there was a copper pipe half-buried under the ground, and I remembered now that there had been a standpipe on the wall around the other side, both fed by the same pipe. And this space next to it must have been where the nuns' office was—here, where there was still a section of brick wall; and these black water stains running down to the ground, must have been from an air conditioner.

I stood in the nuns' office, in the middle of what would have been the room, and I stood by the wall, as if I were looking out the window to the hills behind the house. I had been there before, in that spot. The baby had been here, in a cot by this window. My hands moved as if those same surfaces were still here—the wall, the window, the cot: the room as it was on that night returned fresh and vivid in my mind. The God giveth is the remembering. Because it does seem to me now, as I get older, that to remember the past is its own gift: to be able to return to those past moments—the sorrows and joys—and relive them, even the ones that we don't properly understand.

LATER, WARREN LED ME TO a tree where we were sheltered from the rain. Then we walked around the garden together, him holding up his phone to take photos, and me holding my hands above it, trying to keep the phone dry. I was aware of the minutes ticking past, and I tried hard to soak everything in, so I'd remember every detail. After half an hour or so, maybe a little less, the driver came up saying the pilot had phoned. A discussion followed, about the weather and the roads and the daylight, and then, all too soon, we were walking back down the slope to the church, and getting into the jeep to drive back the way we had come.

On that return journey, in the jeep and then in the dented, rattling airplane, I felt as if something had changed, although I couldn't, at that stage, have fully articulated what it was. Pieces were beginning to settle in new patterns. Maybe my story wasn't: Dawn, who made a mistake and brought shame to her family. Maybe it's: Dawn, mortal woman, who took a wrong turn in life and got lost.

THE NIGHT AFTER THE BABY was born, I slept not in the usual bedroom shared with the other girls, but in a different room on that upstairs floor. There was no curtain over the window, and I have a memory of spending those hours in that small room with only the pale white light of the moon for company. I couldn't sleep. The vinyl sheet on the mattress creaked and rustled every time I moved. Downstairs, the baby cried. I heard footsteps, doors opening and closing, faint voices—I knew that the nuns must be attending to the baby, trying to feed her and soothe her. I kept sitting up, listening. The sound of the crying was unbearable. I put my hands over my ears, but every time I took my hands away, the crying was still there, louder and more urgent than before. I got to my feet then, and for a while I stood facing the doorway aware only of the crying, and seeing the baby in my mind, how her eyes must be squeezed shut, her face turning purple with the effort. I might have been glowing with a kind of electricity; that's what I remember about how I felt in that moment. I felt twice my natural size; ten times as strong. And then I was in the corridor, walking fast in my bare feet, down the stairs, through one door and then another, until I was by the cot.

The baby's little vest had ridden up so it was crumpled under her armpits. Her eyes were shut tight; her face purple with the effort of bawling. I reached my hand under her legs to lift her, and I pulled the shirt down so it covered her soft tummy. It felt strange and yet familiar, like looking at another version of myself. I touched the soles of the little feet, softer than velvet. With my finger, I pushed the cap back from her head so I could stroke her scalp. I saw a reddish glint in the damp hair, a color that I recognized as my own. In her face, I thought I saw something of my grandfather, a cross expression he used to wear sometimes. And the shape of the calves, when the baby's legs stretched out, kicking furiously—the curve of the calf going down to the ankle was the same as the curve of my own legs, and my mother's too.

My hands slid gently under the baby's body, one hand under her hips, the other at the back of her neck. I bent over the cot and used the length of my forearms to scoop the little warm body up. She was purple with distress, her fists clenched, almost choking on her own screams.

And here I think, was my real mistake: what I did next. The one thing any fool could have told me not to do: I pressed her warm little body against my own. I felt the pulse of her heart against my body, thudding and frantic, like beating wings. I kissed her soft, sweet head. I stroked her back, and whispered into her ear. Gradually, her wailing eased. Her little fingers scrabbled at my cheeks, while she grumbled, tiredly, into my ear. Where have you been? she seemed to be saying. I called and called for you! I hushed and kissed her, and gently rubbed her back, until gradually, she laid her tired head against my shoulder, and we were quiet.

Hermana Maria-Theresa came in then, exhausted, her hair uncovered, carrying a bottle of milk. She was gentle, regretful. You are so young, she whispered to me. You have your whole life ahead of you. She meant it kindly. I don't blame her, as I know now not to blame myself. Neither of us could have known what was to come. I allowed the baby to be taken from my arms.

But I remember it now, that for those few moments, she and I were together. The snug warmth of her body melting into my own. The softness of her head against my cheek. We had that time together. We were given that gift.

Acknowledgments

Warmest thanks, firstly, to my rock-star editors and their teams: Alex Bowler, Aisling Brennan, and Emily Fish at Faber; and Parisa Ebrahimi, David Ebershoff, Helen Thomaides, and Maddie Woda at Hogarth. Also to my stellar publicists and production teams; Henry Petrides and Cassie Vu for their beautiful cover designs; and to my mother, Mary Adam, for the use of her art on the U.S. cover.

To my agent, Zoë Waldie, for infinite patience and support—thank you. All the good folks at RCW Literary Agency continue to look after me well, as do Melanie Jackson in New York and Jane Villiers at Sayle Screen.

I owe a debt of thanks to the team at Goldsmiths, especially Maura Dooley, Blake Morrison, Romesh Gunesekera, and Ardu Vakil. Claire Keegan has been a generous teacher, and I've learned so much in her fiction workshops.

Many others have provided invaluable help over the years: my sister, Jennifer Adam, read every word of every draft, and always made time to talk; Rachel Baker kindly let me use her spare room as a writing space, and we had many interesting conversations over coffee in the kitchen; Ken Ramchand and

Zorina Shah in Trinidad chatted with me over Zoom about movements between Trinidad and Venezuela; Kate Clanchy read an early draft of the manuscript and gave very generous encouragement; Veronica Lenz spent several hours talking to me about Venezuela, and Juan Perez read a full draft of the manuscript and diplomatically corrected several errors. And many fellow writers have helped in a myriad of other ways, especially Jane Bryce, Annemarie Cancienne, Divya Ghelani, Nicholas Laughlin, Chetna Maroo, Claire McGlasson, Philip Nanton, Stephen Narain, Monique Roffey, and Bev Thomas. Finally, if I may group all the Trinis together for one huge thank-you—you all are just de bess.

Dear family—in Trinidad, Ireland, the United Kingdom, the Netherlands, the United States, New Zealand, and elsewhere; all those past, present, and to come—much love to you all.

About the Author

Claire Adam's debut novel, *Golden Child,* was published by Sarah Jessica Parker's SJP for Hogarth. It was listed as one of the BBC's "100 Novels That Shaped Our World" and was awarded the Barnes & Noble Discover Prize, the Desmond Elliott Prize, the Authors' Club Best First Novel Award, and the McKitterick Prize. She was born and raised in Trinidad and Tobago. She studied physics at Brown University and later received an MA in creative writing at Goldsmiths, University of London. Adam lives in London.

About the Type

This book was set in Granjon, a modern recutting of a typeface produced under the direction of George W. Jones (1860–1942), who based Granjon's design upon the letterforms of Claude Garamond (1480–1561). The name was given to the typeface as a tribute to the typographic designer Robert Granjon (1513–89).